Spinning Forward

**Center Point
Large Print**

**This Large Print Book carries the
Seal of Approval of N.A.V.H.**

Spinning Forward

TERRI DuLONG

CENTER POINT PUBLISHING
THORNDIKE, MAINE

This Center Point Large Print edition
is published in the year 2010 by arrangement with
Kensington Publishing Corp.

The text of this Large Print edition is unabridged.
In other aspects, this book may vary
from the original edition.
Printed in the United States of America
on permanent paper.
Set in 16-point Times New Roman type.

ISBN: 978-1-60285-694-3

Library of Congress Cataloging-in-Publication Data

DuLong, Terri.
Spinning forward / Terri DuLong. -- Center Point large print ed.
p. cm.
ISBN 978-1-60285-694-3 (lib. bdg. : alk. paper)
1. Widows--Fiction. 2. Mothers and daughters--Fiction. 3. Knitting--Fiction.
4. Cedar Key (Fla.)--Fiction. 5. Large type books. I. Title.

PS3604.U456S65 2010
813'.6--dc22

2009045401

*This book is dedicated
to the memory of my mother,
Alma Leszczynski,
who gave me a love for reading.*

*And to the memory of my father,
Stan Leszczynski,
who passed on a love for words.*

Acknowledgments

When I visited Cedar Key for the first time, in 1994, I knew I was in my element—surrounded by water and Mother Nature. But when I relocated there in 2005, my love for the town deepened because I found that it was the people who were the soul of the island.

The locals made me feel welcome and gave me a sense of belonging. I was inspired by their strength, their compassion for neighbors, and their love for family. Without them, my story wouldn't have been possible, so I owe a huge debt of gratitude to each and every one.

A few in particular touched the writer in me. By sharing their own childhood stories, Cedar Key history, and island folklore, they unknowingly allowed my imagination to create a fictional story. My deepest thanks to Dottie Haldeman, Mary Rain, Frances Hodges, Rita Baker, Jan Allen, Beth Davis, Dr. John Andrews, Marie Johnson, Shirley Beckham, and so many others who enabled me to feel the true essence of Cedar Key.

Thank you to Alice and Bill Phillips, owners of the Cedar Key Bed & Breakfast—for your in-depth tour and enthusiasm for my story.

For Alice Jordan, my high school friend, I can't thank you enough for renewing my interest in knitting, turning me into an addicted knitter, and always being a phone call away to answer any knitting questions. For Bill Bonner, my friend and writing partner, your belief in my work made the tough times easier. And huge thanks to both of you for reading this story and giving me your constructive advice and loyal support.

Thank you to my children, Susan Hanlon, Shawn, and Brian DuLong—for your love and enthusiasm.

Most sincere gratitude goes to my editor, Audrey LaFehr, for your professional support and for making my story a reality. And to the entire team at Kensington for bringing it all to fruition.

Thank you to my husband, Ray, who gave me wings to soar, encouraged my destiny, and has kept me airborne with belief in myself.

And to you, my reader—thank you for including me on your bookshelf.

⟞ 1 ⟝

Whining drew my attention to the fawn-colored Boxer curled up beside the bed. Lilly had been my constant companion for four years and now she was my salvation. With my home, my assets, my life as I knew it taken from me, Lilly was my one factor of stability.

Living on an island off the west coast of Florida wasn't something that I planned to be doing at age fifty-two. Twenty-eight years of marriage to a successful physician provided a lifestyle that I not only enjoyed, but took for granted. Okay, so maybe Stephen wasn't the most passionate and romantic man on the planet, but he created a sense of security in my life. That is, until his Mercedes crashed into a cement barrier on I-495 in Lowell, leaving me a widow with no sense of direction and no knowledge of a secret he harbored.

Two weeks following his funeral, I had been working my way through the grieving process when I was zapped with another shock. I opened the door of my Lexington, Massachusetts, home to find a sheriff standing on my front porch, knowing full well this wasn't going to be good news. My first thought was concern for Monica, my twenty-six-year-old daughter.

"Are you Sydney Webster?" he'd questioned.

"Yes. Yes, I am. What's wrong?" Despite the

chill of the October day, beads of perspiration formed on my upper lip.

He'd cleared his throat and with downcast eyes passed me a large envelope.

"Ma'am, I'm sorry to have to deliver this to you, but it's a certified notice for your eviction."

"My *what?*" I felt lightheaded and gripped the door frame.

"Eviction of premises. You have thirty days to pack up your belongings and vacate the house."

I'd thought it was a joke. Somebody had seen Stephen's funeral announcement in the paper and was playing a prank on me. The house had been paid for years ago. Nobody could just show up and kick me out of my own house. This didn't happen to law-abiding citizens.

Clutching the envelope with sweaty palms, I'd torn it open and removed an official-looking piece of paper. All I saw was a blur of words, making no sense out of what was happening.

"I'm sorry, Mrs. Webster," he'd told me. "I really am. I'll return in thirty days at nine A.M. to make sure your belongings are removed and obtain the house keys from you."

"This is a mistake," I babbled. "A major mistake." Closing the door, I slid down the length of the wall, my sobs shattering the quiet of the house.

And here I was five weeks later on an island off the west coast of Florida. In a quaint but small room at the Cedar Key B&B, and I knew for certain none of it had been a mistake. Stephen's secret vice of gambling and the events that followed were what had brought me to this small town of nine hundred permanent residents, relying on the hospitality of my best friend Alison.

"Come on, girl," I said, swinging my legs to the side of the bed. "Time for you to go out and for me to get some coffee."

The bedside clock read 6:15. At home I never woke before 9:00 and was amazed that in the week I'd been staying at Alison's B&B, I didn't sleep beyond 6:30. Slipping into sweat pants and a T-shirt, I grabbed my pack of cigarettes and with Lilly close at my heels we descended the stairs to the porch.

Opening the door to the small L-shaped dining room, I saw a middle-aged couple quietly conversing over coffee and made my way to the kitchen.

"Mornin'," Twila Faye said as she removed freshly baked blueberry muffins from the oven.

Twila Faye was Alison's right hand running the B&B and I liked her. She'd raised her only son alone after her philandering husband had left town twenty years before with a tourist visiting from Macon, Georgia. Raised in the Boston area, I didn't know much about Southern women, but I knew Twila Faye represented what they called *true grit*.

Pouring myself a cup of dark, strong coffee, I asked if Alison was around.

"Lord, child, she's already out for her walk with Winston."

I should have known. I felt slothful when I had discovered that Ali woke seven days a week at 5:00 A.M. She never varied from her routine. Up at five, she prepared muffins, brewed the coffee, squeezed oranges for fresh juice, and by 6:00, her guests had breakfast waiting for them. Then she rounded up her Scottish terrier for a walk downtown to the beach.

I looked at the clock over the table and saw it would be another twenty minutes before she returned.

"I'm going to sit in the garden with my coffee," I told Twila Faye.

"Take one of these muffins with you."

Patting my tummy, I shook my head. "I'm trying to lose the twenty pounds I packed on this past year. I'll have some cereal later."

Settling myself on the swing in the far corner of the garden, I lit up a cigarette. Blowing out the smoke, it crossed my mind once again that perhaps smoking was another bad habit I should consider discarding.

I watched Lilly sniffing around the artfully arranged flower beds. Bright, vivid azalea bushes in shades of red. Yellow hibiscus gave forth cheer even on a dreary day. And dominating all of it was the huge, four-hundred-year-old cypress tree. I looked up at the leaves creating shade over the garden and wondered about something being on this earth that length of time. Having withstood tropical storms and hurricanes, drought and floods, it stood proud and secure. Right now secure was the last thing I was feeling. I had an overpowering urge to climb the tree. All the way to the top. And maybe absorb some of the positive energy that it seemed to contain. But with arthritis recently affecting my knees, I decided to stay put on the swing.

Physically, I was in pretty good shape for my age. If we discount the extra twenty pounds and smoking, that is. But emotionally, my life was a train wreck.

"Good morning," Ali called, walking through the gate along the brick walkway. "Let me put these shells inside and I'll join you with coffee."

I nodded and smiled. Ali always had a way of cheering me up. Ever since our college days as roommates, she'd always been there for me as a good friend. A no-nonsense-type person, she stepped in when I called her about my eviction. She demanded I drive down with Lilly, a few belongings, and stay with her at the B&B. She apologized that the second-floor apartment in the Tree House was rented till January, but I could stay in one of the rooms in the main part of the house. The Tree House was detached and located on the side of the garden. Ali had her apartment on the first floor and sometimes rented the one above. Feeling like a homeless person—actually, I was—I was grateful to have any space where Lilly and I could stay. But I won't lie . . . going from a 4,500-square-foot luxury home to a 12 x 12 bedroom with adjoining bath was like giving up a BMW 700 for a military jeep.

"I see you still haven't given up those disgusting things," Ali said, settling in the lounge beside me.

I snubbed out my cigarette in the ashtray and remained silent. I could have said plenty. Like she was the one that turned me on to cigarettes in the first place, during our freshman year in college. Everyone smoked back then, until it became a health issue long after our college days. I also could have said, unlike her, I hadn't dabbled in smoking pot. But I let it slide and took a sip of my coffee. The only rule that Ali had imposed when I moved in was no smoking inside the B&B.

Ali flung the long salt-and-pepper braid hanging over her shoulder to her back. She hadn't changed much since our college graduation. Tall and still very slim. Only faint lines beside her eyes attested to the passing years. She was wearing shorts that showed off her long legs, and a crisp white blouse. Her bronze tan reminded me of the days we used to spend (without sunscreen) on the beaches of Cape Cod.

"So what are your plans today?" she asked.

Plans? I was beginning to feel like an inert creature since arriving in Cedar Key. I had ventured downtown a couple of times. Taken a few walks with Lilly. Read a couple books. But other than that, I felt lost. It had even crossed my mind a few times that maybe I should return to the Boston area. Which always led me to question, *to what?* My life, as I knew it, had been snatched away from me.

As if reading my mind, Ali said, "Look, Syd, I know you've been through a hell of a lot these past couple months. Losing Stephen and then the eviction, but you've got to pull yourself together and decide what you'll be doing for the rest of your life. You can't just turn off."

Anger simmered inside of me. "What the hell would you suggest I do? I have no job. I haven't worked as a nurse in twenty-six years. I'm not sure I'd even remember which end of a syringe to use. I have no training in anything else. My bank account is on low. I have no clue what I'm going to do." I swiped at the tears now falling down my cheeks.

Ali reached over and patted my hand. "I don't mean to be hard on you, but it's very easy for a woman in your situation to regress. You're in a funk and you need to do something to get yourself moving forward. What happened to that girl I knew in college? The take-charge, independent woman, who knew where she was going and how she was going to get there?"

"She married Stephen," I said and realized that was true. "He wasn't supposed to die at fifty-five. And he sure as hell wasn't supposed to leave me financially insecure. It's damn difficult not to be angry with the rotten hand life suddenly dealt me."

As soon as I said the words, I felt embarrassed. Alison had gone through similar circumstances twenty years before. Gary had died suddenly after a three-month battle with cancer. Leaving her alone, with no children and no future. Within a year of his death, she had shocked me with the news that she was uprooting. Relocating to an island off the west coast of Florida where she had vacationed as a child. She explained the place was calling to her and she felt certain she could heal there. She had been right. Purchasing the B&B had turned her into a savvy businesswoman, and given her an increased confidence. Something I definitely lacked.

"That's total bullshit and you know it. Life isn't fair, so you move along and make the best of it."

I sighed and reached to light up another cigarette. "Sometimes all of this feels like a dream. In the blink of an eye my entire life has changed. Stephen was well regarded in our community and at Mass General. We had a wide circle of friends and entertained lavishly. Sure, he had been preoccupied recently, but I thought it was his work.

Certainly not illness. When the autopsy revealed a massive coronary had caused the accident, I thought it had been a mistake. Just like I thought the eviction was a mistake. Imagine—he was a compulsive gambler all those years and I didn't realize it."

"You allowed Stephen to run the household financially. He paid the bills, he balanced the checkbook. You're being a little hard on yourself, Syd. I'm not saying it was right, but since you had no idea where money was going, how could you know he'd taken out a second and third mortgage on your house?"

I nodded and felt ashamed. But I should have known. I should have paid more attention, but Stephen made it so easy for me not to. I remembered the conversation with our attorney the day I was slapped with the eviction notice.

"Whose name is on the deed to the house?" Calvin asked.

My mind had gone blank. Whose name? "Our name," I told him, clutching the phone to my ear. "What difference does it make?"

"A big difference, I'm afraid. And Stephen's name is on there."

"Yeah, so? Okay. His name is on there," I'd told Calvin with impatience.

"You're not following me, Syd. *Only* Stephen's name. Your name isn't on the deed. Did he purchase your home in his name only?"

"What the hell difference does that make? I'm his widow and beneficiary. Why would I be evicted?"

Calvin's insistent voice repeated, "Did Stephen purchase the house in his name only?"

"Yes," I had whispered.

I ran a hand through my hair and looked at Ali. "I should have gotten that deed changed years ago. It was the week before Thanksgiving and I was due to deliver Monica any minute. We got an early blizzard that year in Boston and Stephen assured me I didn't need to attend the closing. I guess I always felt we were married and the house was half mine anyway, even though my name wasn't on the deed. Over the years there never seemed a reason to change things. Now it's come back to bite me."

Ali sipped her coffee and remained silent.

"I still find it hard to believe that Stephen mortgaged our house to pay off some large gambling debts. And then, making it worse, he defaulted on the loan and was three months in arrears."

"Syd, sometimes you never know the person you're living with. Really know them. I'm sure Stephen's stress level was off the charts. Knowing that the bank was about to take possession of your home for non-payment."

Anger flared up again inside of me. "And now they'll sell the house for close to a million and I'm left a bag lady. Literally."

Ali smiled. "I'll never let you be a bag lady. You don't need to worry about that. But speaking of bags, where's that spinning wheel and knitting bag you brought down here with you?"

"Up in my room," I replied with no enthusiasm.

"Maybe that should be your plan for today. Sit out here, enjoy the great weather, and do some knitting. That always relaxes you and allows you to think clearly. Try to focus on what you might like to do. Fifty-something is the new thirty—you have the rest of your life ahead of you."

As always, Ali was right. Feeling sorry for myself was getting me nowhere. Maybe I needed to regroup and figure out where I might be going.

Sitting in the garden with the late-afternoon sun creating lacy patterns on the grass, I watched Lilly romp and play with Winston. She sure seemed to have settled in quite well. My eye caught the flashy pink bougainvillea draped along the fence and gate. Circular flower beds held purple lantana with butterflies hovering above the blossoms. It was easy to see why Ali had been drawn to this place. I was captivated with the dramatic green of the old cypress tree. The circumference was at least ten or eleven feet, with thick, knotted roots emerging from the ground. My life was in limbo, but sitting beneath the majestic tree provided me a certain amount of tranquility.

I leaned forward toward my spinning wheel and heard a woman's voice.

"My goodness, I haven't seen one of those since my grandmother's attic."

I recognized her as the guest in room four. "Yeah, it does have an authentic look. That's what attracted me to it. The brochure said it has the look of wheels from the Baltic area of Poland and Scandinavia. In fact, a well-known spinning-wheel historian said that the manner in which the wheel was built is as close to being historically correct as he'd seen."

"Oh, it's absolutely lovely." The woman reached to touch the walnut finish. "And what on earth are you spinning? Is that dog fur?"

I laughed and nodded. "Yeah, this happens to be Winston's fur."

"What a clever idea. So you spin the fur into yarn?"

"Sure. Just like alpaca or any other kind of fiber. Then you knit with it."

Excitement spread across the woman's face. "Oh, my goodness. If I mailed you some fur from my Bailey—he's my Old English sheepdog—would you be willing to spin it for me?"

When I hesitated, she added, "I'll pay you for your services, of course."

Pay me for my services? To spin dog fur? "Well,

uh . . . I've never really done this for other people. I mean . . ."

"I'd need enough to knit myself a sweater. I'd be the hit of my knitting club, I can tell you that. How's two hundred dollars? Would that be adequate?"

I was flabbergasted that somebody would offer me money to do something I enjoyed.

"I'll add another hundred," she said. "I know it's presumptuous of me to even ask you. But I adore my Bailey and he's getting on in years. To think I could have a part of him with me forever. I'd be so indebted to you. By the way, I'm Lucille—Lucille Graystone, but you can call me Lu."

I had no idea if the price was too high or maybe not enough. It did involve a certain amount of work to prepare the fur for spinning. After being properly cleaned, it then had to be carded. Not to mention the labor of spinning it. I knew how I felt about Lilly and couldn't think of the day she'd no longer be with me so it was easy to understand how Lu wanted a keepsake of Bailey. Besides, I was desperate to earn some money.

"Alright," I told her. "I'll do it for you, but I have to explain what you need to do before mailing it to me. Plus, you'll require quite a bit of fur for a sweater unless you want to combine the fur with another yarn."

Lu threw her head back laughing. "Bailey sheds so much, quantity won't be a problem."

"Well, hey girlfriend, you could be on to something here," Ali said later that evening. "You might want to think about opening your own business. Spinning pet fur for devoted owners."

We were sitting on the porch after supper enjoying a glass of sweet tea.

"I don't think so. I haven't a clue about running a business."

"Neither did I when I bought this place."

I shook my head. "No, I'll do this favor for Lu, but I wouldn't know where to begin starting a company. I do need to begin thinking about a job though. Any ideas?"

Alison sighed. "Hmm, not really. Unless you're a merchant, most of the jobs on the island are cleaning, waitress positions, or clerks. Minimum pay."

"Oh, God. I haven't been a waitress since my college days." The emptiness I'd been feeling since Stephen's death overwhelmed me as moisture filled my eyes. "What the hell am I going to do, Ali? It's not like I'm sixteen again and can run home to my parents. They're both gone now anyway. Monica has been extra cool toward me since she found out about the foreclosure on the house. Not that I'd ask her for help anyway."

Ali remained silent, sipping her tea thoughtfully. After a few minutes she said, "I hate to be so brutally honest, Syd, but I guess the time has come for you to figure out what you want to be when you grow up."

I flashed her a nasty look. With raised eyebrows, I said, "What's that supposed to mean?"

"You've always been somebody's daughter, wife, mother. You know yourself you relied on Stephen way too much and as a result you lost your own identity over the years. Haven't you ever wondered about the *real* you? Who you are inside? Not that person created by other people." She paused for a second. "Have you ever thought about searching for your biological parents?"

I sat up straighter in the chair and took a deep breath. Oddly enough, after losing Stephen it had crossed my mind again to wonder if the woman who had given me life might still be alive. Perhaps I wasn't completely alone in the world. I'd shared my adoption story with Ali years ago, but we hadn't discussed it recently. There was nothing earth-shattering about it. Vanessa and Bob Sherwood had been unable to have children of their own. They applied to adopt a child and brought me home when I was three weeks old. I had been told as a young child that I was adopted and it always made me feel special. When I got to be a teen, I became curious and questioned my mother about that other woman. All she could tell me was that I'd been born in New York City, March 19, 1955. I weighed 7 pounds, 12 ounces. I assumed that the woman who had given me away was young and unwed. The typical story.

I reached for a chip from the bowl in front of us and shrugged. "I always wanted to search, but I felt it would be a betrayal to my parents. They gave me a good life. You know that."

"Yeah, but I remember when Monica was born. You questioned if maybe she'd inherited looks or traits from your real parents and it bothered you. I tried to encourage you to begin a search. I think your parents would have understood. It's only natural to be curious and want to know exactly where we came from. Genes aren't everything in forming us, but they do matter."

Ali was right. It wasn't that I felt like a misfit in my adopted family, but I had always felt a void. I used to wonder if maybe my smile was passed on from a cousin or aunt that I'd never met. Had my mother enjoyed knitting like I did? I hadn't seemed to get many traits from my adopted parents.

"Do it," Ali said.

I looked at her with surprise. "Do what?"

"Search for your biological mother," she said forcefully. "You're floundering, Syd. You've lost all that you knew as your way of life. You need to move on and maybe locating some information about that woman will help you to do that. We all need a touchstone. Something to make us feel whole and understand why we're the person we are. I think the time has come for you to discover that."

I recalled shortly after Monica was born that I went so far as to research A.L.M.A. on the Internet. Adoptee's Liberty Movement Association was located in Denville, New Jersey. I never bothered to list my own name though. Maybe I was afraid of what I might find. But now, at age fifty-two, I had a compelling need to search for my roots. Find out where I had come from. And perhaps enable myself to find out where I was going.

"You could be right," I told Ali. "Maybe it's an innate desire in all of us. Whether we admit it or not." I took the last sip of my tea and placed the glass on the table. "Could I use your computer tomorrow to list myself on A.L.M.A.?"

Ali put up her hand for a high five. "Absolutely. And something else I think you should do is scout around town for some space and see about opening a knitting shop. There're a few shops downtown that are being refurbished. I'd bet anything one of them would be perfect for you."

I thought of my bank account dwindling down to nothing after putting a deposit for a lease. And stock? Where would I get the money to order supplies to get me started? After voicing my misgivings to Ali, I was sorry I'd mentioned it.

"I can give you a loan, Syd. You know I would."

"Yeah, I know you would, and I don't want you to. If, and I say *if,* I'm going to do this, it has to be on my own. I'm just not sure I'm ready for that step. What if it falls apart and I lose everything?"

"For Christ's sake, life is a risk. You'll certainly get nowhere if you don't take a chance. It's the same with your search. If you don't even try, you'll never find your biological mother."

Ali always gave me something to think about. She pushed me to pursue things I wouldn't ordinarily do. Like the time in our sophomore year in college she found out I couldn't swim. She insisted I could and after three weeks of her instruction at the college pool, she proved me wrong.

I let out a deep sigh. "I'll think about it," I told her. Wanting to change the subject, I asked when I was going to meet the mysterious Paul.

Ali laughed and then surprised me as a crimson flush covered her face.

"I told you. He works for a large pharmaceutical company in Atlanta. It isn't that easy for him to get down here a lot. And he isn't mysterious at all. We've been seeing each other off and on for a few years now."

"Does he have any plans to get down here in the near future?"

"When I spoke to him the other night, he said he was going to try and come down for a few days at the end of the month."

Feeling like I was back in our dorm room at college, I asked, "So is this serious?"

Ali threw her head back laughing. "Honey,

what's serious when you're our age? I don't have marriage in mind, if that's what you mean. But yeah, we have a kinda sorta committed relationship. We don't sleep with anyone else."

I'd forgotten how outspoken Ali could be. She'd always marched to the beat of a different drummer, and I guess age hadn't changed a thing.

"Don't look so shocked," she teased me. "People over age fifty do continue to have sex, you know. And I can vouch for the fact it's even better as we get older."

Speak for yourself, I thought. I couldn't remember the last time that Stephen and I had had sex. A year? Two? It wasn't something we'd discussed or even brought to a halt intentionally. It had just sort of happened. Or not happened. I guess like most other things in my marriage, I had grown to accept it. And the magazines I'd see at the supermarket checkout seemed to confirm that sex was for the twenty, thirty, and forty year olds. Making love was a taboo subject for those of us over age fifty. But I had to admit that when I was reading a novel and came to a sex scene, it made me pause. Or when I watched a chick flick that involved some hot romping in bed, I felt sadness that that part of my life seemed to be over.

When I remained silent, Ali went on.

"Hell, years ago we had to worry about pregnancy. There's a certain freedom in reaching a point in your life where lovemaking is simply pleasure. Both in the giving and receiving."

I was saved from commenting by the ringing of Ali's phone.

"Cedar Key Bed and Breakfast," she said, in her polished business tone. "Monica. Hey, it's great to hear your voice. Yup, she's right here."

I rolled my eyes as I reached for the phone. "Hi, sweetie. How're you doing?"

"More to the point, how are *you* doing? Have you decided what the heck you're going to do down there? Are you sure you shouldn't have stayed up here? God, Mom, you've got yourself in quite a situation."

As if I didn't know that, and I could always depend on Monica to make me feel worse than I did. Never one to cut me any slack, she always stormed full speed ahead on everything. She made me feel like all of this was my fault. My fault that Stephen died, my fault that I got evicted, and my fault she'd lost her childhood home. Unlike me, Monica had always been sure of herself. Strong willed and independent, she made no pretense of the fact that I should have known better than to leave the house in Stephen's name. She also blamed me for not paying more attention to her father's *hobby* of gambling. Monica maintained I should have been aware that he visited the dog and horse track more than was normal.

28

My anger flared up and I didn't mince words with her. "I have no idea what I'm going to do. But you know what, Monica? You can be assured you will not be called upon to look after your middle-aged mother. I guarantee you of that." Pushing the disconnect button, I slammed the phone on the table.

"Hmm," Ali said, picking up the phone to inspect any damage. "Aren't mother-daughter relationships wonderful?"

～3～

Sitting in the quiet garden was quickly becoming my favorite way to start my days. While my Lexington neighborhood wasn't overly noisy, it did have a fair amount of sound. Car doors slamming, the roar of a motorcycle in the distance, or the faint voice of the WBZ disc jockey floating onto my patio from the radio next door. But here on the island, it was utter and complete silence during the early morning. Occasionally, I'd hear the engine of an air boat across the water. But even that I found to be a soothing hum.

After my conversation with both Ali and Monica the evening before, I'd decided this was the day I'd head downtown and attempt to find some type of employment. I looked up to see Ali and Winston walking toward me. Lilly immediately ran to her new best friend and both dogs took off to explore the garden.

"Feeling better this morning?" Ali questioned, pulling up a chair beside me.

I shook my head. "I don't know. My life is spinning out of control, and I know you're right. I'm the only one that can change that. So first on my list is to beat the pavement downtown and try to find a job."

"It's a good start."

I was feeling extra emotional this morning. "After all that Stephen did to me—the lying, the betrayal, the secrets—I still miss him," I said, as tears formed in my eyes.

"Well, of course you do, Syd. God, you were married to the man more than half your life. Even couples with marriages not made in heaven have a certain attachment and fondness for each other. Stephen wasn't a mean person."

I blew my nose into a tissue and nodded. "You're right. I think he meant well. He just had this terrible addiction to gambling, I guess. But why the hell couldn't he tell me about it? I mean, I knew he loved playing the lottery. I even went with him a few times to Suffolk Downs and to Rockingham for the races, but I never realized he was a compulsive gambler."

"He was ashamed. Admitting this to you would have meant he was . . . well, flawed. And Stephen was a very proud person. He was the doctor. The one to always fix things. People and situations. But this was something he couldn't fix. Not alone. And obviously, he never sought help for his addiction."

"Half of me misses him. You know, the physical presence of him. And the other half of me . . . hates him. I hate him for doing this to me. For leaving me completely alone and on my own." I felt the tears streaming down my face once again as Ali stood up and leaned over to put her arms around me.

Looking down at my face, she said, "We're going to get through this, Syd. It's just going to take time. Like everything else in life."

I enjoyed walking along Second Street in the downtown district. On a weekday, it was quiet with few vehicles or pedestrians. The weekends were when tourists flocked to the island for a respite from city life, but by Monday afternoons, the locals had their town back to themselves.

Lilly trotted along in front of me on her leash as I passed the Historical Museum and then stopped to browse in the corner bookstore. A brand-new release by Debbie Macomber was in the window, and I realized that spending twenty dollars for a book was something I'd never given a second thought to. Twenty dollars now had much more meaning for me. I paused in front of Pelican Realty to browse at photos of homes for sale.

Thinking of my house in Lexington brought a sick feeling to the pit of my stomach. Haven Isle Gift Shop caught my eye with an attractive display of stuffed animals, glass Victorian balls in vivid shades of blue, pink, and lilac, and brass wind chimes. I passed the Jiffy store, the post office, and city hall. And then I saw a sign that made my heart beat faster. HELP WANTED, it said on a piece of cardboard nailed to the post in front of Cook's Café. I took a deep breath and headed to an empty table at the outside patio area.

"I think we might be welcome here," I said to Lilly as she curled up under the table. That was one of the things I liked about this town. It was dog-friendly and outside establishments allowed well-behaved canines to visit.

When the waitress came out, I ordered coffee. Lighting up a cigarette, I glanced across the street to the empty shops and knew those were the ones that Ali had referred to.

"Here ya go, sweetie," the waitress said, placing coffee in front of me and a bowl of water down for Lilly.

"Thank you. I'm sure she appreciates that."

She bent down to pat Lilly and smiled. "She sure is cute. Visiting the island for the holiday?"

In the week I'd been with Ali, I hadn't given a thought that Thanksgiving was on Thursday. My first one in years without Stephen or Monica. My first one alone.

"Yeah, I guess you could say I am. I arrived last week from the Boston area and I'm staying with my friend, Alison Marks. You might know her. She owns the B and B."

The waitress put her hands on her hips and laughed. "I sure 'nuff do. Honey, you'll soon find out that everyone knows everyone on this island. Ain't no secrets here. And you must be Sydney. Alison told all of us 'bout you comin'."

I felt foolishly pleased. I'd lived in Lexington for thirty years and barely knew my next-door neighbors.

"Welcome to the island," she told me. "How long you stayin'?"

I laughed and wasn't used to such abrupt questions. "I really don't know. Maybe permanently. Actually, I need a job and I saw the sign you have looking for help. . . ."

"We sure 'nuff are. I'm Ida Mae," she said, extending her hand. "Me and my husband, Gus, we own this here place. My Gus though, he had a heart attack a few months ago and can't help as much as he used to. Needs to rest, the doctor told him. Rest? How on earth can ya rest when ya have a restaurant to run? Listen to me babbling on. What I need is somebody to open for me at seven o'clock four mornings a week . . . my other girl, she works the other days. So the hours are from seven till two. You'd cover the breakfast and lunch crowd. That would be twenty-eight hours

33

for the week. Nice crowd here too. Mostly locals. You have waitress experience, do ya?"

"Not in over thirty years," I said honestly. "But I'm a quick learn."

"I bet you are. Aw, there isn't much to waitressing. Let me get you an application," she said, heading back inside.

For the first time in weeks I felt a jolt of encouragement. Lifting my coffee cup to my lips, I realized that the woman sitting a few tables away was staring at me intently. At least I thought she was. It was difficult to tell with ebony-shaded glasses covering her eyes. Feeling under scrutiny, I lit up a cigarette and glanced away. But not before I noticed the outlandish outfit the woman was wearing. She appeared to be early seventies, but was valiantly attempting to look thirty. A large, straw crimson hat covered her head and clashed terribly with curly hair that was just this side of orange. Dangling from around the brim were small, white circular things that reminded me of cotton balls. The woman's purple elastic tube top would have been more suited on a younger girl and the tight capri-style pants, with the same dangling white balls down the side, brought a grin to my face. Completing the outfit were assorted gold bangle bracelets that clinked each time the woman took a drag off her cigarette.

Ida Mae returned with the promised application. "Here ya go, honey. You just fill this out and bring it inside when you're finished. Can I give you a call at Alison's place?"

I realized that I didn't even have a phone number to call my own. "Yes. That'll be fine and thank you."

I filled out the application without much hope. I didn't even have former job references to put down. Not unless you counted the hospital where I'd worked years before. I brought the paper inside and left it on the counter. When I unclipped Lilly's leash from the leg of the table and began to walk away, I swear I could feel the eyes behind the ebony glasses following me.

The sound of drills and hammers from across the street caused me to cross and take a peek inside. Contractors were working on a restoration, and I tugged on Lilly's leash to enter one of the empty shops. Long French doors at the corner space were open. I stood in the middle of the brick-walled room and saw tin buckets of paint, various carpentry tools, drop cloths, and ladders. Beyond seeing the construction, I visualized the space being turned into a quaint retail shop. Because of the restoration, it would have a definite Victorian ambiance. I walked over to run my hand along the original brick of the wall and was startled to hear Lilly growl at the same time I heard a male voice.

"Interested in renting some space here?"

Leaning down to quiet Lilly, I looked up to see a middle-aged man standing in the doorway. His height was slightly below the door frame. Wearing tan Dockers and an Irish knit pullover sweater, his curly silver hair contrasted in a pleasing way with the bronze of his tan. Mahogany eyes observed me.

"Oh, I don't think so," I mumbled. Had I ever seen a shade of brown eyes that deep?

His smile only increased his pleasant looks. "Well, that's good. Because I'm thinking of placing first dibs on this particular space. And I've never accepted competition well."

As I was trying to decide if the cockiness in his tone implied humor, he extended his hand.

"Noah Hale," he said.

"Sydney Webster," I replied, surprising myself by not wanting to release his grip.

After a moment, he let go, raising both arms to include the space. "So I don't have to worry about you stealing this from me?"

At that precise moment, I wasn't so sure. An idea had begun to form in my head at the same time I experienced that long-ago sensation when I worked in the emergency room—of being in control to make an important decision.

I ignored his question and asked one of my own. "Why would you want this space?"

"I'm an artist and returned from Key West last year to look after my mother. My family has lived on the island for five generations. I'm planning to open a gallery."

"An artist?" Somehow he struck me more as an outdoors-kind-of-person.

Noah shifted from one foot to the other. "Do you have something against artists?"

"Not at all," I replied, heading toward the door. "As long as they don't think being a native and an artist gets them superior treatment. See ya," I tossed over my shoulder, as I tugged on Lilly's leash and crossed the street.

"Noah Hale?" Ali repeated, as we finished up dinner.

I had explained my afternoon encounter with him. "Yeah. Why? Do you know him?"

"Not personally, but I know *of* him and Paul kind of hangs out with him when he's here visiting."

"Hmm. Well, he seems a bit arrogant to me. Just his tone of voice and implying that I'd better not even think of renting that space because he wants it."

"His family has been here on the island since the eighteen eighties. You know that huge, gorgeous house on the corner of Fourth and F Street? It's called the Hale-Johnson House. He lives there with his mother."

I got up to help Ali clear the table and begin the dishes. "Still lives at home with mom? Is he gay?"

Ali laughed. "I doubt that very much. In case you failed to notice, he's pretty damn hot. Very good looking and I'd say Cedar Key's most eli-gible bachelor."

"He's never been married?"

Ali placed dishes into the sudsy water. "I'm not certain, but I heard rumors that he was married years ago. To a French girl. That was when he was painting and teaching in Paris."

When I remained silent, Ali said, "So . . . are you interested?"

"In Noah Hale? Don't be ridiculous."

Ali looked at me with raised eyebrows. "Actually, I was referring to being interested in the retail space."

It's for you," Ali said, passing me the phone.

Expecting to hear Monica's voice (who else would call me?), I was surprised to hear a Southern drawl.

"Hey, there, sweetie. Ida Mae here. I have your application and I'd like to hire you."

"Me?" I replied, stupidly.

I heard Ida Mae's laughter come across the line.

"Sure. You. I think you'd be reliable and dependable. Not like those teenagers who say they want to work and then lounge around. So . . . tomorrow's Thanksgiving. That means a very busy weekend. Could you start on Friday? And your days would be Friday, Saturday, Monday, and Tuesday? This way you'll have two pretty busy days and then two slower ones. How would that be?"

Be? I never thought I'd be so excited to gain employment as a waitress. We discussed salary, and I was surprised to hear she'd be paying me a little more than minimum wage, plus my tips, of course.

I clicked to disconnect the phone, grabbed Ali, and proceeded to dance her around the kitchen, both of us giggling and laughing like we used to in college.

"I take it you got the job?" she teased.

"Can you believe it?"

Slowing down to catch her breath, she said, "Of course I can believe it. You have a lot to offer in any position, Syd. Believe in yourself."

I felt good. The best I'd felt in months. "Here," I said, sitting her down at the table. "Let me practice and pour you some sweet tea."

Just as I'd placed the glass in front of her, the phone rang again. My confidence evaporated as I prayed it wasn't Ida Mae changing her mind.

"Monica," Ali said, passing the phone to me again.

"Hey, sweetie," I said, feeling more positive than I had in ages. "Guess what?"

"You're coming back up here?"

Why couldn't that girl get it through her head that *up there* was a dead end for me? "No, I'm not. But . . . I did get myself a job today. I'll be a waitress at Cook's Café downtown. Four days a week."

"Oh, God, Mom. Are you serious? Doing waitress work at your age? What about your bad leg veins? How the heck are you going to stand on your feet for hours, carting heavy trays?"

I have to admit . . . my daughter certainly had a way of bursting my bubble. "My age? Christ, Monica, I'm hardly ready for a nursing home. I'm still ten years away from Social Security. No, it won't be easy. But I have to do something for income." I found myself apologizing to my daughter. For what, I wondered.

"Well, I didn't mean to imply you're over the hill, but . . . whatever. I just wanted to call and wish you a Happy Thanksgiving a day early. Jen and I are heading out tomorrow morning for the White Mountains. They've had snow and the skiing should be good."

"You and Jen? Aren't you spending Thanksgiving with Russ?" My daughter had been dating the Boston attorney for almost a year. He'd written a book and they'd met at a party the publishing company she worked for had given.

There was a brief silence and then she said, "Russ and I are finished."

That was it. No explanation. Nothing.

"Oh," I replied, not knowing what else to say.

"Right. So anyway, have a good day tomorrow.

I'll be back on Sunday, so I'll touch base with you next week."

I hung up the phone, looked at Ali and shook my head. "I don't know what it is about Monica and me. We got along so well when she was younger. But lately . . . we're like oil and water."

"Is she giving you a hassle again?"

"I think it's safe to say she's not enthused at all about her mom working as a waitress. Probably ashamed. And I just found out that she and Russ are over. I don't understand that either. She gets into, what seems like, serious relationships and then before a year has passed, they're history."

"Well, she's twenty-six and still has plenty of time to find Mr. Right. Girls today stay single much longer than we did."

"Hmm, true. She might not be happy for me, but I'm going to take Lilly and go for a nice walk downtown to the beach to celebrate getting back into the work force."

"Good for you. I think you'll enjoy working at Cook's. Ida Mae's from another family that's been here forever on the island. Some of the people you'll meet will be a bit quirky, but they're good people, and I think you'll enjoy them."

"Speaking of quirky," I said and proceeded to tell Ali about the woman with the dark glasses I'd encountered the day before.

Alison laughed. "Oh, yeah. That would be Sybile. Sybile Bowden—a real character. Lived here all her life. Rumor has it that she left the island at age eighteen for the big lights of New York City. But after a very lucrative divorce settlement, she came back. The prodigal daughter, I guess."

"Was she an actress?"

"Into modeling, I think. I'm not really sure. She keeps pretty much to herself. Has a sister here on the island, but they're like night and day. You'd never know they were sisters. Sybile lives in a very unusual home—the Lighthouse. It's on Rye Key. I think when it comes to marching to the beat of a different drummer, Sybile has me beat by miles."

Based on what I'd observed the day before, I had to admit Alison was probably right.

Unlike the cold and gloomy New England Novembers, afternoons on the island were perfect for walking and soaking up the semi-tropical climate. I stood on the bridge heading to Dock Street and paused to watch airboats cruising out from the marina into the Gulf. Their loud motors reverberated through the otherwise silent air. Mullet jumped in the water below and further away, I could make out the silver fins of dolphin jumping. Yeah, each day it was becoming easier to see what drew Ali to this place.

Walking along Dock Street, I ended up at City Park and the beach. Unclipping Lilly's leash to let her run, I went to sit on a bench and sip my afternoon coffee. The yipping of a small poodle drew my attention to an elderly man entering the park. He raised a hand in greeting as he took the bench next to me and his dog ran off to play with Lilly.

"Beautiful afternoon isn't it?" he said.

I nodded. "It sure is. Coming from New England it's hard to believe that tomorrow's Thanksgiving."

"You visiting here?" the man inquired.

"An extended visit, you might say. My friend Alison owns the B and B, and I'm staying with her."

The man turned to face me. His baseball cap stated he was a member of Eagles Aerie 424 and his T-shirt, suspenders, and baggy pants reminded me of Jeb on *The Beverly Hillbillies*. A weather-beaten face showed too many years of sun and caused deep furrows in his forehead and cheeks. But these features faded when he smiled.

Extending his hand to accompany a grin, he said, "Why, I know who you are. Yup, you're that friend of Ali's she said was comin' from the Boston area. Nice to meet ya, ma'am. I'm Saren. Saren Ghetti."

I accepted his handshake and laughed. "Are you serious? That's really your name? Like the Serengeti Plain?"

He joined my laughter. "Yup. My mama and daddy, they thought if they gave me a different kinda name, I'd go on to do great things in the world."

I couldn't resist. "And did you?"

"Well, now, that depends what ya think great things are. I'm an artist. Nah, not as great as Picasso or Monet, but I've gotten by. Sold a lot of paintings around the world over the years." He nodded his head emphatically. "All those sales have provided for me in my old age. So I guess I did okay."

I detected a resiliency in the man's demeanor. "Do you still paint?"

Saren removed his cap, scratching his head before replying. "Yeah, guess ya could say I do. But not as much. The old fingers don't work like they used to. Damn arthritis tightens them up."

I glanced at his hands that were twisted with swollen joints.

"But ya gotta keep movin'. What's that they say? If ya don't use it, ya lose it. Well, I don't intend to lose it. I turn eighty-two on my next birthday and I say life is what ya make of it."

Good philosophy. The man obviously took the bad with the good. "Cute little dog," I said, watching the black poodle dash into the water to catch Lilly.

"Ah, that's my Aggie. Me and her, we go way back. She's fourteen. Never know it though, would ya? That's 'cuz I keep her as active as I am. We walk three times a day. Don't know what

I'd do without my Aggie. She's my best friend."

The simplicity of his words touched me. "All of your love for her shows. She looks great."

Saren waved his hand to somebody in back of me and I turned to see the strange woman with the sunglasses walking past the park.

"Hi, Saren," she called in greeting and kept walking.

Today she was wearing bright orange slacks, an orange tank top, and spangled wedge-heel sandals. A white bandana with orange polka dots covered her head. I could see she did have an enviable figure for an older woman.

Saren nodded toward the departing figure. "Have ya met Miss High and Mighty yet? Thinks she's queen of the island, she does. Ain't no better than the rest of us, but she doesn't know that. Comes back here a failure and thinks she's a celebrity."

"I saw her at Cook's the other day. Alison said she left the island years ago to become a model."

Saren pursed his lips and grunted. "She wasn't no Christie Brinkley, that's for sure. I don't know what all she did up there in that fancy town, but if it was so great, what'd she come back here for? Probably to bury her secrets, that's what I say. She only speaks to me when she has a mind to."

I was beginning to realize that fishing wasn't the only pastime on the island. Gossip flowed as easily as the water.

Saren stood up and whistled. The poodle came running without hesitation. "This here is Miss Aggie."

I leaned over and let the dog sniff my hand. "Well, you sure are cute and it looks like my Lilly has found herself another new friend."

"Sure 'nuff she has and we'll see you tomorrow for dinner. You take care," he said, walking away with the poodle close at his heels.

I remembered that Alison had said she'd be cooking for five other people, but was surprised that Saren Ghetti was to be one of the guests. I smiled as it occurred to me that the dinner conversation would probably be pretty lively.

5

When I returned to the B&B, I found Ali surrounded by bowls, pots and pans, and pie plates in the kitchen.

"Geez, Ali, I had no idea you were such a Martha Stewart. Can I help?"

She swiped a stray piece of hair from her face with her forearm. "Not at the moment you can't. But don't worry, I'll keep you busy tomorrow morning setting the table and assorted chores."

Four pies sat lined up on the counter ready to go into the oven. Bowls of sweet potato and green bean casserole were on the table.

"There, that'll take care of ole Tom," Ali said, as

she finished filling the cavity with cornbread stuffing. "I like to get as much done the day before, then we can all enjoy tomorrow."

"I met one of the guests at the beach. Saren Ghetti. He seems really sweet."

"Yup, Saren's the salt of the earth. He's somebody that could tell you all about this island. Born and raised here. Left during his mid-thirties to pursue his painting career, but by the time he was fifty, the island drew him back like a magnet."

"Who else will be here tomorrow?"

Wiping her hands on her apron, Alison took a deep breath. "Ah, let's see. It sometimes changes from year to year. But I think tomorrow I have Saren, Miss Dora, Miss Polly, and Officer Bob coming. Lots of people on the island have no family or anywhere to go on the holidays, so most of us put out an invitation. Miss Dora is Sybile's sister and for some strange reason, Sybile called a little while ago and canceled. But she's an odd duck, so I'm not going to worry about it. Miss Polly owns the hair salon on the island and lives alone. Same with Officer Bob. Never married and no family. And you met Saren."

"I'm looking forward to meeting all of them," I said, pouring myself a cup of coffee. "I think it'll be fun. I'll be outside spinning the rest of Winston's fur. Did you manage to brush him and get any more?"

"Yup and I did what you said and put it into the plastic bag. It's on the porch table."

I began spinning the fur and the thought occurred to me this would be the first time in over thirty years I wouldn't be preparing Thanksgiving dinner. When Monica was a baby, we had my parents to our house and I did the cooking. It became our tradition. I also realized that for the first time since leaving high school I had no plan—no direction, no commitments and, except for Lilly, no responsibility. It was both frightening and exciting.

Worrying about lack of money was the scary part, but finding the job at Cook's helped me to feel a little better. The possibility of discovering *me* was exciting though. Ali had been right. I'd never had a chance to be alone and figure out that in addition to being a daughter, a wife, and a mother, I was a woman. Somehow my own identity had been squashed as I took on the roles expected of me. I had listed myself on the A.L.M.A. Web site and wondered if I'd ever be contacted by a woman thinking I could be her daughter.

I continued to spin Winston's fur and thought it might be fun to own my own business. I was an expert knitter. For years I'd taught girlfriends how to knit and suggested different patterns and yarns. It would be fun to be doing this and actually pull in a salary.

My mind wandered to the retail space downtown. I probably had enough in my bank account to put a deposit on it. But I didn't even know if a knitting shop would be a lucrative business in such a small town. Ali had mentioned I should pay a visit to the bank and speak with Dorothy. She could give me some tips and suggestions about opening a shop. I decided that after I finished my first shift at Cook's on Friday that was exactly what I'd do.

I wondered about Noah Hale. Although I wouldn't admit it to Ali, he *was* pretty damn good looking. I smiled, trying to recall the last time I'd thought that about a man. Other than a TV or movie star. Momentarily, I felt ashamed thinking such thoughts less than two months after losing Stephen. Well, not to worry, I thought. He may have been quite handsome, but I'm not sure I cared for his attitude. Besides, a man was certainly the last thing I needed in my life.

Polly Tyburn was the first to arrive at the B&B for Thanksgiving dinner.

"Yoohoo," she hollered, entering the hallway off the kitchen. "Anybody here?"

"Just us turkeys," Alison called out while checking the oven temperature.

Laughing, Polly placed a bowl on the table. "I made my special cranberry chutney," she said, walking over to give Alison a hug. "Happy Thanksgiving."

"And to you. Thanks for your contribution. You make the best on the island."

"You must be Sydney," Polly said. Her eyes squinted, as she adjusted her glasses for a better look. "Welcome to Cedar Key."

"Thank you."

Polly was a petite woman, barely five feet tall. She appeared to be late sixties and had brunette curls framing her face.

Leaning closer, she stared into my almond-shaped brown eyes, making me feel a bit awkward.

"You look familiar to me. Have we met before?"

"I don't think so, but I've been here over a week. You may have seen me around town."

"Hmm, could be. Well, welcome again. I hope you'll like it here."

The woman then reached to finger my hair, which I'd pulled back into a limp ponytail.

"Oh, my. You could really use a good conditioner, and a cut would add wonders to your looks."

I was shocked by the woman's candor, and my hand went protectively to my hair.

"Honey, you come see me tomorrow. We'll get you all fixed up. A widow today has to do everything possible to snag herself a new man. Lord knows there's enough competition out there. Look at me—my Harold's been gone ten years and I'm still alone."

A man was the last thing on my mind. How dare she insinuate I was looking for a replacement? Unsure whether to laugh or be offended, I stood there mute.

"Lighten up on her, Polly." Alison grinned. "But if you do want a makeover, Syd, Polly's the one to see. She can work miracles with a pair of scissors. Not that I'm a very good advertisement for her."

"Happy Thanksgiving," a male voice called from the porch.

"Officer Bob, come on in," Alison hollered.

I had questioned the informality of calling a police officer by his first name when Ali told me he was coming to dinner. That was unheard of in New England, but Ali assured me that in the South, it was quite common. I turned to see a heavyset man in a police uniform walk into the kitchen carrying a beautiful bouquet of orange mums.

"For the chef," he said, handing them to Ali.

"Thank you so much," she told him. "They'll look lovely on the table. Bob, meet my best friend, Sydney."

"Nice to meet ya," he said, extending a large, calloused hand.

"Same here," I replied, thinking the man was a dead ringer for Ernest Borgnine.

"I hope you'll enjoy your stay on the island, and if you need anything at all, why you just let me know. I'd be happy to help you."

His sincerity came through in his words. "That's very nice of you," I told him. "Thanks."

Alison was pouring apple cider into glasses arranged on a tray. "Do me a favor, Syd. Take this out to the porch. Dinner will be ready in about forty-five minutes, so we'll have some cider first."

Placing the tray on the table, I glanced up to see an older woman coming down the walkway. Silver hair was pulled back into a fashionable chignon. Wearing a two-piece beige pantsuit, she carried herself with an air of elegance.

Walking up the steps, the woman's eyes met mine, but she didn't speak.

"I bet you're Miss Dora," I said, smiling.

For a fraction of a second, the woman scrutinized my face before replying.

Clearing her throat, she nodded. "Yes. Yes, I am. I'm Eudora Foster and you must be Sydney." Her hand flew to her hair smoothing stray pieces from her chignon.

"Yes, I'm Alison's friend. Happy Thanksgiving. Would you like a glass of cider?"

"That would be very nice. Thank you," she said, as the rest of the crowd filtered out onto the porch.

"Ah, Miss Dora, welcome." Alison greeted the

woman with a hug. "Is that your famous squash pie?"

"It is," Dora said, not taking her eyes from mine as she passed the covered plate to Ali.

"Thank you. I'll put it in the fridge. Hey, Saren, just in time for cider."

The elderly man nodded to everyone. I noticed that the baseball cap from the day before was missing and strands of white hair covered his head. In place of the T-shirt was a crisp blue-and-white striped shirt, but the suspenders remained.

"Some of my mullet dip," he said, passing the bowl to Alison.

"Saren still goes fishing almost every day," Ali explained to me. "And his mullet dip is to die for. I'll get some crackers and we'll have some with the cider."

I finished handing out the glasses and pulled up a chair with the guests.

"Are you planning to stay on the island long?" Dora questioned.

"I'm not really sure what I'm doing yet. Alison was kind enough to extend an open-ended invitation."

"I see," Dora said, continuing to inspect my face. "Where is it that you're from? The Boston area?"

I nodded. "I grew up in Concord, northwest of Boston, but when I married, I moved to Lexington, which is nearby."

"I'm sorry to hear that your husband passed away," Dora told me. "Please accept my condolences."

"Oh, I remember Lexington from history classes," Polly said with pride. "The battle of Lexington and Concord."

"Yeah, we have a lot of history in that area."

"And your family?" Dora questioned. "They're still living there?"

"My parents passed away and I'm an only child. I have a daughter, Monica, that lives in Boston. Do you have children?"

"I do. I also have one daughter, Marin. She's married and lives in Gainesville. She and Andrew have two grown sons. They spend Thanksgiving with Andrew's family in South Carolina and come here for Christmas."

"That makes it nice to share the holidays. I was sorry to hear your sister couldn't make it today."

"Oh, you've met Sybile?" Dora seemed surprised.

"Well, no, not formally. But I've seen her a couple times and people told me her name."

Alison joined us and passed around a plate with mullet dip and crackers. "Yeah, what happened to Sybile today, Dora? Isn't she feeling well?"

"Nothing serious. A bit under the weather with a cold."

"That turkey sure smells good, Miss Ali," Officer Bob said.

"And there's plenty of it, so I hope you're hungry."

"Anyone know what's to become of those restored shops downtown?" Polly questioned.

"From what I hear, Noah Hale's interested in renting one of them," Saren said with excitement.

I had a feeling he enjoyed being the first to spread any island news.

"Hate to burst your bubble, Saren," Ali told him, "but we already knew that. Syd was downtown and ran into him at the corner shop."

"Well, that's nice," Polly said. "This place has always been a selling point for artists and writers. Seems they get what they call 'inspiration' here."

"I can understand that," I said, biting into a cracker. "It's really beautiful."

It didn't escape me that Dora remained silent.

Officer Bob reached for another cracker, popping it into his mouth. "How's Miss Elly these days, Saren?"

The elderly man's face lit up with pleasure. "Fine, just fine. Thank you for asking. I told her I'd be home by evening so we can have our cognac together."

Now I was confused. I thought Saren Ghetti had no family and lived alone. "You have a wife?" I asked.

My question was followed with Polly clearing her throat, while an expression of embarrassment crossed Bob's face.

"Saren has a live-in ghost," Alison explained to me, like it was the most natural thing in the world. "Miss Elly has been with Saren for over thirty years."

The man's face flushed like a schoolboy and he nodded his head. "Yup, that's right. I couldn't believe it myself the first time I saw her. There I was, sitting in my parlor enjoying a cigar and cognac and Miss Elly walked into the room. Dressed in one of those long, frilly, old-fashioned dresses she was. And a more beautiful sight, I'd never seen. Wears her dark hair all piled up on top of her head. She's a vision, she is. Told me I wasn't much of a gentleman not offering her a bit of cognac. So I jumped up to get her a glass and since that night, she joins me every evening." He smiled fondly as if just the thought of her brought him pleasure.

I stifled a giggle. Surely, he was kidding. Wasn't he? But nobody in the group was disputing his story. "Do you talk with her?" I asked, unsure what to say.

"Oh my, yes. We have delightful conversations. Now you're probably thinking I'm a crazy old man, 'cuz that's what I thought at first too. Thought maybe I was gettin' one of those mind problems old people get, 'cept I was only in my fifties when she first paid me a visit. It's all pretty simple to understand. See, Miss Elly, she was married to a fisherman, and they lived in the house that my family bought in the thirties. Her husband, that would be Mr. Cecil, he drowned at sea. Never did find his body. Miss Elly died shortly after. The town said she died of a broken heart. You believe in that sorta thing?"

My marriage to Stephen had probably been as satisfying as most other couples. Certainly not any more so. When I recalled stories like *The Notebook,* where Nicholas Sparks weaved a love story of passion that was ageless, my relationship paled in comparison.

I felt uncomfortable with Saren's question, but managed to say, "Well, yes, I imagine that could happen."

"Darn right it can. Ya meet that one great love of your life and nothing else equals."

I wondered if he was speaking from experience. "But then why hasn't Miss Elly gone on to join him?"

"Well, that's the strange part. She's stuck *between.* Says because Cecil's body was never found, he could still be here on the island. So I guess she's still lookin' for him, but she comes every evening to sit and keep me company."

Alison was right. The island had its fair share of eccentrics.

"Okay, everyone, dinner is about to be served. So bring your appetite and find a place at the table," Alison told us, heading to the kitchen.

"I'll help you carry things out," I offered,

grateful to get off the subject of Miss Elly. "Is he for real?" I whispered.

Alison laughed as she placed the turkey on a platter. "He's very much real. Can't prove it by me that Miss Elly doesn't visit him. Sometimes a little belief goes a long way," she said, shrugging her shoulders.

"But everyone out there acts like she's real too—well, like she's a ghost."

"We don't know that she isn't. There's a lot of good energy on this island—some souls might not ever wanna leave. You've always been too cynical. Get those bowls and let's get this feast on the table."

Surrounded by my best friend and new acquaintances, I clasped Polly's and Dora's hand as Alison said grace.

"Lord, thank you for another beautiful day on Cedar Key. Thank you for all that you've given us and thank you for the wonderful friends that grace my table."

"Amen," we all said in unison.

I had survived my first week as a gainfully employed woman. Sure, my legs ached from all the walking and carrying trays of food. And I had to admit, it was pretty menial work, but I felt good with a sense of accomplishment. Making it enjoyable were the customers—mostly locals, all of whom were friendly. But even the tourists were chatty and appeared happy just to be on the island visiting.

Stepping on the bathroom scale, I was thrilled to discover I'd lost five pounds since arriving in Cedar Key. Even workouts at the gym in Lexington hadn't brought about the loss of weight I'd hoped for.

I looked into the bathroom mirror and frowned. "God, maybe Polly was right. I'm a mess," I said, pulling my hands through hair that refused to do anything but droop like wilted flowers.

Lilly was sitting in the doorway, staring up at me with furrowed brow.

"I've managed to lose five pounds," I told her. "Maybe it's time for a new hairstyle."

After pouring myself a cup of coffee, I wondered if Polly could squeeze me in. It was my day off and I had no plans.

"Come on, girl," I told Lilly. "We'll phone her and find out."

Polly confirmed a 2:00 appointment for me.

Walking to the salon along Third Street, I was still grinning at the name of the shop—Curl Up and Dye. I hoped that Polly Tyburn showed the same creativity with styling hair as she did with words.

Opening the door, I noticed that the buzz of chatter ceased as I stepped inside.

Polly was putting the finishing touches on an older woman's hair. The silver bouffant style was similar to what my mother had worn in the fifties, and I wondered if perhaps I'd made a mistake booking with Polly.

"Come on in, sweetie," she told me. "I'll just be a sec. Hey, everyone, this is Sydney. Alison's friend from Boston."

Murmurs of hello accompanied smiles as everyone looked me up and down.

Feeling like I was on display, I nodded and slipped into a chair. Glancing around, I saw that even the shampoo bowl and dryers had a vintage look. God, I'll probably walk out of here looking like Little Orphan Annie.

A few minutes later I was enjoying the most relaxing and invigorating shampoo I could remember. I recalled the high-priced salon I had frequented before Stephen died and thought that shampoo girl could take a lesson from Polly.

Following twenty minutes with conditioners on my hair, I sat in front of the mirror as Polly stood with her head cocked this way and that. Finger to chin, she pursed her lips and then nodded her head. "Yup, I think I know what will look great on you."

Deciding to leave the fate of my hair in Polly's hands—literally—I sat back and took a deep breath.

One hour later I peered into the mirror with a

huge smile on my face. "My God, Polly. I look fabulous."

"Told ya you needed a change."

Turning my head from side to side, I couldn't believe I was the same woman who had walked into the salon earlier. Gone was the limp ponytail and in its place was a chic cut—chin length, it was swept behind my ears with long bangs covering my forehead. I swear Polly had removed ten years.

Feeling embarrassed for my prior anxiety, I said, "Polly, I can't thank you enough. I just love it."

"Thought ya would. Next time you might want to consider some foil. You know, a few highlights here and there to brighten it up a bit more."

This woman walked on water as far as I was concerned. "I think you're right. We'll do it."

Walking from the salon to the post office, I couldn't resist catching my image in each shop window I passed. Amazing what a new hairdo can do for a woman.

"Hey, Miss Sydney," the postmaster greeted me. "I almost didn't recognize you. Very nice."

"Thanks, Sam. I kinda like it myself."

"Have a big package for you in the back. Hold on a second and I'll get it."

I looked around the small post office. All of my life mail had been delivered to my front door, but

61

I loved coming here to pick up mail from the numbered box. It had a small-town feel to it which was beginning to grow on me.

"Have ya got the golf cart with you? It's pretty hefty to walk with," Sam said, putting a good size carton on the counter.

Glancing at the postmark, I saw the return address of Lucille Graystone in Connecticut. "Hmm, I think you're right. I'll have to go back to the B and B to get the cart. This is the dog fur."

"Dog fur?" Sam questioned, scratching his head in bewilderment.

"Yeah, dog fur. I'll be back in a little while." I chuckled, leaving Sam to ponder the contents.

Walking out of the post office, I figured it wouldn't be long before Sam would add me to the list of quirky island residents.

The following Monday I was doing my shift at Cook's when I heard a male voice behind me say, "Well, I guess you changed your mind."

I turned around to see Noah Hale sitting at one of the outside tables. "Excuse me?" I questioned.

"Since you're now working here, I guess you changed your mind about renting the space across the street."

Damn, but this guy was good looking. Wearing jeans and a T-shirt with *And Your Point Is?* across the front, he had a youthful appearance. Which made me wonder how old he was. Late fifties?

"Don't be too sure of that," I shot back. "What can I get you?"

"Hmm, a woman of few words." He chuckled and then said, "I'll have the meatloaf special."

As I was scribbling the words on my pad, I could feel him staring up at me. "Anything to drink?"

"Sweet tea, please. Hey, I know why you look different today. Did something with your hair. Looks nice. I like it."

My hand trembled and I could feel heat creeping up my neck. Damn. Another hot flash at a most inopportune moment. In thirty years of marriage to Stephen, I couldn't recall one single time he'd commented on my hair. Good, bad, or indifferent.

"Thanks," I mumbled, feeling like a flustered high school girl. "I'll get your order in."

I laid the slip of paper on the shelf for the cook, and then peeked through the window. Noah had opened up a newspaper. Putting on a pair of small glasses, he began to read. I wasn't sure if I was more disturbed over the fact that he'd scrutinized me close enough to notice a change in hairstyle or that it felt oddly reminiscent of flirting.

I managed to busy myself with other customers until Noah's meal was ready. Setting it in front of him, I started to walk away.

"Hey," he called. "Come on, you can tell me if you're still interested in that space. I won't say anything."

"Are *you* still interested in it?" I asked.

He shrugged his shoulders. "I'm not sure. I think it would be perfect for a studio with all the windows for lighting. But I was up in St. Augustine recently and found a great shop for lease there too."

"Oh, so you'll be leaving the island?" Why did this matter to me? I wondered.

"Well, that's just it. I love this place. I left years ago for college and then came back. Then I left again in my late twenties. That time I was gone about thirty years—to Paris."

He paused, waiting for my reaction, I guess. I recalled that Ali had mentioned that to me and I remained silent.

Stirring his tea, he said, "So, I don't know. I think at sixty-two, my roots are now firmly planted here."

Sixty-two? He didn't look his age. "Then it seems you're the one that will be taking the lease on that space."

"If you were to open a shop there, what type of business are you considering?"

I smiled. "A tattoo parlor," I said and walked away laughing. For the first time in a long time, it felt good to laugh.

Rummaging through the fridge in Ali's kitchen, I found the bottle of chardonnay I'd purchased a few days earlier. Pouring myself a glass, I went to sit in the garden with my feet up. Another seven-hour shift behind me and on Friday, I'd be receiving my first paycheck in years. My tips were adequate, but all of it was a far cry from the financial freedom I was used to.

Taking a sip of wine, I thought about my meeting with Dorothy at the bank. She'd told me that just a knitting shop probably wasn't a great venture for a small town. But since I was going to specialize in spinning dog and cat fur, she thought it had a lot of potential. She advised me to get a computer, set up a Web site, and begin doing mail orders via the Internet. She felt that like most businesses on the island, my weekends would bring in tourists and also day-trippers from Gainesville and nearby towns. Dorothy also explained that I could apply for an American Express Small Business Card and that would enable me to order some stock and begin selling yarn and accessories right away. Hopefully, I'd make enough to pay the monthly installment charge the card required.

God, who would have thought I'd be starting over like this at fifty-two? I felt a wave of nausea at the same time a throbbing began in my right temple. All of the stress of the past few months seemed to hit me full force. I'm financially insecure, I have a mediocre relationship with my daughter, and I have a solitary future ahead of me.

I glanced up to see Eudora Foster crossing the garden toward me.

"I really hate to bother you," she said, clutching a canvas tote bag. "But Ali told me you were an expert knitter. I have a bit of a problem with this sweater I'm working on. I wonder if you could help me?"

"Sure, have a seat," I said, gesturing to the chair beside me. "Let's see what you have there."

Dora removed a professional piece of work from her bag. "It's these instructions here," she said, pointing to a paragraph in her knitting book.

I had a strong suspicion the knitting wasn't what brought her to speak to me. But I looked it over and explained the stitches to her, and then waited to see what else she had to say.

"So you're enjoying it here on the island? How's your job at Cook's going?"

"I like it here a lot. It's certainly different from living in a much larger town. And yes, I really enjoy working at Cook's and meeting all the locals. But I won't lie, being a waitress was much easier on the body when I was in college. Doing physical work at my age, when you're not used to it, can be exhausting."

"Oh, you're still very young," Dora said. "I bet you're about the same age as my Marin. When were you born?"

"March of 1955."

Dora nodded. "Yes, I was right. Marin was born in 1957, so there's just two years' difference."

She seemed to think about this for a few minutes and then asked, "You were born in Boston, right?"

"Actually, no. I was born in New York City." I had a feeling this was pertinent information for Dora. "I was adopted as an infant," I added.

She was inordinately interested in my birth. "Why are you so interested in when and where I was born?"

Dora shifted in her chair, looking uncomfortable. "How rude of me. I'm sorry to be so inquisitive. I hope you'll forgive me," she said, standing up. "Thank you so much for helping me with the knitting. I really appreciate it. And Ali tells me you might be opening a shop downtown. I can assure you, I'll be your first and best customer."

I smiled. "Thank you," I said, as she walked away.

Is she just another quirky resident on this island? I wondered. *Or was there much more to that conversation?*

That does seem a bit odd that Dora asked so many questions," Ali said a few nights later. "I've never known her to be a nosy person."

"So, what do you make of it?" I asked, and took a bite of my juicy apple.

"I'm not sure."

"Maybe it's an island thing. People just naturally ask a lot of personal questions?"

Ali laughed. "Could be. I know when gossip spreads around here, they refer to it as the coconut pipeline."

Living in a small town was definitely different from one with more than thirty thousand people. I realized that I'd been here less than a month and already many people knew who I was. I did enjoy the feeling of welcome it gave me though, to be walking down the street and have somebody wave to me. Reminded me of the TV series, *Cheers,* where everybody knew your name.

"Heard anything from the adoption Web site?" Ali asked.

"Not a thing. I checked again this morning. It's highly doubtful I'll ever find out any information."

"Don't be so sure of that. Give it time."

I took another bite of my apple. "So is Paul arriving tomorrow? I'll finally get to meet him?"

Ali smiled. "Yes. He should get here around six tomorrow evening."

"How long will he be staying?"

"He's never sure, but I penciled him in for a month."

"Penciled him in? He stays in the main house?"

"Yeah, we both still kinda like our space. But trust me, he wakes up in my bed most mornings. By the way, the couple in the Tree House—

they're checking out earlier than they planned. The day after Christmas, rather than January. So you can move in there when they leave."

"Oh, no, Ali. Really. You could rent that again and right now, I couldn't afford to pay you very much."

"Don't be silly. I want you there. It'll be so much nicer for you and Lilly. So that's the end of it—be prepared to move within a few weeks."

Damn this menopause. Emotion gripped me again as I felt tears forming in my eyes. "Ali, I don't know how to thank you. You're truly the best friend a woman could have."

"Nonsense," she said, reaching over to pat my hand. "I'm just being selfish. I love having you here with me."

A few days later, I walked outside at Cook's to collect dirty dishes and was surprised to see Sybile Bowden taking a seat. It looked like I was finally going to meet the mysterious woman. Walking to her table, I smiled. "Can I help you?" I asked in a friendly tone.

Without removing her sunglasses, she glanced up at me. "Well, I imagine you can, since you're the waitress here."

When she neglected to say any more, I asked, "What would you like?"

"Two eggs, boiled for three and a half minutes. One slice of toast. Dark, but not charred. Do not bring me any butter, because I won't use it. If the coffee has been brewed within the past thirty minutes, I'll have a cup. Otherwise, forget it."

I couldn't help but feel she rattled off her order like she was a customer at the Ritz-Carlton. When I neglected to move, she glared up at me, sunglasses still on.

"Well?" she demanded. "Get to it."

What a nasty woman. It was impossible to believe that she was Eudora's sister.

I walked inside the restaurant shaking my head. Sandy, the cook, saw the look on my face and bent down to peer out the window.

"Oh, we should be honored. Miss Sybile has decided to grace us with her presence."

When I attempted to pass her the order slip, Sandy shook her hand in the air.

"I know exactly what she wants. She never deviates."

"Not very friendly, is she?"

"Nope. That woman has an attitude with a capital A."

"Wonder why she's so miserable?"

"Have no idea," Sandy said, preparing to boil the eggs. "Never known her to be any different. My mom tells me Sybile left this island years ago and came back a changed person. And not for the good."

"Interesting," I said, going to tend to my other customers.

When I placed the meal in front of Sybile, I didn't even get a thank-you. So she's not only unfriendly, she's rude.

After she'd finished eating, I put the check beside her and was about to walk away.

"Hold on there," she hollered after me.

"Did you want something else?"

"I hear you're a friend of Alison's and staying at the B and B. Planning to be in town long?"

I was beginning to find it amusing that complete strangers were so interested in my comings and goings. "Probably," I said, refusing to share my plans with her. But it seemed she'd already gotten wind of that coconut pipeline.

"I hear you might be opening a knitting shop. And that you do something with dog and cat fur. Does the Humane Society know about this?"

Who the hell did this woman think she was? Obviously, she didn't know a thing about spinning fiber, and she was making me feel like an animal abuser.

"It's perfectly legal to spin pet fur. It doesn't injure them at all. Collecting excess fur that would be thrown away doesn't harm dogs or cats."

She made a sound that resembled a snarl. "Well, it doesn't sound right to me. And I can tell ya right now—if you think a business like that would be successful here, you've got another thought comin'."

What a nerve. I hadn't asked for this woman's opinion and here she was knocking me down before I even started. Damn her. I was sensitive enough right now and didn't need her adding to my problems.

Removing her glasses and staring up at me she said, "Well, just don't say I didn't warn you."

She sniffed and replaced her sunglasses, but not before I had the distinct feeling we'd already met.

Had I not been waiting on her as a customer, I would've had some choice words to fling back. But instead, I said, "Guess we'll see what happens," and I walked back inside.

"Oh, yeah, Sybile can be a bitch," Ali related to me. "But don't let her get to you. Sometimes I wonder how poor Miss Dora puts up with her. She seems to carry sisterly love to a whole new level."

I nodded. "Yeah, why would Dora put up with such behavior?"

"Have no clue, but . . . Now, I know you won't say anything, but somebody mentioned to me that they saw Dora and Sybile at the Medical Center in Gainesville last month."

"So you're saying she's ill?"

Ali pursed her lips. "I really don't know, but I guess that would explain why Dora seems to cater to her. Sybile has always acted like a prima donna. But she's gotten worse this past year."

"Is Dora her only relative? Sybile never had children?"

Ali paused for a moment before answering. "God, I feel like a guest on *The Jerry Springer Show*. I don't enjoy gossip, but I know what I tell you won't go further. Although, most of the town probably knows this rumor."

"What is it?" I asked with curiosity.

"I'd heard from a number of different people that Sybile did have a child years ago. But nobody knows for certain what happened. If the child died or she gave it up for adoption . . . or what."

The word *adoption* jumped out at me. "How the heck would anybody know something so personal? You mean it happened here when she was a teenager?"

"No, I guess she was drinking at the Eagles years ago and got to talking. It seems whatever happened occurred when she lived in New York City."

As soon as Ali said the words, I could see by the look on her face she was headed on the same track that I was. "New York City?" I repeated.

"Yeah," she replied slowly, nodding her head. She remained quiet for a few moments. "Oh, Syd, don't let your imagination run away with you. I know what you're thinking."

She was right. Both about what I was thinking and about the thought being ludicrous. It was insane to even consider that Sybile Bowden could

73

be my biological mother. Wasn't it? The age would be about right though—Dora told me that Sybile was seventy-two. She would have been twenty when she gave birth. And why was Dora so inquisitive about my birth date, where I was born, and that I was adopted? No. Absolutely out of the question, I told myself. Get a grip, Sydney.

"Yeah, you're right," I told Ali. "God, what would the chances be? That I'd end up here in Cedar Key and find my biological mother? That's the kind of stuff they make movies about. It's just not possible. Besides, I can't stand this woman. No way could she be related to me."

Ali laughed. "Your chances are probably about a billion to one. So I don't think you need to be concerned."

A group of six women came into Cook's for lunch and took a middle table inside. I recognized a few from the hair salon. They were friendly, and it made me feel good that they remembered me.

One woman in particular kept staring. When I stood next to her for her order, she made no effort to switch her gaze from my face. "I'm Raylene Porter," she said. "I don't think we've met, but you sure do look familiar to me."

I recalled Polly saying those exact words on Thanksgiving and gave my standard answer. "No, I don't think we have, but you've probably seen me around town. I've lived here a month and I stay with Alison at the B and B. She's a good friend of mine."

"Hmm, no, I don't think I've seen you around. I live in Rosewood, off island, and I don't get into town that much. Strange. I could swear we've met before though. Oh, do you have some relatives in Cedar Key? That's probably what it is. You resemble somebody that I know."

A lump formed in my throat as another hot flash raced up my neck, causing me to break out in a sweat. Running a hand across my forehead, I shook my head. "No. No relatives here at all. Just a coincidence, I guess. What would you like to order?"

For the first time since encountering Sybile and hearing her story from Alison, I wondered if any of what I was experiencing was merely coincidence.

Sitting in the garden, sipping a glass of cabernet, I observed the interaction between Ali and Paul. From the moment she'd introduced us, I liked him. Five years older than Ali and about four inches taller, silver streaked his dark hair and provided a nice contrast to his smiling blue eyes. His sense of humor had kept us laughing, and he seemed to be one of those men who were at ease in their own body.

He sat comfortably relaxed in a lawn chair, one hand resting on Alison's knee. A natural aura of warmth and caring floated between them. Ali's persona had changed the moment he'd arrived and embraced her. She appeared different in a subtle way. More relaxed, brighter—youthful.

"Alison tells me you're giving some consideration to opening a business," he said, moving his hand to begin kneading Ali's forearm.

I nodded. "I'm doing some research. Since I've never owned a shop before, I'm a real novice. But I've been to the bank to sort out financial details and . . . I actually stopped in at Pelican Realty yesterday to find out more about leasing the space I'd like to have."

"I didn't know you'd taken that step," Ali told me. "That's great, Syd. And you're now beginning to get orders from Lu's friends. That's a great start to your mail-order business."

I laughed. "Yeah, if Lu keeps this up, I'll have to put her in charge of publicity and advertising."

They both stood up. "Are you sure you won't reconsider and join us for lunch?" Paul questioned.

"No, but thanks for the invite. I think I'll hang out here for a few hours and get some spinning done. Then maybe I'll head downtown and browse around."

Later that afternoon, I found myself peering inside the empty retail space once again. I allowed my imagination to take over, and could visualize an antique desk in the corner where I'd conduct purchases. Stepping inside, I saw that the large wall would be perfect for wooden cubby-holes filled with rainbow colors of yarn. And the lighting—Noah had been right about that. It would be ideal for women who wanted to sit and knit. The small brick fireplace provided a focal point where I could place two wing-back chairs on either side. My spinning wheel would add a nice touch, and the wide window seats in the front windows would allow me to display various yarns and accessories.

I looked around and realized that the remodeling was almost finished. Opening a door off the main room, I discovered a medium-sized back room that would be perfect for storing stock and taking breaks.

"Can't seem to stay away from this place, can ya?"

I spun around to see Noah Hale standing in the doorway. Was that annoyance I detected in his tone?

"Guess not, but I could say the same of you."

He nodded. "Yeah, I'm guilty of being indecisive."

Walking past me, he inspected the back room. "This would be perfect for storing art supplies."

Heading toward the door, I paused and turned around. "Maybe. But it would also be ideal for storing knitting supplies."

"Knitting?" He said the word like he couldn't comprehend the definition.

"Yeah, like in knit one, purl two."

Noah threw his head back laughing. "I thought your joke of a tattoo parlor was humorous . . . but knitting?"

"Something wrong with that?" I questioned and heard the edge to my tone.

A sheepish look crossed his face. "Well, uh . . . no. But I'm having a hard time seeing this place filled with the sound of knitting needles clacking."

"And I fail to see that it's any of your business," I retorted, as I stormed out of the shop.

Before I even realized what was happening, I found myself standing in the office of Pelican Realty. Twenty minutes later, I was sitting at Ruth's desk, pen poised in my right hand, reading over the lease papers carefully. Adjusting my glasses, I wondered for the hundredth time if I was doing the right thing. Not only was I embarking on a new adventure, I could be risking my financial situation forever. I was terrified of taking such a major step, but the chronic fatigue and blisters on my feet told me I couldn't be a waitress for the next ten years.

"Anything wrong?" Ruth questioned. "You realize the lease will begin on January fifteenth. The contractors will be finished with the shop by then. You're really lucky to be getting one of the first spaces that'll be ready to open."

I nodded. "Everything seems to be in order," I said, unable to control my spidery penmanship as I realized I hadn't been this anxious when I signed my marriage license.

Ruth smiled, took the papers, and went to the copy machine. She returned a moment later, passing the copies to me, along with a set of shiny gold keys.

"Here you go. Feel free to visit your shop anytime between now and next month. There're only minor things the contractors will be finishing."

I felt the coolness of metal in my palm and stood up to shake Ruth's hand. "Thank you so much. You've been very patient with me while I tried to make up my mind."

"It was my pleasure and I wish you much success in your business. I plan to be one of your first customers. I'm already collecting fur from my Muffy. She has the most beautiful cat fur that I'll love knitting into a sweater."

"You come by anytime," I told her, walking to the door. "The coffee will always be on."

I walked out to Second Street and inhaled the crisp December air. Looking at the red velvet bows decorating Haven Isle, I realized that Christmas was only a week away and within a month, I'd be joining the ranks of other merchants lining the street.

Clutching the keys in my hand, I stood in front of the library and looked across to my shop. *My shop*. Giggling, it occurred to me that I hadn't even thought of a name for the business. I saw that the contractors were finished for the day and the door was closed. Crossing the street, I placed the key in the lock and stepped inside. Sunlight streamed through the long French doors, creating rays on the brick walls.

"Didn't I just see you in here an hour ago?"

Once again, Noah Hale was leaning against the door frame. But this time it was *my* door frame. I also noticed arrogance in his tone.

"Ah, yeah, you did," I said, and then paused for effect. "And since I'm now the official lessee of this shop . . . you'd better get used to seeing a lot more of me here."

The look of surprise on Noah's face was followed by an indignant stare. "Excuse me? I'm afraid you're way off base. I have an appointment at nine tomorrow morning to sign the lease with the realtor in Gainesville."

"Really? Well, I'd suggest you contact that realtor and make him earn his money, because he neglected to let the realtor on the island know he had a potential lease. Not that it would have mattered anyway." I removed the signed lease from my handbag, waved the pages in his face, and nudged him out the door in front of me. Checking the knob to make sure I'd locked it, I took a few steps, then turned around. "You know the old saying—he who hesitates, is lost. I'd say you lost this one."

Without looking back, I walked up Second Street to the B&B.

Sitting in Alison's apartment, a glass of champagne in front of both of us, I doubled over with laughter. "Can you believe it? That arrogant SOB. Telling me he was getting that shop. The look on his face was priceless."

Alison's laughter matched mine. Shaking her head, she said, "I'm so proud of you, Syd. Joining the ranks of businesswomen. You're on a journey to discover your feminine soul."

When the state trooper had shown up at my Lexington home to inform me of Stephen's accident, I had become numb. And when the sheriff had confronted me with my eviction, I truly thought my life was over. I now realized that coming to Cedar Key had been the first step along a journey I'd never traveled. A journey that was both frightening and exhilarating at the same time. But I failed to see what my *feminine soul* might have to do with any of it. "All I know is I feel like I'm being pulled along to a whole new place in my life."

Ali smiled, clinking the rim of her glass to mine. "Exactly. It'll all make sense to you eventually. Here's to your reawakening and mega success in your new shop."

After taking a sip, she questioned, "Hey, have you thought of a name yet? And how about your hours? Will you still be working at Cook's?"

"I have a few ideas on a name, but nothing definite. I have to keep working for a while. It'll help pay the lease. I doubt I'll be super busy at first, so I'm thinking of only being open a few hours in the afternoon, after I finish my shift at Cook's. Like from three till six and on Wednesdays and Thursdays, I could be open in the morning."

"Whew, so Sunday will be your only day completely off work?"

I massaged the back of my neck and nodded. "I don't think I'll have a choice."

"Oh, forgot to tell you . . . when I stopped by the post office earlier, Sam gave me three more boxes for you. I imagine it's more fur to spin for customers."

I smiled. "Bless Lu. She's really keeping me going."

Alison nibbled on a chip. "See, I told you. Just wait till word gets around this area. Why hell, they'll be coming from Gainesville to our island for your spinning."

"I'm here," I heard Twila Faye call as she came up the walkway. Loaded down with a basket, she placed it on the counter and came to hug me. "Congratulations. I'm so happy for you."

"Thank you," I said, wondering what Twila Faye was doing here. Alison had told me this would be just a little celebration for the two of us.

"Hello," Polly said, stepping into the kitchen, followed by Dora.

Both women had bowls of dip to go with the chips.

I accepted their hugs and good wishes, while I laughed and pointed a finger at Alison. "You lied to me."

"That's what's known as a white lie. I'll open another bottle of champagne. I know we're a little cramped here, but you gals pull up a chair."

When the glasses were filled, four women raised the amber bubbly toward me.

"Here's to my best friend. May she be as successful a businesswoman as I am."

Laughing, the other three shouted, "Hear, hear."

I shook my head and swallowed hard to hold back tears. "Thank you. You guys are the greatest."

Twila Faye laughed as she placed plates of cheese with crackers and mullet dip on the table. "The dip is compliments of Saren. He said to congratulate you, Sydney. But he wanted to know if it was a lady gathering, why you didn't invite Miss Elly."

"Well, that's simple," Alison said. "She never leaves his house."

"Most of the time, I think that ghost is a figment of his imagination. But I admit, there're times he has me convinced," Dora said, laughing.

"Well, no matter." Polly reached for a handful

of popcorn. "Poor Saren's lonely and if Miss Elly keeps him company, then so be it."

"Hey, Syd," Twila Faye leaned forward conspiratorially. "What's with Noah Hale giving you trouble about the shop you leased?"

Four heads turned toward me. "Typical, controlling man," I said and shrugged my shoulders in dismissal.

"Might be that," Polly said. "But he sure is one good-looking man."

"If you like that type," I retorted.

"What type is that?" Dora questioned.

"Spoiled and used to getting what he wants. Arrogant, cocky, and thinks he's superior."

"Oh, *that* kind." Dora nodded her head knowingly.

"So is he going to lease another shop downtown?" Twila Faye asked.

"I'm sure I wouldn't know," I replied. "Nor do I care."

I saw the women raise their eyebrows and look at Alison for a hopeful explanation.

"Supposedly, he considered leaving the island and relocating to St. Augustine. But you know Nellie—his mother has him back here now and I don't think she's about to let him go again. Plus, at eighty-four, she's not in the best of health. I think Noah feels a certain responsibility toward her."

"Oh, yeah," Polly said. "If Nellie had had her

way, he never would have left the island for Paris. I always felt she was a borderline control freak."

"Well, that's why he stalled on committing to a lease on the shop," Ali explained. "But I guess he waited too long and Syd beat him to the punch."

"So—will he be staying?" Twila Faye asked again.

Ali nodded. "Yup, guess so. I heard he signed a lease on another shop that's being restored."

I could feel four faces staring at me for a reaction, but I lowered my eyes, reached for a slice of cheese, and remained silent.

9

I opened my eyes and my glance was drawn to the calendar hanging on my bedroom wall. January fifth already. I looked around and saw that Lilly was still curled up on her bed, sleeping. I had moved into the second-floor apartment in the Tree House over a week ago, and it didn't take long for both Lilly and me to adjust to our new residence. It may be only three rooms, but it felt like the Taj Mahal compared to the tight quarters in the main house.

I yawned and stretched. The bedside clock read 5:30. Even on my days off work at Cook's my body was acclimated to waking up early. I plumped the pillow under my head and luxuriated in the fact I had the whole day to myself.

The sound of water drew my attention to the window and I realized it was pouring outside. Not only raining, but it sounded like the wind was howling.

Smiling to myself, I felt a sense of accomplishment. It had been a tough few months, but I seemed to be sitting pretty now. Well, as pretty as a widow with a shaky future can be sitting.

I had ordered a computer and Ruth told me I could have it delivered to the shop. Even though technically my lease didn't begin for ten more days. Dora had volunteered a lovely antique desk (exactly like what I'd pictured) and insisted it had been sitting in her garage collecting dust. She also supplied a mahogany captain's chair and I felt like I was in business. Only three items in the shop— but, it was a start.

Then I surprised myself by setting up a Web site for mail orders. And I was able to enter all the names and information about my customers. Yup, I was feeling mighty proud of myself. I had also hired a local contractor who would begin building my cubbyholes within the next few days. And best of all, I'd secured the American Express card and had ordered a sufficient stock of yarn and accessories to get me going.

I felt wet, slobbery kisses on my arm. "Hey, Lilly. Yeah, it's going on six o'clock. Guess we should get up. You might not like the weather out there today though."

After throwing on sweats and a heavy sweater, we made our way down the stairs outside. Shielding myself with a large umbrella, I realized it was probably useless. The wind threatened to blow the material inside out. Lilly peed quickly, and we both dashed into the kitchen of the main house.

"Good morning," Ali greeted us. "Well, it looks like you're in for your first tropical storm on the island."

I poured myself a cup of coffee. "Really? How bad will it be?"

"Not a hurricane this time of year. But heavy rain and wind for a few days according to the local forecast."

"I guess it won't affect me. I plan to spend the day working on the computer at the shop."

"Did your phone service get turned on yesterday?"

"Yes. It's nice to have my own phone again. I even gave Monica a call yesterday."

"Hmm. And how is the little darling?"

I smiled. "More accepting of the fact I'm opening the shop. Not ecstatic, by any means. But at least she's not bitching at me that I'm making a mistake."

"Maybe she'll come to realize that her mother isn't so helpless after all. Stay firm with her, Syd. It's your life, so don't allow her to make you feel it isn't."

I knew she was right. But I dreaded stirring up more animosity with Monica, so I had learned to tread lightly.

"Oh, I meant to tell you. A woman named Carrie . . . can't remember her last name. Anyway, she dropped into the shop yesterday while I was there. Really sweet elderly woman. She wasn't in there five minutes and she said she thought I looked familiar. This is getting downright eerie. Do I have a twin on this island?"

Alison continued to squeeze oranges and remained silent.

A shiver came over me. "Ali? Did you hear what I said?"

She turned around to face me, wiping her hands on a towel.

"Yeah, I did hear you." A deep sigh escaped her. "No, I don't think you have a twin here, but . . . after thinking about it, and I'm not sure why I never noticed it before—there is a striking resemblance between you and Sybile."

My shiver reverted to a cold sweat. "What are you saying?"

"I don't know. Thinking out loud, I guess. But have you seen Sybile? Really looked at her? Didn't you notice or feel any recognition there? Especially the eyes?"

I had really only seen Sybile once at Cook's face-to-face. And I did recall that when she briefly removed her dark glasses, I'd felt *some-*

thing. Like I'd known her before or had met her and it tugged at me now.

"You think we look alike? You think Sybile Bowden could be my mother? Are you nuts?"

Ali turned around and resumed squeezing oranges. "I know," she said softly. "Don't pay any attention to me. I mean . . . Christ, never mind a billion to one—the chance of this being true is probably a *trillion* to one."

I couldn't define why, but I felt angry. "Probably even higher, I'd say. This is really insane. And don't you think somehow I'd *know* if she were my mother? That we shared the same DNA? That her blood ran through my veins? I can't stand that woman. She's mean and rude and . . . nothing at all like me."

Struggling with Lilly's leash and my umbrella, I managed to unlock the door of the shop and get inside out of the wind and rain.

"Whew," I said, shaking drops of wetness from my hair. "They're not kidding about tropical storms. They can be pretty fierce."

I unclipped Lilly's leash and she promptly went to her bed in the corner and curled up. She loved coming with me to the shop. Maybe it gave her a sense of purpose like it did for me. I measured out coffee into the filter, poured the water in, and then turned on the computer.

Nothing. I got a black screen. Hmm. Getting up,

I checked the plugs and thought perhaps we'd had a power outage. But no, the electricity was on. After fooling with it for twenty minutes, I gave up and called Ali.

"A totally black screen?" she asked.

"Yeah, it's really weird, because it was working fine yesterday."

"I hate to tell you this, hon, but I think your computer crashed on you. But there's good news. You have all your info on disk, right?"

Crashed? Disk? What the hell was she talking about?

"What kind of disk?"

"You backed up all your important information on a CD. Right?"

"No," I said, slowly, as it dawned on me that was something I should have done. Oh, my God . . . how could I have been so stupid?

"Oh," Ali said. "Well, ah . . . let's see. Why don't you try to shut it down? Unplug it. Plug it back in and start over. Sometimes computers have silly little glitches. Maybe the weather has something to do with it and it'll work fine for you when you turn it back on."

Why did Ali not sound very optimistic about these instructions?

"Oh, shit," I said. "I think I'm doomed. What the hell am I going to do if I've lost all my customer information and contacts? I won't know who ordered what or even where to send it."

Unable to control them, tears flowed down my face splattering onto the keyboard in front of me.

"Geez, Syd. Do you want me to come over? See if I can figure something out?"

"No," I said, staring dumbly at the monstrosity in front of me. "I knew I never should have relied on this damn thing to help me. I would have been better off to keep records the old-fashioned way. With pencil and paper. No, you and Paul are heading to Gainesville for the day. I'll be okay. Thanks."

Yeah, I'll be just fine, I thought as I hung up the phone. Now what? Shaking my head, I pushed away from the desk. Lilly sat looking at me, a puzzled look on her face.

"It's a wonder I can take care of *you*. What the hell am I thinking? That I can run a business. No wonder Stephen handled everything—he probably had no faith in me either."

After spending an hour working with the computer, I gave up. There was no way that puppy was going to come to life for me again. Breathing out a deep sigh, I saw it was 1:00. The post office had reopened after lunch. Lunch—no wonder my stomach was growling.

I nibbled on the sandwich I'd brought and gave Lilly a biscuit. After finishing, I decided to walk over to the post office. Maybe I had some new orders and at least I'd know who those were from and what their information was.

As I was about to leave, the telephone rang. "Spinning Forward," I said, in my best professional voice. I had gotten a lot of compliments on my final decision to name the shop. Not only did it fit perfectly for a yarn and spinning shop, I thought it was a great metaphor for my present life.

I heard Jeremy Wilkinson's voice.

"Miss Sydney, I do hate to bother you again. But Mr. Hale insisted that I try one last time to get you to change your mind. You don't begin to actually lease the place for ten days and as you know, a couple of other spaces will be available by then. Won't you please reconsider?"

Hearing what Jeremy had to say convinced me that I was at the end of my proverbial rope. Anger bubbled up inside and I took a deep breath. "Look, Jeremy, I know this isn't your fault and it's all simply a matter of bad timing. But I've had it with Noah Hale trying to use his clout just because his damn ancestors came from this island. I also have a real problem with the fact that with all his money and prestige he could open a gallery anywhere in the world. Why the hell is he so insistent on having *my* shop?"

I heard Jeremy clear his throat.

"Yes, I understand your feeling, Miss Sydney. But it all has to do with lighting."

"Lighting?" Were we back to that stupid subject again?

"I'm afraid so. Your corner space has the very best natural lighting and so, of course, this would only enhance the placement of his paintings. Mr. Hale feels the other spaces simply will not be adequate."

"Well, isn't that just too damn bad. All I want is to be left alone. You can tell Mr. Hale for me that if he continues to pursue this matter, I'll consider a harassment case against him. I'm not changing my mind or moving to one of the other spaces. That's my final word. Good-bye, Jeremy."

I slammed the phone down so hard, I was certain I broke it.

I stood with hands on hips and screamed to Lilly and the room, "Damn him to hell. How dare he try to intimidate me like this. Big deal—he's a Hale. Well, I'm a Webster."

By the time I came out of the post office, water sluiced onto the street. Looking up at the black sky, I thought perhaps I should have left the mail where it was. Wind was whipping the oak trees full-force. Palm trees across the street were bent almost in two. No pedestrians were on the street and nobody was out driving cars in this weather.

Well, I thought, clutching mail and a box against my chest, while trying to balance the umbrella, may as well make a dash for it.

"Damn," I said, trying to juggle the package and run toward my shop.

Thankful for the overhang above the door, I placed the box on the pavement while rummaging in my jeans pocket for the key. Lilly sat on the other side of the glass, tail wagging. Panic washed over me as I realized I'd rushed off in anger and left the keys on my desk.

"Oh, just great," I wailed, as Lilly now began whining.

I did have another set of keys at the apartment, but it was now pouring buckets. I'd be drenched by the time I reached D Street. My wet jersey was already clinging to my skin causing me to shiver. Looking up and down the street to figure out a solution, I saw Noah Hale walking toward me, huddled under an umbrella.

"Jesus," I muttered. "Just what I don't need."

"Having a problem?"

There was that sarcastic tone again.

"Ah, no," I said, pushing closer to the building to keep dry. "Not really."

A grin crossed his face. "Hmm, seems to me you might have locked yourself out of your shop."

Damn, why did he have to have such a sexy smile? Lilly's whining had now turned into full-blown barking.

"Hush," I hollered through the door. "Actually, I did lock myself out." The shivers from a few minutes before were now replaced with the heat of embarrassment creeping up my neck. "But I'll be just fine," I told him, as I tried to muster some confidence.

"Ah, then you have another set of keys with you?"

I was certain that was smugness covering his face.

Lilly was jumping on the door, demanding to be attended to. "It's okay, girl. I'll get the door open." Running a hand through my drenched hair, I spun around to face Noah. "No, I don't have any keys with me. They're at my apartment. Which is where I'm going right now to get them."

"And I bet you walked to work and don't have a vehicle here." Without waiting for an answer, he said, "Come on. I'll give you a ride to the B and B."

Double damn, I thought. "No, that's okay. Thanks anyway."

Noah shrugged his shoulders and began walking down the street. "Okay, suit yourself."

Swallowing my pride, I called after him, "Well, if you really wouldn't mind."

When he turned around, the sexy smile had returned to his face. "Wait here. I'll go get my car."

"Leave it to me," I said, when I knew he was out of earshot. Turning to the door, I attempted to placate my whining dog. "Lilly, be a good girl. I won't be very long. Go lay down."

A few minutes later Noah pulled up in a black Lexus.

I slid into the passenger seat, but remained silent.

"I'm opening my gallery in a few weeks," he said.

"Oh, found a spot, did you? I hope you'll be happy there."

"Not as happy as I'd be in your shop, but it'll do. How're you doing getting set up?"

"Very well. Thank you."

Noah chuckled. "You're a woman of few words, aren't you?"

"When I want to be. Yes."

He turned the car onto Third Street and pulled into a spot alongside the B&B. "Get your keys. I'll wait for you."

"Oh, that won't be necessary. I can take Ali's golf cart back to the shop." As soon as I said the words, I remembered the cart was in Ocala being repaired.

"Okay."

When I made no attempt to leave the car, Noah stared across the seat at me.

"Well, uh, I just remembered the golf cart isn't here. It's being repaired."

"Get your keys," he repeated as a grin crossed his face. "I'll wait."

Without another word, I jumped out of the car, ran through the rain across the garden, and up the stairs to my apartment. Stepping into the kitchen, I shook off the wetness. Rushing to the bathroom,

I grabbed a towel rubbing it back and forth across my hair before I ran to the bedroom, opened a bureau drawer, and retrieved my keys. Taking a deep breath, I stood in the middle of the room and caught a glimpse of myself in the mirror.

"Oh, just gorgeous," I said, leaning closer. "Even if you did like him, there's no way in hell he'd be interested in a drowned rat like you."

Spying the tube of lipstick on my vanity, I quickly ran some color over my lips. Flinging off the wet jersey, I replaced it with a dry sweater. I then grabbed an umbrella and raced back to the car.

"I see you're now prepared," Noah said, gesturing to the umbrella.

"My other one is locked inside the shop," I replied, hearing distinctive bitchiness in my tone.

"Hmm, a lotta good that does you."

A few minutes later he pulled up in front of Spinning Forward. I reached for the door handle and then turned toward him. "Thanks for the ride."

"My pleasure. But next time, maybe you should tie those keys around your neck. Then you won't forget them."

How dare he speak to me like a child, I thought as I slammed the door harder than necessary.

⟫⟪10⟫⟪

If I thought my computer problem was a catastrophe, that was mild in comparison to what I found the next morning at Spinning Forward.

Although the wind had diminished a little, rain continued to soak the island. All seemed well in the shop until I entered the back room and realized I was squishing in my sneakers.

"What the hell!" I looked down to see about two inches of water covering the floor. The floor that held three boxes of my newly purchased yarns. Yarns that were no doubt water damaged.

"Oh, no," I said, as I stared at a virtual pool beneath me. "My stock is ruined."

"Hello," I heard and turned around to see Eudora Foster entering the shop. "I hope you don't mind, but I was at the post office and thought I'd peek in."

"Have you got your water wings with you?"

Dora came to the doorway and gasped. "Oh, Lord. You got some water in here. Unfortunately, many of the shops downtown get some flooding with heavy rains. I guess nobody told you not to store anything on the floor?"

"I should have known better. I thought the yarn would be safe there until my cubbyholes are built. Obviously, I was wrong."

"Well, not to worry," Dora said, reaching for a

broom in the corner and opening the back door. "We'll have this water out of here in no time."

I was amazed at her willingness to help. "That's so nice of you, but I don't want you doing that."

"And why not? You don't happen to have one of those shop vacs, do you? That would suck it up faster than a broom."

I shook my head. It was becoming more apparent to me that not only didn't I have a shop vac, perhaps I was very ill-equipped to think I could run a business.

"All the merchants downtown have one, so I'll run over to the book store. I know Tom wouldn't mind letting you borrow his."

Before I could protest, she was out the door and on her way.

I picked up the broom and continued to sweep water out the back door, but I could see it was a lost cause. So I lugged a box down the step and into the front room. That step is what prevented the water from going any further.

I slit the box and was thrilled to see the top layer of yarn was dry. What a break. Carefully removing the skeins, I placed them on the desk. Out of a box of twenty-four, I was able to save half. The other twelve would end up in the trash or once they dried, maybe I could discount them.

"Here we are," Dora called cheerfully, as she entered the shop followed by a middle-aged man pulling a canister vacuum behind him. "Have you met Tom yet?"

"No, I haven't. I can't thank you enough for helping me out. You're a life saver."

"Aw, I'm glad I can help. But, just for future reference, you really might want to invest in one of these," he said, reaching down to plug it into the wall. "Heavy rain always seems to find a way of getting into the downtown shops."

I could vouch for that.

"How's the yarn?" Dora asked, as the miracle machine began sucking up the culprit.

"Actually, not quite as bad as I feared. The top layers are fine and once the others dry, I guess I could sell them at a discount. Thank God this was the shipment of my worsted yarn and not the alpacas and cashmere."

Dora helped me empty the remaining boxes while Tom made my back room dry.

When we finished, I shook my head. "I really don't know how to thank both of you. Dora, that was quick thinking on your part."

"Well, let me know if you need this again until you get your own," Tom said, heading to the door.

"I guess I'll be scooting along too," Dora told me.

"Wait a minute," I said, as a thought formed in my head. "I really would like to do something to thank you. Dinner. Let me cook a nice dinner for you. I have my own apartment now with a proper kitchen."

"Oh, no. Don't be silly. But's that's very nice of you."

"I'm serious. You live alone. Join me tomorrow evening. I'll prepare dinner for us."

Dora hesitated and then said, "Well . . . That would be nice. I think I'd enjoy that."

"Great. You know where I live. Let's say seven."

I admit I had an ulterior motive inviting Dora to dinner. She's Sybile's sister. I thought maybe I could find out more about this woman.

It was Ali who told me I should call Lucille Grayson. Many of my customers had been referred by her. So she'd know who had placed recent orders with me.

"Do you think that'll help?" Ali asked when I hung up the phone.

"Well, at least it's a start. She said she'll speak to all her friends and any that placed orders, she'll have them get in touch. I guess if people don't receive their yarn after a decent amount of time, they'll be calling me. And then I can explain what an idiot I was."

Ali laughed. "Okay, so now tell me how you came to invite Dora to dinner tomorrow evening."

I explained my latest fiasco at the shop and the help Dora and Tom had given me.

"Well, if there's any truth at all to our suspicions about Sybile, maybe Dora can fill in some missing pieces. It'll all depend on how much she's willing to share secrets with you."

"Let's have a glass of wine while the biscuits are in the oven," I told Dora while uncorking a bottle of Pinot Grigio.

Dora sat at the table and smiled. "My Marin would like you. You remind me of her."

In which way, I wondered? "I'd love to meet her. Will she be coming to visit soon?"

"She's planning to come for the weekend some-time next month. Just her. She likes to do this a few times a year. She calls it 'girl time.'"

I smiled. "That must be nice. Mother-daughter time. I used to spend a lot of time with my mom before she died. When Monica was small, we'd just pop over for lunch or to go shopping. Girl time is good."

"Even though you were adopted it seems you had a special relationship with your mother."

"Yeah, I did. They brought me home at three weeks old, so they're the only parents I ever knew. And they told me at a young age that I was adopted."

"Did it bother you?"

"Not in the least. They made me feel pretty spe-cial—that not only was I wanted, but that I was chosen."

"I've heard it's natural for adoptees to search for their birth mother. Did you ever attempt doing that?"

I stared at Dora's face, but her expression remained neutral. "Actually, just recently I decided to pursue the search again."

"Again?"

"Yeah, when Monica was born I had an overwhelming curiosity about the woman who'd given birth to me. But I didn't put a lot of effort into the search. Now I'm listed with an organization that helps adoptees search."

Dora fingered the edge of the tablecloth and remained silent.

I got up to remove the biscuits from the oven and then began spooning stew into the brightly colored ceramic bowls. After placing salad plates on the table, I joined Dora.

"This looks delicious," she said, taking a bite. "Hmm, very good. You'll have to give me your recipe."

"Thanks, but it's pretty easy. It cooked all day in the crock pot."

Dora continued eating and then surprised me by asking, "Have you thought about what you'd do if you located your birth mother?"

I buttered a biscuit. "Do?"

"What I mean is, would you want to meet her? What if she isn't like you envisioned? Wouldn't that be disappointing?"

"First of all, I have no preconceived notions about her. I've never done an in-depth search, so maybe curious is a better word."

"Are you angry that she gave you up for adoption?"

Call me silly, but I was beginning to feel most people wouldn't be asking the questions that Dora was. But I shook my head. "No, I've always felt she was probably unwed and in 1955 that was a difficult position for a young girl to be in. Now that I'm older and have a grown daughter, I can only imagine how devastating it must be to part with your child. It's not a natural thing to do, you know?"

Dora nodded. "Yes, I quite agree. I suppose each woman that's relinquished a child has a different story. It must be a terrible decision to have to make."

"I think it takes an enormous amount of courage, so I'd like to think the main ingredient for that action is love."

"Love for the baby?"

"Yeah, giving up the child to assure he or she has a much better life than the birth mother could provide."

"You could be right," Dora said, wiping her lips with a napkin. "And your daughter . . . you have a good relationship with her?"

I grinned. "Well, that depends on which day you're asking me. I'd say we get along okay, but

Monica is very self-involved. I suppose part of that is my fault—a bit of spoiling, since she was an only child. We've had some warm moments but since her father passed away, I think she's taking her anger out on me." I paused to take a sip of wine. "I get the feeling that she feels had I been more independent and a stronger woman, I could have fixed her father's addiction with gambling."

"Hmm, I understand. Sometimes children only see things through their eyes. Marin and I have had our moments also. Mothers and daughters have a very mysterious type of relationship."

"What about you, Dora? What was it like growing up on this island during the thirties and forties?"

My question brought a smile to her face. "I thought it was the best place in the world for a child to grow up, but we were pretty isolated. We didn't have the things available that kids in large cities had. Yet we had other enjoyments they couldn't begin to understand. Most of our time was spent on or near the water—boating, fishing, crabbing. We didn't have to worry about crime, so after school or during the summer we just ran free. And of course, everybody knew everyone else so the kids behaved for the most part. If you didn't, you could be assured that by the time you got home, your mama already knew what you'd done."

I laughed. "Yeah, small towns are like that. So both you and Sybile loved growing up here?"

Dora hesitated before answering. "I love it— I'm not sure I can say the same for Sybile. We didn't have much, but then everybody back then was poor. Clothes were passed around to wear and getting something new was pretty exciting. Once Sybile turned about twelve, it bothered her a lot. I believe that's when she made the decision that as soon as she turned eighteen, she was leaving the island. Our daddy used to tell her she had pipedreams and his nickname for her was Cinderella." Dora shook her head. "But nobody could ever tell Sybile a thing and sure enough, the June she graduated high school, she was gone. She'd worked at the local fish houses and other odd jobs for five years saving money to make that happen."

I took a deep breath. "But she did make it happen, and I guess that's what counts. So she found her happiness."

"I wouldn't be too sure of that. Maybe in her own way, she did. I'm not one to judge."

I declined Dora's offer to help and began clearing the table.

"I have some oatmeal cookies for dessert, but I can't claim credit. Alison made them for me."

"Oh, my, no. I'm stuffed. That was a delicious supper, Sydney, and I'd like to have you over to my house soon to repay the invitation."

"I'd like that. How about some tea?"

"That would be a perfect ending to such a nice meal."

For the first time since moving to the island, I had trouble falling asleep. Thoughts swirled in my head. Would I ever get my business up and running? And more important, would it be a successful income for me?

And Sybile. Based on what Dora had told me, there certainly wasn't much evidence to think she could be my birth mother. The time frames would fit, but beyond that . . . no proof whatsoever.

Floating in and out of all my thoughts was the image of Noah Hale's face. What was it about him that drew me in? Sure, he was good looking. And if I were honest with myself, I had to admit I did feel a certain attraction. Some of the things he said to me also felt like flirting, but since it had been over thirty years since I'd indulged in that act, I probably couldn't be depended on to know the diffcrence.

~11~

"I didn't really learn much of anything from Dora," I related to Ali a few days later.

"And I wasn't going to say anything to you, but this is getting downright bizarre."

"What?" I questioned, sitting up straighter in the lounge chair while lighting a cigarette.

"I bumped into Miss Sophie at the post office the other day. Said she met you at Cook's recently."

I was meeting so many different people, it was becoming difficult to keep everyone straight.

"She told me she couldn't get over the resemblance you had to Sybile Bowden and asked if you were a niece or something."

"Are *you* serious?" I could feel the hairs on the back of my neck stand up. "Do you think I look that much like her?"

"Apparently not as much as other people seem to think. But as I'd told you, yeah, I do see a similarity in your eyes."

I shook my head. "I'm beginning to feel like I'm living in a sci-fi movie. Even if this were true, and I still can't believe it is, I mean, what? I can't just approach Sybile and say, 'Hey, are you my mother?' Wouldn't that be a pisser though? I don't even *like* her as a person. Maybe I don't want to know the truth."

Ali nodded. "Yeah, I know what you mean. But remember the old saying, the truth can set you free."

I could feel the tingling of annoyance setting in. "I don't recall saying I wanted to be set free."

"Look, Syd, I know you've never bought into my feminist ways, but at some point in our life we're all searching for that inner mother. That deepest part of us that fulfills our completion. Maybe finding the woman who gave you life is what you need to take you where you need to be. But it's entirely up to you. And I do have to partially agree—you could be opening quite a large can of worms. I mean, God, what if it *is* true? Would Sybile want everyone on this island to know that not only did she give birth years ago, but that she gave that daughter away? She has a right to her privacy too."

"So you're saying I should just forget about it? Not try and find out?"

"I'm not saying that, Syd. I'm just saying be careful. You might want to ask Saren some discreet questions. They might not get along today, but there was a time when they were pretty tight."

"Really? I had no idea."

"It's just another piece of island info that isn't mentioned much. But yeah, people say that when Sybile left for New York, she and Saren were involved. Some people thought they'd end up getting married. But she stayed in New York and he left the island for Paris and his painting. I do know they continued to keep in touch via letters though. Dora told me that once."

I was surprised about this revelation and was beginning to feel that eventually all secrets have a way of coming to the surface.

"According to the little that Dora told me, he

was pretty sweet on her. Saren never did marry, so maybe he still is. That's what was so surprising when Sybile returned to the island—guess everyone thought they'd get together again, but she kept her distance from him."

"Interesting," I said. "Hmm, maybe you're right. Maybe I need to pay a visit to Saren Ghetti."

Sipping tea in Saren's living room the following day, it was easy to see the man was lonely. No wonder he jumped at my offer to pay him a visit.

"You have a lovely place," I told him. "And your artwork—I feel like I'm in a gallery."

Saren's living room was like stepping back in time. I sat on a horsehair sofa that was similar to one from my childhood. White crocheted doilies rested on the arms and back. Small mahogany antique tables held wide-base lamps with white fringe dangling from the shades. I was certain my grandmother had had the same pattern rug that covered the center of the hardwood floor. Many people decorate with antiques, but I knew this house was Saren's childhood home and the furniture was what he'd grown up with—all lovingly and meticulously cared for.

"Thank ya, Miss Sydney. There's something comforting about growing old in the home you grew up in. Oh, don't get me wrong, I sure did enjoy living and working in Paris—but I always

110

agreed with what Dorothy said about Oz." He chuckled while reaching for his tea cup.

"Yeah, there's no place like home." Unsure exactly how I should broach the subject of Sybile, I questioned, "And you never married? In small towns many people end up marrying childhood sweethearts."

Saren nodded his head slowly. "That's true, but no, I never married. Too busy workin' on my painting, I reckon. Had a sweetheart though— yup, I loved her for a long time."

I remained silent.

"Betcha you'd never guess who it was." Without waiting for my answer, he said, "It was Miss High and Mighty. Yup, Sybile Bowden."

"Oh, Miss Dora's sister. She's quite a character. So you grew up together, huh?"

"We sure did. Many a day we spent out on my daddy's boat. Sometimes catching fish and some-times just smoochin'." A crimson flush spread up his neck. "She was a looker, she was. Downright gorgeous. But it was those looks of hers that took her off the island."

"Yeah, I'd heard she went to New York to become a model. So I guess you lost touch then?"

"Nah, we wrote to each other. Not what you'd call love letters. Just news about her modeling and my painting, and we'd exchange information about New York City and Paris." Saren took another sip of his tea. "We'd had a big fight the

111

night she told me she was leaving Cedar Key. I told her she was nuts—nuts to think she'd make the big time in the big city. Oh, not because she wasn't beautiful enough. But I knew how hard it was to make it in painting, and I knew modeling would be even tougher. But she didn't listen—off she went, with her head in the clouds. Saw her briefly in New York before I left for Paris and a couple months later her first letter arrived. So we wrote back and forth for years. By the time I came back to the island, she was already back. Thought maybe we could pick up where we'd left off. But oh no, she wanted nothing to do with me. I knew she'd been married for a short time, but she was divorced. She'd bought herself that fancy dancy lighthouse and blew me off like she never knew me." A sigh of sorrow escaped him. "Still got every darn one of her letters, I do," he said, as an afterthought.

"You do?" I asked with excitement, but the sorrow of the doomed love affair now seemed more important than the letters. "I'm really sorry it didn't work out for the two of you, Saren. Believe me, it was Sybile's loss."

A look of gratitude crossed his face. "Why, thank you, Miss Sydney. What a kind thing to say." For a few minutes he appeared lost in the past and then he focused his eyes on me. "I know this is silly, but is there any chance you'd like to look at those letters with me? I've been thinking about them a lot lately. They're packed away and it'll take me a couple days to find them, but I'd sure enjoy going through them with you."

The letters might contain some relevant information—but even more important, Saren considered me worthy of sharing an exceptional part of his past.

Reaching over to touch his hand, I said, "I'd be honored, Saren. Call me when you've located them."

I realized it had been over a week since I'd heard from Monica and dialed her number. I also thought the time had come to tell her I had begun a search for her biological grandmother.

The minute I heard her voice I knew something was wrong.

"No, everything is okay," she told me.

Call it mother's intuition, but I knew different. I let it go and said, "Well, I thought you should know—I'm beginning a search for your biological grandmother."

I heard a gasp on the other end of the line and then silence.

"Are you still there, Monica?" I questioned.

"Yeah. Yeah, I am. I can't believe you're finally going to do this."

"Does that mean you think it's a good or a bad idea?"

"I've always thought it was a good idea. I never

could understand why you didn't pursue this years ago. It might be too late now."

She was right. "I know that and it's a chance I'll have to take. But I think the timing is right." I paused, not sure whether to mention Sybile and decided what the hell. "There's a little more to this . . . It's actually too bizarre to be believable, and I know you'll think I'm a definite candidate for a nursing home, but . . ."

I went on to explain about Sybile Bowden. The comments from people in town, Alison's agreement on a similarity in looks, and the fact that Sybile was in Manhattan during the time I'd been born there. I also told her about Sybile's self-imposed exile and isolation on her return to the island.

"Oh, my God," Moncia exclaimed. "This is stuff movies are made of."

My sentiments exactly.

"Could it be possible?" she asked. "What does she look like? Do you really look like her? Are you going to just ask her?"

"Whoa, slow down. I guess it *could* be possible, but it's highly improbable. And don't get too excited. Her personality is a cross between Rosie O'Donnell and Joan Rivers. In all honesty, Monica, I don't even *like* the woman. And no, of course not, I'm not going to ask her. What I'll probably do is question her sister, Dora, and an old friend of hers, Saren. I'll have to be discreet, so I'm not sure how much information I'll even get." I paused before asking, "Do you think I'm totally insane?"

"I admit it's a long shot, Mom. But all of what you told me does seem a bit of a coincidence. And you have to admit, all of this sure puts a whole different slant on your life."

That was putting it mildly. "So I'll play detective for a while, I guess. Okay, enough about me. Tell me what's wrong."

Reminding me of the fourteen-year-old Monica, she blurted out, "As of next week, I'm without a job. The publishing company is downsizing, and I'm one of the unlucky ones. And added to that . . . On the ski trip last weekend, I had a nasty fall and broke my arm, so I'm in a cast for the next six weeks." Without missing a heartbeat, she questioned, "Mom, can I come down there and stay with you for a little while?"

Before I had a chance to answer, sobs came across the telephone line.

My God, was the broken arm more serious than a fracture?

"Monica, are you alright?"

"No," she said, between hiccups. "No, I'm not alright. I miss Dad. I visited his grave this morning and . . . I still can't believe he's gone. That I'll never see him again."

I'd been so caught up in my own drama that I'd failed to pay attention to my daughter's loss. She was grieving for the death of a parent and while I missed Stephen, I resented the situation he'd left me with. My grief had quickly been replaced with survival.

Moisture filled my eyes and I wished I could pull her into a comforting embrace. "I do understand, honey," I told her. "He was a good father and you were so close to him. Focus on all the good memories you shared. That's what he would want."

"I know," I heard her say, followed by the sound of sniffles. "And I know I've been tough on you, Mom. Dad wouldn't have wanted that. It just . . . It just hurts so much to have him gone. I *do* love you."

My throat tightened with emotion. "I love you too, Monica."

⋙12⋘

I've always been a believer of that saying *life is what happens when you're busy making other plans*. From the moment I got the news about Stephen's accident, my life seemed to be going in directions that were totally foreign to me. And once again I was being subjected to something that I neither wanted nor welcomed.

When Monica moved out of our home at age eighteen to attend college, while I may have felt a bit sentimental, I certainly wasn't one of those empty-nest mothers. Around the time she turned sixteen, we'd found it difficult to agree on much of anything. The sweet, calm personality of Monica's youth had been replaced by an opinionated and strong young woman. Many college break visits back home found us barely speaking to each other.

I loved my daughter. I was proud of her education and her intelligence, her ability to make decisions, and her self-confidence. But live with her again? Oh Lord . . . This was more than my life suddenly going awry . . . this was the supreme sacrifice as a mother. And of course I told her yes.

Monica assured me it would only be until she could get back on her feet . . . or more accurately, resume the use of her right arm again. She thought she'd return to the Boston area at that time, but then again, she wasn't sure. Knowing that Gainesville was only an hour's drive away, she hinted at doing some job hunting there. So all in all, her dilemma was solved. Mine was only beginning.

It would be tight, but I assured her she could stay at the Tree House apartment with me. We'd manage somehow. She was planning to arrive in about two weeks—just about the time I was hoping to open Spinning Forward.

The telephone interrupted my thoughts and I briefly wondered if it might be Monica calling back to change her mind, but I answered to hear Ali's voice.

"You about ready? Paul and I will meet you in the garden in an hour."

I'd completely forgotten I'd agreed to have dinner with them at the Island Hotel. "Yes," I lied. "I'll need the full hour though. Just got off the phone with Monica."

"Not a problem. See you at seven."

After dressing, I appraised myself in the full-length mirror. Black slacks and a pale pink cashmere sweater. Twirling this way and that, I smiled. Not bad. The few pounds I'd lost and hours of exercise were beginning to show. Guess it was worth giving up the ice cream. Grabbing my handbag, I bent down to give Lilly a hug. "You be a good girl," I told her. "I'll be back later."

Paul and Alison were waiting in the garden when I came down the stairs.

"It's so nice out this evening, let's walk downtown," Ali said.

I nodded and fell into step with them.

When we arrived at the hotel, we were seated in the dining room at a table for four. For the first time since Stephen's death, I felt out of place. Like that proverbial fifth wheel. After ordering a glass of cabernet, I asked Paul if he was enjoying his visit.

"Very much so. I love coming here to the island. I only wish my job allowed me to get here more often."

I caught the squeeze he gave Alison's hand resting on the table.

"You've been coming for quite a while, so you've made some friends here?"

Paul nodded. "Yeah, there's a group of fellows I enjoy fishing with. We always get together while I'm here." He lifted his hand in greeting over my head and beckoned somebody to the table.

I turned around to see Noah Hale approaching, his face lit up with a smile. Oh, God, that's right. Ali said they knew each other.

Paul stood up to shake Noah's hand. "Good to see you again. You know Alison," he said, and then gesturing toward me, he said, "This is Ali's friend, Sydney Webster. She'll be opening a yarn shop here in town."

Alison cast a furtive glance at me as she nodded to Noah. "Nice to see you."

"Same here," Noah replied.

I neglected to acknowledge the introduction, making no attempt to speak.

"Sydney and I have met," Noah said. "On a number of occasions actually."

"Yes, we have," I mumbled.

"Well, that's great. Noah, if you haven't had dinner yet, why don't you join us?" Paul asked.

I couldn't believe what Paul had just done. Bad enough to have Noah standing there, staring down at me, but to sit beside him through an entire meal?

Pulling out the chair next to me, Noah smiled. "If you guys don't mind, thanks. I'd like that."

I glared across the table at Alison, who raised her eyebrows in apology. A trace of exotic spices floated in the air as Noah settled in beside me. Squirming in my chair, I desperately wished I were anywhere rather than a few inches from Noah Hale.

The waitress returned to take Noah's drink order and I stole a sideways glance at him. Was that smugness in his expression? How dare he horn in on our dinner and sit there looking like the Cheshire cat.

"I purchased one of Noah's paintings over twenty years ago at a showing in Chicago," Paul told us. "It was great to actually meet the artist face-to-face a couple years ago here on the island."

Alison nodded and took a sip of her wine. "Which piece was that?"

"The Parisian street scene that hangs over my sofa."

"One of my favorites," she said. "Guess I'll have to stop by your gallery, Noah."

I shot her a glance that clearly yelled, *you traitor.*

"I'm having my opening next week. I'd like to extend a personal invitation for you both to attend." Turning his head sideways, he grinned at me. "That includes you too."

Three faces waited for my answer. Shifting uncomfortably in my seat, I said, "I'm not sure what my plans are." The waitress arrived for our dinner order and saved me from further comment.

"How's your mother doing, Noah? I heard she had bronchitis a few weeks ago."

He nodded. "The doctor put her on an antibiotic and she's now as feisty as ever. Bounced right back."

"Nellie is another native of the island that never left," Alison said. "Her family has been living in the Hale-Johnson house for generations. It's such a lovely place. Do you use that widow's walk very much?"

"I do," Noah said. "It's great to sit up there on a summer evening sipping a glass of wine and enjoying the sunset. The view from that vantage point is spectacular."

"How'd that remodeling go last year?" Paul questioned.

"They did a great job, but my mother was happy to see the last of the workmen leave. I've been tossing around the idea of using a couple of the rooms upstairs for teaching art. The lighting up there is perfect for painting." Looking directly at me, he said, "Lighting is very important for an artist."

"So I'd heard," I mumbled, not bothering to conceal the edge in my tone.

Paul looked sharply from Noah to me, probably

121

picking up on the tension. Not sure what was going on, he said, "I heard you were looking for a boat."

Noah nodded. "Yeah, I had one years ago and sold it. Might be nice to just take off on the water again when the mood strikes me and do some fishing."

Glancing at Noah's hand on the wineglass, I saw it was large, with carefully groomed nails—a masculine hand that made me briefly wonder what it was capable of. The waitress arrived with our dinners, preventing me from further thought.

"Syd, you've got a birthday coming up next month," Ali said, in an obvious attempt to keep the conversation going. "We'll have to plan something special."

I felt Noah's eyes on me and wished Alison would just eliminate me from the conversation. "Now that I'm over fifty, I was thinking of just skipping birthdays."

"So you're a Pisces like me," Noah said, reaching for the salt at the same time I did.

In the process of doing so, I hit Noah's wineglass sending the red liquid onto his lap. Jumping up, he began dabbing his tan slacks with a napkin.

"Oh, God. I'm sorry," I stammered, standing up with a napkin in my hand. I was about to assist him with the wipe up until I realized that the wine had landed perfectly on his crotch area. Whipping my hand back as heat floated into my face, I said, "I really am so sorry."

Noah threw his head back laughing at my obvious discomfiture. "It's quite alright. Really. I'd been meaning to toss out these slacks and now you've given me a good reason."

I felt like a teenager on my first date. What was it about this guy that brought out my clumsy, awkward side?

Alison and Paul had sat mutely observing our scene. Paul now cleared his throat. "How about some club soda? They say that removes red wine stains."

Noah raised a palm in the air, grinning. "No, no. It's fine. Nothing to be concerned about." Proving the incident was forgotten, he picked up his fork to begin eating.

Alison buttered a roll and glanced across the table at me. "So what date is your birthday?" she asked Noah.

"I'm March eighteenth. How about you, Sydney?"

"Mine is March nineteenth."

"Well, it seems like you have *something* in common," Paul replied with a grin.

The rest of the dinner conversation was between Noah and Paul. All of us passed on dessert. Noah reached for the check, insisting it was his treat.

Paul concurred, saying, "We'll do this again soon and next time it's on me. Thank you."

Yeah, right. When pigs fly, I thought. But I also thanked Noah.

We stood in front of the hotel as I reached into my handbag for a cigarette. Lighting up, I realized I was the only smoker and caught a disapproving look on Noah's face. Challenging him, I said, "Something wrong?"

Shrugging his shoulders, he said, "Nothing at all."

I didn't miss the smirk on his face. Damn him. What business is it of his if I smoke? Longing to be away from his company, I mustered up my most priggish tone. "Thanks again for dinner." Then turning toward Ali, I said, "I'm going to pass on going to Frogs with you guys for a drink. I'll see you in the morning."

Turning on my heel, I headed up Second Street at a brisk pace.

Settling into bed, thoughts and concerns swirled in my mind. I wondered how it would go with Monica and me living in the same space together. Would Saren's letters provide me with any information about Sybile and the possibility she could be my birth mother? My mail orders for spun yarn were doing fairly well, but how would my sales be once I opened my shop? And throughout all of these thoughts one image kept jumping to the surface—Noah Hale's handsome face.

≈13≈

"Oh, you didn't have to do this, Miss Sydney," Saren exclaimed, taking the plate of blueberry muffins from me.

"Alison insisted," I said, stepping into the living room.

"Well, they sure will go good with the tea I'm about to brew. Let's go in the kitchen while I get that ready. Then we'll go through those letters I found."

After setting out the tea and muffins, Saren sat opposite me at the old Formica table. "Heard some talk that Miss Syblile isn't feeling so well," he said, avoiding eye contact.

"Really? I don't know her that well, but Dora hasn't mentioned anything. Maybe she has a cold that's turned into bronchitis. I heard Nellie Hale recently had that."

"Hmm, could be," Saren replied thoughtfully.

Finishing up the tea and muffins, I helped to clear the table.

"Okay, now let's get to those letters," he said, leading the way to the living room.

Saren settled himself in a chair while reaching for an old wooden box. Lifting the hinged cover, he drew out a packet of letters held together with rubber bands.

"These were the first ones she sent," he said and proceeded to read aloud about a young and dream-filled Sybile Bowden arriving in Manhattan to stay at the Barbizon Hotel for Women. "Yup, June of 1953, that's when she left."

"Do those letters cover all the years she was there?" I questioned.

Picking up another stack, he nodded. "Yeah, pretty much they do." He hesitated. "But ya know, something always had me wondering. There was a period of time that Sybile left the Barbizon. Said she had a chance to share an apartment with another girl she'd met. Those letters should be in here too, but she didn't write much during that time and then shortly after that she went back to the Barbizon." Peering closely at the postmarks, he held up another bundle. "Ah, here they are," he said, removing the first one. "Maybe you'd like to read through these and I'll read some others."

I reached for the packet with sweaty palms. I knew Sybile certainly hadn't shared her pregnancy with Saren, so it was doubtful they'd contain any evidence of my birth.

Removing a thin, parchment sheet from the envelope, I began reading.

August 18, 1954
Dear Saren,
As you'll see from the new address, I'm no longer residing at the Barbizon so please send your letters here. I'm living in an apartment on the Lower East Side with another model that I

met. The rules aren't as strict as the hotel and it allows me more freedom to enjoy the city.

I've been feeling a bit under the weather recently, and therefore, I'm not able to work quite as much. So Molly has been very generous in allowing me to stay with her. I hope all is well with you in Paris. Such an exciting place to be. Maybe someday I'll visit you there. Please keep in touch.

Fondly,
Sybile

I replaced the letter into the envelope. Under the weather? Could she have been experiencing bouts of morning sickness? The dates would add up, but other than that no concrete evidence that Sybile was pregnant with me. Glancing over at Saren, I saw he was lost in time reading the words of the woman he loved. Searching through the bundle I found the year 1955. Saren had meticulously organized the letters according to years and months. Finding March, I was surprised to see that the packet contained only one letter. Removing the rubber band from the envelope, I began reading.

March 5, 1955
Dear Saren,
I have the most marvelous news. My friend Molly has invited me to her family home in the

Hamptons for an entire month. After so much work, she feels we both need a rest and I'm very much looking forward to being there.

So please don't write me again until I'm in touch with you, as I'm not sure exactly when I'll return, and I'd hate to see your letters get lost.

Spring has arrived in New York and it's a delightful time to be here. I hope all is well with you and I'll be in touch sometime next month.

Fondly,
Sybile

Interesting, I thought. The month that I was born Sybile refrained from corresponding with Saren. Could it be because my birth was approaching that she wanted no contact with him during that time? Possibly. And possibly this is all pure speculation on my part.

"Ah, these letters are from when she was dating her husband," Saren said, interrupting my thoughts.

"What year was that?"

"Nineteen fifty-seven and then six years later, the marriage was over and she was back here on the island. She sure did make out alright in that divorce settlement though. It allowed her to live here all these years."

"What kind of work did her husband do that provided for her so well?"

"He was her agent for modeling. Not long into the marriage Sybile had told me he had a rovin' eye, if ya know what I mean. So I think he wandered once too often and that was when she called it quits."

I got up and stretched, glancing at the time on the grandfather clock in the corner of the room. "Oh, gosh, I really need to get going, Saren. I have to meet the carpenters at the shop. I'm hoping they've finished up all the work over there."

"I sure do thank you for coming here this morning. I think I needed a bit of encouragement to take these letters out again."

"It was my pleasure. And thank you for sharing them with me."

Walking me to the door, that faraway look returned to his eyes. "I think I'll just spend a bit more time reading through some more of these."

I was thrilled to arrive at the shop to find the workmen finishing up my cubbyholes. "Oh, they look great," I said, standing just inside the door to admire the holes that could now be filled with rainbow colors of yarn.

Within twenty minutes they were finished and I had written them the check. *Well, this is it, kid. There're no more excuses. You're ready to open in a couple days and begin doing business.*

I was surprised to glance toward the door and see both Dora and Sybile coming in.

"I hope you don't mind," Dora said. "I just wanted to check and see when you might be opening."

"My carpentry is finished." I gestured toward the empty holes against the wall. "So I'd say probably this Thursday."

I stifled a giggle as I saw that Sybile was clad in skin-tight hot pink capris and a fuzzy crimson jacket, with a most unusual hat. The exact shade as the pants, the toque tightly hugged Sybile's head showing only a few wisps of red hair on the forehead. I couldn't help but wonder where Sybile purchased these outrageous head coverings.

"Oh, that's great. I hope you don't think I'm a pest, but I'm so happy we'll be having a yarn shop here on the island. We have a nice shop in Gainesville, but I don't relish the drive, and many times I do order from companies online, but the shipping costs are high."

"Well, I hope many others will feel the way you do."

It didn't escape me that Sybile had remained silent.

"How're you doing today?" I asked.

Replacing her sunglasses, she said, "Just fine. Well, at least I was until I got dragged out of my house to go to lunch with my sister. I was watching a good movie when she called."

Before I could respond, Dora said, "Oh, for goodness sake. Wouldn't hurt you once in a while to get away from that TV set. You spend entirely too much time watching those old fifties movies."

"That's right, I'd heard you were a model," I said, hoping to entice the woman into a conversation. "I would think you'd enjoy seeing the fashions of that era."

For the first time since I'd met her, Sybile seemed to perk up and become animated. "I was pretty near a top fashion model in New York City during the fifties and early sixties. It was the most exciting time of my life and then those hideous mod fashions appeared. That wasn't for me. They called that style—they had no idea what style was."

Based on Sybile's current mode of dress, I was at a loss for words and merely nodded in agreement.

"I could have gone on to be like those other top models. But Twiggy hit the scene and everything changed in modeling." She flung her large leather bag over her shoulder. "That was a lifetime ago. Are you coming for dinner this evening?" she asked her sister.

Dora nodded. "Yes, I'll be there about six and don't forget to call your doctor."

Flashing Dora a deadly look, she retorted, "You need to worry about yourself, Dora." And without even a good-bye, she left the shop.

Unsure what to say, I remained silent.

"That sister of mine is a handful," Dora said, shaking her head.

"She's had that cough for quite a while, hasn't she? I hope it's not serious."

"She'd kill me for saying anything, but I'm afraid it *is* serious." She paused for a moment. "The doctor suspects lung cancer."

"And she's not doing anything about it?" I gasped.

"Not yet. But her coughing is getting worse and now she's getting short of breath, so I don't think she has a choice. She promised me she'd call for an appointment this week."

"That's terrible."

"As I'm sure you've gathered, Sybile has always been her own person. Does what she wants, when she wants. So illness is no different. She's in control. All I can do is try to steer her in the right direction."

"Since she has no children or other family, she's fortunate to have you."

Dora laughed. "I'd bet she wouldn't always think that. But I try to look out for her."

"I'm sure you missed her years ago when she left the island."

"Yeah, she's only eighteen months older than me so we were pretty close growing up. It took a while to get used to her not being here."

"I've been talking to Saren Ghetti. I guess he was pretty fond of her back then too."

A look of surprise crossed Dora's face. "Did he tell you that?"

"Yeah, he did actually. Told me he and Sybile exchanged letters the entire time she was gone. Then when she came back here she pretty much ignored him."

Dora smiled. "That's Sybile. Never did know what was good for her. She would have had a nice life with Saren, but no, she wanted those bright lights of New York. Got herself into a situation and now she's left alone."

"A situation?" I questioned.

Embarrassment crept across Dora's face. "Oh, well, I meant with marrying the wrong man." Clearly wanting to change the subject, she said, "Well now, I'd just better get moving along. I'm sure you have plenty to do for your opening."

Realizing the conversation was over, I said, "Yeah, and I have some spun yarn to package up for customers. But thanks for dropping by, Dora. I look forward to seeing you again."

≈14≈

Standing in front of my spinning wheel with arms crossed, I surveyed the room in front of me. It looked like a bona fide knitting shop. And it was mine. I took a deep breath as I walked to the wall and rearranged some skeins of yarn. Lilly and I had gotten to the shop at 8:30, well before my 10:00 opening time. Alison was ten minutes late bringing home-baked muffins for my customers. Where the hell was she? Not that I had one customer in the shop.

I turned around to see her pull up in the golf cart and felt guilty. That was nice of her to even offer to do the baking.

"Here, let me help you," I said, taking a large tray from her. "God, Ali, I think you made too many."

"Don't be silly. Think positive."

After arranging the muffins, while I brewed the coffee, she said, "I love what you've done to this place. It looks so cozy for a knitting shop. Makes ya just want to curl up on that sofa there with knitting needles. Well, maybe not me . . . but somebody."

I laughed. "You could knit as well as anybody. You've just never tried."

"Is the reporter still coming out from the *Gainesville Sun* to cover your opening?"

"Yeah, said she'd be here this afternoon."

"Terrific. I think you're going to do well, Syd."

"I sure hope so. My mail orders have slowed down though."

"Everything goes in fits and spurts. Hey, what time is Monica due to arrive?"

"She said about four. She'll get her rental car when she lands, and it's about a three-hour drive from the Tampa airport."

"I feel so bad that I'm booked solid for the next couple months. Otherwise, she could stay in one of the rooms in the main house."

"It's certainly not your fault she's decided to come down here. We'll be fine."

"Well, it's going to be tough sharing a small apartment with your grown daughter. God, you won't have any privacy at all."

I laughed. "What on earth do I need privacy for?" When Ali didn't say anything, I turned around. "Well?"

"You just never know. You might want to . . . ah . . . you know. Invite a male friend back to your place sometime."

"Oh, yeah, right. There's all kinds of *male friends* breaking down my door for the pleasure of my company."

Ali shrugged her shoulders. "Well, I happen to know there's one in particular that might enjoy your company."

"Noah Hale? Are you nuts? Don't even think it. He hates me. I doubt he'll ever forgive me for taking his precious gallery space here. And I get the feeling he thinks I'm a total ditz."

"Don't be too sure of that," Ali said, as she poured herself a cup of coffee.

"Do you know something that I don't?"

Ali pursed her lips. "All I'm saying is, be open, Syd. Give the guy a chance. Losing Stephen doesn't mean your entire life is over."

She was right. Lately, I'd given some serious thought to that topic.

"You were young when you married Stephen.

135

You had a decent marriage, yes. But it doesn't mean you won't ever have feelings for another man again. But you need to allow yourself to be open to that possibility. Even Paul agreed, there's a certain chemistry between you and Noah."

"What? Are you guys talking about me behind my back? Chemistry? This isn't a high school science class, Ali."

"Just don't isolate yourself in regard to a male companion. That's all I'm saying."

At 4:15 I glanced up when the wind chimes sounded on the door. "Monica," I said, coming from behind the desk to hug my daughter. I spied the cast on her right arm and felt bad for not being overjoyed about her arrival. "How's your arm doing? I'm glad you made it here okay."

"At least there's no pain. Yeah, it was a good drive. I'm glad Ali suggested coming up that Suncoast Parkway. No traffic. And the ride onto the island was spectacular. I hit that Number Four bridge, and it was like a postcard. All those patches of green and the sun hitting the water. God, you were right, Mom. This place is like paradise."

Her stylish cut bobbed around her cheeks as she spoke. Monica had always been animated, and perky was one of the adjectives they'd used in her high school yearbook. Despite her skiing mishap, she looked great.

"So this is Spinning Forward," she said, looking around. "I like it. Perfect for a knitting shop. So how'd your first day go?"

Trying to sound optimistic, I said, "Well, a bit slow really. I had some of the locals drop in, but beyond that . . . it was quiet. I'm sure it'll pick up."

I noticed that Monica refrained from giving me any encouragement.

"So what time will you be finished here?"

I glanced at the clock. "I don't think a bus will be pulling up with any customers, so why don't I close up and we'll get you settled in at the Tree House."

"Great. Where's Lilly? I thought she came to the shop with you."

"Yeah, normally she does. But for today, I left her home. Come on," I said, grabbing my handbag and keys. "She's waiting for you at the apartment."

A week later I sat at the desk in my shop, chin in hands, as disappointment washed over me. Besides Dora, I'd only had a handful of sales. Lots of lookers, but not many buyers. I recalled what Dora had mentioned that morning about knitting classes. Maybe she was right. Many of the locals had dropped by, admired the beautiful yarns, and then admitted they didn't know how to knit. Offer it and they will come, Dora had said. If they purchased their yarn from my shop, that purchase would include assistance and suggestions. Monday was a slow day for business and I didn't open until 4:00 after I finished my shift at Cook's. Doing a knitting class from six till eight might work.

Jumping up with a bit of renewed enthusiasm, I found a poster board in the back room. With colored pens in hand, I made a sign promoting the classes. Capping the pens and stepping back to observe my work, the sight of a couple hugging on the sidewalk caught my attention. Looking closer, I realized it was Noah Hale. The very attractive female was tall, slim, and sported a stylish blonde cut. She threw her head back laughing, as Noah embraced her once again. They stood talking for a few minutes and before departing, Noah leaned over to kiss her cheek.

Oh, right, Ali. There's no doubt he's interested in *me*.

A moment later, the chimes sounded on the door and the woman walked inside. Forcing a smile to my face, I said, "Welcome to Spinning Forward."

"Hi, there. Thanks," she said, as Lilly raced over for her requisite pat.

You traitor, I thought, while maintaining the smile. "Anything in particular you're looking for?"

Walking to the wall of yarn, she said, "Yes. Alpaca in a soft shade of blue. It's to make a sweater for a special person with the most incredible brown eyes, and I thought blue would be a nice contrast."

Obviously the sweater was for Mr. Noah Hale and obviously this female had a vested interest in him. Well, la di da to both of them. "We do have a few shades of blue in the alpaca," I said in my most professional voice and pointed to the yarn.

"Oh, yeah. This is perfect," she said, scooping up an armful of skeins. "You have a lovely place here."

"Thanks." I wasn't sure why I felt awkward that my shop was empty. "Do you live on the island?" I asked and then wanted to bite my tongue. What do I care where she lives?

"No, I flew in from Savannah yesterday. I'm only here until tomorrow. We have a great yarn shop there, but I see you also do spinning of dog and cat fur. That's really different. I have a Maltese and I'd love to get some yarn from his fur. How would I go about having that done?"

I explained the procedure to her and handed her a card. "My address is on there and you can just mail it to me."

After paying for the purchase, she extended her hand. "Thanks so much. I'm Tori, by the way." Glancing at the business card in her hand, she said, "And you're Sydney?"

"Yes, and thanks for stopping by."

I watched her leave the shop, but not before

noticing how well she wore the gray woolen slacks and matching blazer. Two things crossed my mind—that woman had made my till for the day, and I recognized a pang of jealousy toward this person who was clearly involved with Noah Hale. Why the hell should I care? Without warning, a flash of the years ahead crossed my mind—alone and possibly lonely. Pushing aside these thoughts, I grabbed the poster and taped it to the front window.

Walking home with Lilly, I felt every day of my almost fifty-three years. Doing the shifts at Cook's and rushing to open the shop was beginning to take its toll on me. What I'd give to have a Jacuzzi bath like I had in my old home. To ease away the aches with a nice glass of wine. Climbing the steps to the apartment, I realized that thinking about Lexington and Stephen and my old lifestyle felt like it was another person that had experienced all of that.

Opening the door, I gasped. Looking around my normally very neat and organized kitchen, I took a deep breath. It sure as hell did not look like this when I'd left in the morning. Coffee cups were piled in the sink, along with a stack of dishes. A frying pan with caked-on eggs sat on the stove. Inching its way down my cabinets from the counter was a stick of butter that had turned from solid to liquid. Newspapers covered the table.

Walking into the bedroom, I saw the still-unmade bed and clothes heaped in a pile on the chair. I opened the bathroom door to find balled-up towels on the floor with remnants of makeup covering the vanity.

Tears stung my eyes. What the hell had I gotten myself into? I swung around to see Monica coming in the door, clutching shopping bags in her left hand.

"Hey, Mom. I hope you weren't worried. I met a new friend last night at Frogs and we've been in Gainesville shopping all day." She saw the look on my face and stopped. "Oh, sorry about the mess. But Bree called at nine and I didn't have time to clean up before we left."

I had been up since five, stood on my feet for seven hours serving food, opened my shop, and worked another three hours. All of this while my daughter slept in and then gallivanted around Gainesville shopping for the day. Something was wrong with this picture.

My normally calm way of dealing with things slipped away. "This is unforgivable, Monica. There is no way in hell I'm going to allow this in my house. You didn't do this when you were six-teen. For Christ's sake, you weren't brought up to live like a pig." I heard my voice going up a few decibels. "And you damn well will clean it all. *Now.*"

Grabbing my cigarettes, with Lilly close on my heels, I stormed out of the apartment, down the stairs, and out to the garden. I was glad to see it was empty and plunked down into the lounge. Lighting up a cigarette, I blew out the smoke and wondered how much longer I could tolerate living under the same roof as my daughter.

≈15≈

By early March, my business hadn't increased dramatically. I had visions of still waiting tables at Cook's, my walker in hand, years from now trying to make ends meet. The weekends were a little busier with tourists on the island, but sales during the week were slim. While mail orders were beginning to increase again, it wasn't enough to give me a sense of security. I was beginning to question why I thought I could make a go of a yarn shop.

Monday evening knitting classes were also bringing in some additional income, but all of it had me worried. One of the snags I was now encountering was not enough time to tend to the daily chores in the shop and maintain a prompt schedule of spinning fur for customers. Coming into the shop earlier allowed me some time to catch up, so lately I was lucky to get six hours' sleep at night. I sat spinning a champagne-colored fur from a cocker spaniel in Fort Lauderdale, and wished I could take on an assistant. But that was out of the question. And making everything even more discouraging was the fact I'd come down with a nasty cold. I had to admit—my energy level was on low and I was running out of steam fast.

A soft tapping on the glass door caused Lilly to bark. I looked up to see Eudora Foster standing on the pavement. Glancing at the clock, I saw it was 10:05 and time to remove the CLOSED sign from the door.

"Oh, I'm sorry. Am I here too early?" Dora inquired.

"No, not at all. I'm afraid I lost track of time. I'm getting pretty behind on my mail orders, so I've been coming in early to catch up. What can I do for you?"

"I need to purchase some yarn to make that Aran sweater I'd been talking about. I made them years ago when Marin was small, and she's been hinting for another one."

I sneezed and reached for a tissue from the box. "Sorry," I said, and led the way to the yarn Dora was looking for.

"You sound terrible. And you don't look so good. You need to be home resting."

I chuckled. "Yeah, right. Don't I wish. I'm afraid that's not possible. I'm here till five. You never know when a bus will pull up out front—all women wanting yarn," I said with sarcasm.

"Well then, what you need is an assistant. Somebody who can fill in for you. You know, like on days like this."

"That would be great. Except I can't afford to pay anybody."

"The business isn't doing so well?" Dora questioned.

I let out another sneeze and shook my head. "Certainly not as well as I hoped it would. It takes time to build a business. The thing is, I'm short on time. Right along with short on money."

Nodding, she began fingering the wool. A few moments later, she turned around to face me. "I have an idea. Now just tell me if I'm butting in and I'll mind my own business. I have plenty of time on my hands and I love to knit."

I wasn't following where Dora was leading. I raised my eyebrows and waited for her to continue.

"What I'm saying is I'm a pretty good knitter, and you wouldn't know this, but it was always my dream to have my own knit shop." She paused while fingering the wool. "I'd love to help you out, Sydney. I wouldn't expect to get paid. I don't need the money. But I'd love to be here in the shop and helping you at the same time."

Had I misunderstood? This woman, who just happened to be an expert knitter, was offering to assist me for free? "I don't know what . . ." I began hesitantly. "What to say. That's so incredibly kind of you."

Dora laughed. "Not kind at all. Incredibly selfish on my part. I'd just love being in here surrounded by all the different yarns. And it's easy to

144

see, you could use a little help. Like today. You should be home in bed sipping hot tea."

I smiled. Dora was right—on both counts. I should be home resting, and I certainly could use her help on the weekends. I also really needed to devote more time to advertising. Ali had kept nagging me to do this and assured me it would increase my business. There just hadn't been enough time. Working both day and night was beginning to catch up with me.

"Well," I said, taking a deep breath. "I'd be honored if you'd help me out in here. You're an expert knitter and would be a great asset to me. However, I can't let you do it for nothing." I thought for a moment. "I tell you what. How about if I give you a fifty-percent discount on any yarn or items you purchase in here. I get it at cost, so I really wouldn't be losing anything. And it would make me feel better for the time you're giving me."

A broad smile crossed Dora's face. "Deal," she said, extending her hand. "And how about if I start right now? You go home and get some rest."

I glanced at my watch. It was only 10:30. "Are you sure?" I questioned.

"Positive," Dora said. "Just explain the cash box to me and I'll be fine. If you don't mind, I'll purchase that Aran yarn right now and I can start the sweater. Anything in particular I need to know about the shop?"

I couldn't believe my good fortune. "Well, if, and I say if, there's any mail order deliveries, Clyde usually shows up between two and three. And if any stock comes in, you can open the box and just put the yarn and stuff in the bins."

"I think I can handle that. I know my way around this shop pretty well. Just one request," she said. "Could I run over to Cook's and get myself a sandwich to go for my lunch? And then I'll be all set."

"Of course you can," I said with a smile and watched Dora cross the street.

Bending down to pat Lilly, I shook my head. *People really are kind,* I thought. With a little help maybe I *could* make this business into something.

Surrounded by a box of tissues, a mystery novel I couldn't seem to get involved in, and a cup of tea, I sat in bed propped up with pillows. By the time I'd arrived home with Lilly, I was grateful for Dora's offer. I was running a low-grade temp and the pressure in my face had increased. No doubt the cold had settled in my sinuses.

"Come in," I hollered to a knock on the door.

"I thought some nice hot soup would help," Alison said, walking in with a tray.

"I'm not an invalid. I could have fixed something later."

"I know you could have. But you don't have to. Stay bundled up and you'll be over this quicker."

"Thanks," I said, straightening up to take the tray. "I never get colds. Hell, I'm never sick. I can't imagine where I caught this."

"Gee, could it be all the stress of the past year finally catching up with you? You were a nurse. You know what stress will do to your immune system."

I nodded, taking a sip of the homemade chicken soup. "Hmm, yummy."

Ali pulled up a chair. "Things going any better with Monica?"

"Well, I haven't had a repeat performance of what I witnessed last week. She didn't say much, but she cleaned up the mess and has managed to pick up more after herself. It's just tough—living with somebody else again."

"And where's the little prima donna today?"

I smiled. "Off to Gainesville again with Bree. Shopping, I imagine."

"Where the hell is she getting the money for all this shopping, and what the hell is she buying?"

"She's buying clothes. Says it's been a while and she needs an *island* wardrobe, whatever that means. Monica's not hurting for money. She's been working at a well-paying job since she graduated college and doesn't normally shop so much."

Ali shook her head. "Maybe there's a reason I never had kids. She knows you've been sick with this cold—has she offered you any help at all?"

"No. But guess what?" I told her about Dora offering to help me in the shop.

"That's great. Dora's a special person. I've always liked her. Anything new with Sybile?"

"Not a thing. It's hard to try and get information without being too obvious. I don't want to offend Dora or Saren. Monica is certainly showing an interest in the search though."

"Has she met Sybile yet?"

I shook my head. "No, but she's met Dora and likes her a lot. I told her Dora and Sybile are like day and night. Just in case it's true, I want her to be prepared. I sure can't see Monica caring much for her either."

I awoke on the morning of my birthday feeling considerably better. Spending two days in bed helped with getting over the cold.

I walked into the yarn shop at noon to find a huge set of brightly colored balloons tied to my spinning wheel. "Happy birthday!" Dora said, coming to embrace me.

"Thank you and I suppose you provided those beautiful balloons?"

"I did and I hope you'll enjoy them."

"Dora, you didn't have to do this."

"I know I didn't—I wanted to."

We both turned to the sound of the door opening. A young fellow approached me almost hidden behind a huge bouquet of yellow roses. "Sydney Webster?" he asked.

"Yes," was all I could manage to say.

"Then these are for you."

I reached for the crystal vase full of flowers. "Thank you."

Sybile? Could Sybile have sent them and was this was her way of telling me I was her daughter?

"My, my," Dora said. "Those certainly are gorgeous. Open the card and let's see who they're from."

I pulled the card from the envelope and mouthed a silent "oh."

Dora looked at me expectantly.

"They're . . . they're from Noah Hale."

"Oh, my. Now what a thoughtful thing for that man to do. How did he know it was your birthday?"

I couldn't believe he'd remembered, much less taken the time to send flowers. "It came up in a conversation recently. Actually, yesterday was his birthday."

"I see. Well, they're just beautiful," Dora said, leaning over to inhale the fragrance.

I left them sitting on the desk and walked into the back room. Now what the hell was I supposed to do? Send him a thank-you note? And why did he really send them? A man sending flowers normally indicated a certain interest. And this man had another woman in his life. I'm certainly not about to get involved in a triangle. Damn, I wish he hadn't sent them.

An hour later, Dora was waiting on a customer and I headed to the front door. "I'll be back in a little while. Are you okay here?"

"Sure, take your time," Dora replied and I headed down Second Street to Noah's gallery.

Walking into the shop I found it was empty and began browsing some of the artwork hanging on the wall.

"See anything that interests you?" Noah said, stepping from the back room.

I spun around. "Not really. Well, what I mean is I don't know that much about art. But I'm sure yours is good." Why did I always sound like a flustered teenager with him?

Noah laughed. "Based on sales, yeah, I'd say it's pretty good."

He never cut me any slack either. "I just wanted to thank you for the flowers. You really shouldn't have done that."

"Why? Don't you like them?"

God, this man had an irritating streak. "Yes, of course I like them. They're beautiful."

"Then good. They accomplished what I hoped they would."

"Which might be what?"

"A visit from you."

"Oh," was all I could think of to say.

150

"Happy birthday," Noah said, a grin spreading across his face.

"Thank you and to you as well. A day late."

Noah acknowledged the wishes with a nod. "So do you have big plans to celebrate tonight?"

"Alison and Paul are taking me to dinner."

Noah leaned against the counter, arms folded across his chest. "Speaking of dinner. I'd like to take you out for dinner sometime when you're free."

"Me?" I asked stupidly. "Thanks but I don't think so."

"You don't think so?" he asked in surprise. "Why is that?"

Why was he pressuring me? He had a damn girlfriend. What was I supposed to be, a replacement? "Well, uh . . . I just don't think . . ." I was uncertain what to say and took a few steps backward. As soon as I did, I heard the sound of glass hitting the tile floor and spun around to see that I'd knocked over jars of water with paintbrushes in them.

Bending down to try and pick up the glass, I stammered, "God, I'm so sorry. I didn't realize that table was there."

I felt my wrist being snatched by Noah's hand.

"Don't touch it. You'll cut yourself. Let me get something to clean this up."

He disappeared into the back room and returned with a roll of paper towels and a broom and dust pan. Soaking up the water first, he then swept up the glass.

"I'm really terribly sorry," I said, feeling like an errant child.

"You seem to say that a lot to me," was all Noah replied.

Anger fused with embarrassment. "Well, for Christ's sake, I didn't do it on purpose. So crucify me. And let me know if I owe you anything for the broken glass," I tossed over my shoulder before stomping out the door.

At 6:00 I flipped the sign on the yarn shop to CLOSED. "Now, Dora, it's time for you to go, so scat," I said, waving my hands in the air.

Dora laughed. "Okay. I'll be on my way. You enjoy the rest of your birthday. Are you leaving now too?"

"I will be shortly. I have a few accounts to look at and then I'm outta here. Have to get ready for my birthday dinner."

Dora reached for her sweater and handbag. "Okay, and have a lovely celebration this evening."

Twenty minutes later tapping on the glass door caused me to look up from the accounting I'd been working on. Noah Hale stood outside waiting. Oh God, what the hell does he want now?

Getting up, I unlocked the door. "Can I help you?" I asked with a curt tone.

"May I come in?"

Blowing air through my lips, I stepped aside but said nothing.

"Thanks. Nice flowers," he said, nodding toward the desk.

"Hmmm."

"You and I seem to be like oil and water."

I sighed. "Then why do you keep contacting me?"

"Because I like you, that's why."

"You coulda fooled me." He likes me? Did he just say that?

"How about if we call a truce? Are you willing?"

"A truce? Sure."

Noah smiled. "You don't sound all that certain about it."

"Well, what does this truce involve?"

"Nothing too strenuous. Just have dinner with me some evening."

Okay, I thought, I've had enough of his game playing. "Look, I don't want to be rude to you, but . . ." I took a deep breath. "I'm fifty-three years old. This isn't high school. And at my age I don't play games, nor do I get involved in other people's relationships. Do you understand?"

Noah raised his eyebrows. "What games? What relationships?"

This man was truly dense. Why was he forcing me to spell it out? "The cheating game, that's what I'm talking about and the relationship you obviously have with another person. There. That's what I'm referring to."

Noah ran a hand through his curls. "Forgive me for not understanding, but I don't. Could you be a little more specific?"

"Tori. Is that specific enough? She's your girl-friend and I'm not about to go there and be in the middle."

Noah threw his head back laughing. "Tori? You know Tori?"

Why did he think this was a hilarious joke? "I don't think it's the least bit humorous. Yes, I know Tori because she's one of my customers. I saw you a couple weeks ago in front of my shop hug-ging and kissing and then she came in here to pur-chase yarn for, and I quote, 'a special person with the most incredible brown eyes.' I assume that special person would be you."

Noah shook his head while continuing to laugh. "I apologize for laughing. Yes, I guess I am that *special* person, but Tori . . . We've known each other since college days. She's happily married to my friend Stan. There's never been anything romantic between us. Not ever. We're just very old and good friends."

At that moment I wished the floor would swallow me up. College friends? Never anything romantic? Oh God, I must have sounded like a shrew and worse yet . . . like a shrew that had some feelings for him. I could feel heat burning my face and was certain it wasn't a hot flash. "Oh . . . I thought . . ."

"I'm pretty sure I now understand what you thought," he said as the laugh diminished to a smile. "No, there's nothing like that between Tori and me."

I ran my tongue along my upper lip and nodded. "Okay, so I guess I owe you an apology."

"And I'll collect on that apology with an acceptance to dinner some evening. Then we can call it even. How's that sound?"

It sounded much better than I could have hoped for.

≫16≪

Seated at the Curl Up and Dye, I leafed through the latest issue of *Vanity Fair* while waiting for my color to process. I enjoyed the luxury of being pampered and, not for the first time, was grateful I had Dora to cover the shop for a little while.

I glanced up as an elderly, white-haired woman entered the salon. Greetings were exchanged with Polly and the other customers and then the woman turned to me.

"I don't think we've met, but aren't you the new owner of the yarn shop downtown?"

"Yes. I'm Sydney Webster."

The woman pushed her glasses up the bridge of her nose and peered closer. "And I'm Margaret Johnson. You sure do look familiar to me. You have kin on this island?"

Here we go again. What is it about these people thinking I'm related to somebody here? But I smiled and said, "Nope. Afraid not. I only moved here five months ago. You've probably just seen me around."

Shaking her head slowly, the woman raised an index finger to her chin. "Hmm, could be. But no . . . I know what it is. You sure do bear a striking resemblance to Sybile Bowden. Are you two related?"

Goose bumps rose on my skin, as a deep-seated emotion glided to the surface. Once again, I remembered staring into Sybile's almond-shaped eyes while something familiar tugged at me.

The chatter in the salon dwindled to a hush as the other women also waited for my answer. Feeling like a child being admonished by a teacher, a sense of unease came over me before I replied. "No, I'm not related to her at all. I'm originally from the Boston area and have no ties to anyone on the island."

Shrugging her shoulders, Margaret went to sit down. "Sure could fool me. I've known Sybile since we were born—although the high and mighty phony would probably deny it. Same age we are, ya know. Anyway, you sure do remind me of her."

Polly prevented any further conversation. "Well, they say we all have a double. Come on, Syd, let's get that color rinsed off."

I returned to the shop to find Twila Faye talking to Dora.

"Hey, Sydney. I'm doing so well with Chelsea's sweater, I'm going to make another one." Reaching into her bag, she removed pale pink yarn that clearly resembled a child's sweater.

"It's gorgeous," I told her. "See, and you thought you'd never learn to knit."

She smiled with pride. "I never thought I could do something like this. Now I'd like to buy some multi-color yarn for the next one. Do you have that?"

After choosing what she wanted, she brought the skeins for me to ring up.

"Oh, did you know they're having a Bloodmobile here on Monday? They'll be doing it in front of City Hall."

"No, I hadn't heard about that. With my blood type, I suppose I should donate."

"I'm Type B. What're you?"

"Type AB. It's a bit rare. Only four percent of people in the world are AB and the blood banks are always wanting mine."

Twila Faye laughed. "Think you're descended from royalty?"

"Oh, I seriously doubt that," I said, filling a small shopping bag with yarn.

After Twila Faye left, Dora questioned, "Are you really Type AB? Is that true?"

The serious look on her face caught my attention. "Yes, why?"

She concentrated on filling the shelves. "I was just wondering. It's fairly uncommon, as you said."

I had a feeling there was more to this subject than Dora was willing to discuss.

Later that afternoon I sat at my spinning wheel while casting furtive glances at Dora. The shop was empty and she was working on the Aran sweater. I recalled Margaret's conversation and for the first time began to seriously consider the possibility that Sybile could be my mother. Could that be possible? Highly unlikely. Or is it? While I had to agree that the chance wasn't even remotely possible—there *was* still a chance. I realized that my mother could be anybody. But Sybile Bowden? It was inconceivable to think that I'd come to a small island in Florida and end up finding my birth mother.

Feeling compelled to bring up the subject, I broke the silence in the shop. "I haven't had much luck in searching for my birth mother since we last discussed it," I told Dora.

She put her knitting in her lap and looked over at me. "I've been meaning to ask you about that. That's a shame, because it seems like you're interested in finding her."

I nodded. "Well, yes, I think I am. But Monica has shown an interest in meeting her biological grandmother."

"I can understand that. Family is important. I may not see Marin and the boys as much as when my grandsons were small, but I know all of them are just a phone call away. So besides Monica, do you have any family left?"

"Not really. A few elderly aunts that I was never close to, but that's it."

Dora remained silent and in that moment, I blurted out, "Do you think I look like Sybile?"

Surprise covered Dora's face. Chewing on her lower lip, her eyebrows formed two perfect arches, while her fingers rubbed the knitting needles in her hand. "Well, now, that's quite a question. They do say everybody has a twin."

In that moment, I knew. Dora's reaction confirmed the suspicion more than any birth certificate could. Neither affirmation nor denial. Without anything more concrete, I sensed puzzle pieces tentatively sliding into place. The room began closing in on me, making it necessary to grip the edge of my spinning wheel. Despite the cool air, perspiration formed on the nape of my neck and when I spoke my voice sounded unfamiliar. "Your sister gave birth to a baby years ago, didn't she?"

Without looking up from her lap, Dora nodded and whispered, "Yes."

"It was a baby girl?"

Once again, Dora nodded.

"And what blood type is Sybile?"

After what felt like hours, I heard her say, "She's also Type AB."

That night in bed I tossed and turned for hours. Glancing at the bedside clock I saw it was 3:05. Giving up on sleep and trying not to wake Monica, I put on a robe and sat on the balcony. Lilly came out, plopping down by my feet.

"I'm sorry I'm keeping you awake, girl," I said, lighting up a cigarette.

Blowing the smoke into the night air, I replayed the afternoon again in my mind. I'd had no intention of being quite so blunt in the conversation with Dora. But I felt like I was on a roller coaster and there was no turning back—none whatsoever. And each question that Dora confirmed had pushed me further ahead.

"You think I'm that daughter too, don't you?" I had asked her.

"From the first moment I laid eyes on you, yes, I felt you were my sister's child. I never even knew of your existence until Sybile was back on the island at least five years. For some reason, she broke down and told me about your birth and made me promise that I'd never mention it again. And I didn't. Not until I saw you."

"What does Sybile think?" I'd asked Dora.

"I'm pretty sure she thinks you're her daughter but she won't admit it to me. Won't allow me to even discuss it with her. Said it's all insane and I'm crazy to even consider such a thing."

Dora and I discussed the improbability, the denial of Sybile, and where to go from here.

I looked up at the star-studded night sky and sighed. I heard Dora asking, "Do you want to pursue this? Do you want Sybile to know that you figured it out and based on the evidence you want her to confirm that she's your birth mother?"

With those questions I contemplated the word *rejection*. Rejection was never an easy emotion to deal with, but in those few moments I knew I'd come too far not to take the risk and replied, "Yes, talk to her and let me know what she says."

Mashing out the cigarette in the ashtray, I stood up. "Come on, Lilly. Time to go back to bed. I've set the wheels in motion and all we can do now is wait."

"God, do you think Sybile really could be my grandmother?" Monica buttered a slice of toast while waiting for my answer.

"I have no clue. She's certainly not going to own up to it easily. She went to great lengths to keep me a secret."

"And your father? Who could it be? The modeling agent she was married to?"

"No, the dates wouldn't be right. I have no idea.

He was probably a married man she was seeing and didn't have a choice. It has to be horrible to be faced with something like that—young, no means to support a child and yet, no other choice but adoption."

Monica nodded. "Yeah, thank God for birth control today. I mean they didn't even have the pill back in the fifties."

"Well, all we can do is wait and see what Dora is able to find out from Sybile. What's your plan for today?"

"I have a couple of job interviews in Gainesville. I don't want to get my hopes too high, but one is with the university for a teaching position."

"You're finally going to use your English degree and teaching credentials?" I asked with hope.

"Could be," was all she said before getting up to head into the shower.

After I locked up the shop on Friday evening, I returned home, had supper, then put on Lilly's leash for a walk around the neighborhood. I approached Noah's house and realized he was clipping bushes out front. He turned and saw me.

Giving a wave of his hand, he hollered hi. Damn. Why didn't I go in the other direction? I had no choice now but cross the street to where he was standing with clippers in his hand.

"Hi," I said. "It's a nice evening to be outside." Was I giving him a reason why I was out walking? Unsure whether it was the warm air or another hot flash, I felt my face heating up. Once again he managed to make me feel like a silly teenager.

"Yeah, I like the fact it's staying lighter a bit longer. Gives me a chance to catch up on outdoor projects," he said, bending down to pat Lilly.

Making an attempt to be more personable than our previous encounters, I nodded toward the house. "Ali was right. It really is lovely."

Noah ran a hand through his curly hair, looking up at the house with pride. He paused for a moment before asking, "Would you like to come in and see it?"

Feeling like I'd hinted at the invitation, I shook my head. "Oh, no, that's alright. Besides I have Lilly with me."

"I do allow dogs in the house—especially well-behaved ones. Come on, I'll show you around," he said, leading the way up the front steps.

I followed, with Lilly on the leash.

Stepping inside, Noah closed the door. "You can let her loose in here. She can't hurt anything."

I leaned over to unclip Lilly's leash, whereupon the dog walked over to the Aubusson carpet in the middle of the living room floor, squatted, and peed.

"Oh, my God! Lilly! What on earth are you doing?" I ran over, grabbing the dog by the collar.

"I'm so sorry. She never does this. I don't know what got into her. Do you have some cleaner? I'll clean this for you." Embarrassment suffused my face with crimson while perspiration covered my upper lip.

"Well, I must say that's a first," Noah replied, humor absent from his tone. "I'll get some cleaner," he said, walking to the back of the house.

Kneeling down beside the dog, I took Lilly's face in my hands. "You bad girl. What's wrong with you? Why did you do such a thing?"

Lilly showed no remorse. Her tail began thumping the carpet as she licked my face.

"We'll see if this takes the stain out," Noah said, attempting to spray the carpet.

"No, give it to me." I reached for the cloth and bottle and began spraying the circular wet spot, attempting to remove the traces Lilly had left. "I think it'll be okay. If you find the stain is still there tomorrow, please let know. I'll pay to have the carpet cleaned." Standing up, I clipped the leash to Lilly's collar. "Come on, we've done enough damage for one night," I said, heading toward the front door.

"Why don't you stay and let me show you around?" he replied with a lack of conviction.

The coolness of his tone made it clear Noah wasn't happy about Lilly's escapade. "No, thank you anyway. Maybe some other time. Without Lilly."

Noah followed us to the door. "Have a good evening," he said.

I heard the door closing before I reached the pavement.

⮡17⮠

The next afternoon I was busy in the back room when Dora called to me. "Somebody to see you out front."

I walked into the shop to see Noah standing near the desk. Oh great, he's probably here to collect the exorbitant price of the carpet cleaning. Smiling uncertainly, I said, "Hi, what can I do for you?"

"I just wanted to let you know there was no damage to the carpet. The stain is gone."

I breathed a sigh of relief. "Oh, good. I'm really sorry about that. I can't understand why Lilly would do such a thing." When Noah remained silent but made no attempt to leave, I said, "Thanks for letting me know."

"I was wondering if you'd like to try that tour again this evening? Like around seven-thirty?"

Caught off-guard, I glanced over at Dora, who was busying herself sorting skeins of yarn. "You don't have to do that," I told him.

"I'd like to. Really. So come on over about seven-thirty," he said, walking toward the door. The wind chimes tinkled and he turned around.

"Do me a favor though. Leave Lilly home this time."

I stood in the middle of the shop as Dora stared at me.

"He seems like a nice man," Dora said, continuing to sort through the yarn.

"You think? I'm not sure what to make of him." I went on to explain the incident of the previous evening. When I finished, Dora started laughing. "You think it's funny?"

"Well, you have to admit, it does have a touch of humor to it. Poor Lilly. Is she still in the doghouse for her transgression?"

Hearing Dora laugh about the story made me grin. "No, I've forgiven her. And since I got another invitation, I guess maybe Noah has forgiven her too."

"I'm sure you'll enjoy seeing the inside of that house. I'd been in there years ago. It's quite lovely. It gave Noah a good reason to have you over anyway."

"Have me over? He was just being polite."

"Oh, I see," Dora said, turning her back on me to resume sorting yarn.

At 7:25 that evening I wagged a finger at Lilly, who was sitting in the middle of the kitchen floor. "I'm going out. You be a good girl, hear? Go lay down on your bed and I'll be back in a little while."

Lilly's head drooped as she walked to her bed, made the ritual circle, and plopped down.

I walked up Noah's front steps and rang the bell. What am I doing here? I wondered.

Noah answered the door immediately. "Hi," he said, friendliness in his voice. "Come on in." When I stepped into the foyer, he leaned out the door looking to the right and left. "Just making sure the pooch isn't here."

Damn, this man could be irritating. What the hell *was* I doing here?

Noah led the way toward the back of the house and an oversized kitchen. A large wooden counter with stools occupied one end and designer appliances completed the other side. Beyond the kitchen was a sitting room and informal dining room combined. A bottle of red wine sat on the counter with two glasses. Noah poured the red liquid and offered me a glass. "No tour is ever complete without a glass of wine."

Reaching out my hand brushed his, and I looked up to see a smile on his face. "Thanks," I said, accepting the glass.

"Here's to family ancestry," he said, touching the rim of mine. "Welcome to the Hale-Johnson House."

I took a sip and smiled. Little did he know that my own family ancestry could have had its beginnings on this island as well. "Hmm, very good," I said.

"Come on." Noah indicated for me to follow. "As you can see, this is the kitchen and sitting area. It's where I spend most of my time." Walking into the next room, he said, "And here's the formal dining room. My mother and I don't use this as much as when I was growing up."

"Is she here?" I asked.

"No, she's gone over to the East Coast to spend a couple weeks with an old friend."

I noticed the highly polished wood floors and the beautiful molding above doorways. The furniture was antique and looked comfortable in the spaces.

Walking back toward the front of the house, Noah waved an arm to his left. "You've seen the living room and over here are the bedrooms."

I followed him into the front bedroom. A beautiful wood sleigh bed dominated the center of the room. Nicely appointed furniture and decoration completed the master suite. I felt awkward standing in his private sleeping quarters and was glad to follow him to the bedroom in back.

"And here's my mother's room," he said.

Another antique bed with a beautiful floral quilt was the focal point of the room.

"It's very nice."

I followed him up the intricately carved oak staircase. From the landing I could look down to the foyer. The front of the second floor was dominated by an etched glass window and a cushioned window seat took up the center space. A large open area comprised the midsection and two more rooms flowed off the main one.

"These could be bedrooms too, but we've left them empty. We don't need any more and this is where I'm considering having my art classes. As you can see, the lighting is great up here."

I nodded. The fading sunlight lit up the open area.

"And up here," Noah said, leading me up the final staircase. "This leads to the widow's walk."

I climbed the steps into a glass-enclosed area and then up a few more steps through a door outside. A railing encircled a porchlike space. Two cushioned chairs sat facing the water, a small table between them.

Walking to the west side, I gasped. "Look at this view." My eyes took in the blue water, the dotted islands, and the bright red of the sun setting beyond. Shaking my head, I said, "Cedar Key is really the place to watch the sun set. This is magnificent."

Noah came to stand beside me. "Yeah, Key West was nice, but this . . . this is a slice of paradise. I come up here every day to watch the sunset and I haven't tired of it yet."

I inhaled the fragrant spring air. "I wouldn't understand anybody getting tired of this view. It's beautiful from down below, but from up here . . ."

I found there were no words to adequately describe the beauty I was witnessing.

Noah nodded. "What makes it even more special is the fact this is the house where my ancestors spent their days."

I surprised myself by asking, "Why does that matter to you?"

Noah took a slow sip of wine, gazing out at the water. "It never did, really. Not until recently. I can't quite explain it. I grew up here as a kid until I left for college. I lived in Paris for many years. During that time I never gave a thought to ancestry or heritage." He shrugged his shoulders. "I don't know. Maybe it's the passing of each year that makes us want to go backward, rather than forward? Maybe blood really is thicker than water? Maybe some of us instinctively want to go full circle and return to our roots if we have the chance? I don't have an answer." He pressed his lips together and sighed. "All I know is I'm exactly where I'm supposed to be."

I envied him. That need to find out if Sybile was my birth mother seemed to be growing stronger. I might never find out. I might never have the luxury that Noah had, knowing precisely where he came from. A strong urge to share my story with Noah consumed me, but I forced it down. Taking a sip of wine, I inhaled deeply. Standing there, I'd never felt so alone in my life. Suddenly that void—a void I'd never been aware existed—

was aching to be filled. That need to know where my beginning had started.

"Are you alright?" Noah asked.

I nodded. "Yeah, I'm okay." I finished off the last of my wine. "Thank you so much for this tour," I said, passing him the glass. "It's a spectacular house." I headed to the staircase. "You're fortunate to have it."

Noah followed me down the stairs. "How about another glass of wine? I have some cheese and crackers to go with it."

I walked to the front door and shook my head. "Thanks, but I need to get back. I enjoyed seeing the house."

The following morning I arrived at Spinning Forward to find Dora waiting on the doorstep.

"I spoke with Sybile yesterday," she said, as I unlocked the door.

Placing her handbag in the desk drawer, she turned to face me.

"She didn't seem surprised at all about your suspicions. All she asked me was if you knew the hospital and time of your birth."

"Saint Vincent's at two thirty-five A.M."

"And then she said she needed time to think. She gave me no further information, only that I wasn't to raise this subject with her again. I didn't want to push it. With her illness, I don't like upsetting her."

I nodded. "You did the right thing. She may never acknowledge me as her daughter—and that's okay. There's another part of this equation that we've neglected to discuss."

"What's that?"

"That I'm your niece."

Without hesitation, Dora enveloped me in her arms. Moisture filled her eyes as she said, "I acknowledge you. You never have to question that. I'm proud to be your aunt."

I hugged Dora tighter. "I hope Sybile knows what a great sister she has. Too bad she didn't get more of your genes." Swiping at the wetness on my cheeks, I said, "And this means I've also acquired a cousin."

Dora broke the embrace to grab a tissue and blot her eyes. "Marin has been hoping this would all prove to be true. She's very anxious to meet you."

"So even if Sybile refuses to tell me the truth, you and I know what that truth is."

"I suppose it would be best to protect Sybile's privacy. What I mean is, as much as I'd love everyone in town to know—I don't think it's a good idea to talk about this."

I nodded. "I absolutely agree. If Sybile went to such lengths to keep her secret quiet, it's not up to us to divulge it."

"But between you and me—I *am* your Aunt Dora."

• • •

Alison leaned forward in the lawn chair touching her glass to mine. "Here's to family and most of all, here's to Aunt Dora."

I laughed. "I was never close to the few older aunts and uncles I had. I didn't have cousins, as they had no children. Imagine—I'm fifty-three—and I'm a long-lost niece and I have a cousin."

"You'll love Marin. She reminds me of you in some ways. Let's see, she must be about fifty or so now."

"Yeah, Dora said we do have similarities and Marin turns fifty-one next month."

Alison shook her head. "It's pretty hard to believe, isn't it? You came here hoping to heal and get your life back together. You're sure getting a helluva lot more than you bargained for."

I laughed. "Very true and to think, I may never have come down here if I hadn't lost Stephen and been forced to relocate."

"Oh, don't be too sure of that, Syd. It's that searching for our feminine soul that I've told you about—sooner or later, all of us feel compelled to find it. In one way or another."

"Possibly."

Alison reached for a pretzel. "Have you heard from Noah lately?"

"No, was I supposed to?"

"Well, you had the tour of his house and everything. I just thought he might be in touch."

"Ali, there's nothing going on between us."

"Hmm. Well, as I said before, you never know what's ahead for you."

"Since when did you become the matchmaker of the island?" I asked, standing up. "Come on, Lilly, time to get to work."

∾18∾

I sat at the spinning wheel turning dog fur into yarn as my mind wandered. Maybe Ali was right. Maybe it was okay to feel an attraction toward another man. And I had to admit, since finding out that Tori was only a friend, I was pleased. Why couldn't I be Noah's friend too? But I knew that since finding out he was available, that attraction had grown.

I glanced over to see Noah enter the shop, stooping down to pat Lilly.

"I see she's forgiven you," I said.

"Forgiven *me?* She's the one that peed on my carpet."

"Ah, but you're the one that made her feel bad about it."

"Since it seems we called a truce, I'll let you get away with that statement."

I grinned. Chalk one up for me. "Are you here to purchase yarn?"

"No, I'm here to ask you to dinner. Friday evening? About seven-thirty?"

My grin grew into a smile. "Hmm, I'll have to check my calendar," I said and resumed spinning fur.

"Well, do you think you might do that now so we can make plans?"

"I imagine I could," I replied, continuing to spin a few more moments before getting up.

Walking to the desk, I flipped open a Day Runner and saw blank pages filling the week. "This Friday evening? Yeah, I think I'm free. Did you say seven-thirty?"

Noah walked to the desk attempting to gaze at the book but not before I snapped it shut. "Right, seven-thirty. I'll pick you up at your apartment about seven-fifteen? I thought we could go to the Island Room. It'll be warm enough to sit outside for dinner, if that's alright."

"That's fine, but I can meet you there. You don't have to pick me up like it's a . . ."

"Date? It *is* a date. Be ready at seven-fifteen," he said, and walked out of the shop.

At 7:00 Friday evening I lit up a cigarette and stood on the balcony of my apartment. God, what am I thinking? A date? I haven't had a bona fide date in over thirty years. Is it too soon after Stephen's death? It was going on a year. I took a few quick puffs off the cigarette, walked back inside, and plopped two breath mints into my mouth. Stopping in front of the mirror, I smiled.

The beige slacks fit perfectly and complemented the black cotton long-sleeved sweater. Leaning closer I observed my makeup for final approval. Satisfied, I stood back, tucking hair behind my ear. Lilly barked and my stomach lurched. He's here. Am I really ready for this?

"Hi," I said, producing a wide smile while stepping aside to let Noah in.

"What a cute place. I've never been in here before."

"There isn't much to it, but I'll show you through. Obviously this is the kitchen and in here," I said, waving an arm around the room, "is the bedroom/sitting area. But out here, this is the bonus."

Stepping outside, Noah nodded. "Very nice. I like it."

"I'm afraid it can't compare to your view, but I love sitting out here," I said, leading the way back inside. "Now, Lilly, I expect you to be a good girl while I'm gone."

"Right," Noah said, patting the dog's head.

Lilly let out a groan before lying down.

"All set." I opened the door to find Monica coming up the stairs. Oh, terrific!

"Hey," she said with a smile that vanished when she saw Noah standing in back of me. I had neglected to share that I was going out for dinner. With a man.

"Ah, this is a friend of mine, Noah Hale."

Turning to him, I said, "And this is my daughter, Monica."

If looks could kill, I would have been dialing 911 for poor Noah.

"Nice to meet you," she mumbled, edging her way into the kitchen.

Attempting brightness, I hollered, "I won't be late," and headed down the stairs with Noah behind me.

After our dinner orders had been given, he leaned back in his chair and took a slow sip of San Genovese. "So tell me about yourself."

"There isn't much to tell. Married for twenty-eight years, now a widow—I'm still having a problem with that word. One grown daughter, that you just met. Originally from the Boston area and before I married, I was an RN. That's about it."

"An RN? I didn't know that. And you own a yarn shop?"

"After I had Monica, I never returned to nursing. I let my license lapse. Probably not a very smart thing to do at all. But how could I know then that I'd desperately be needing a well-paying profession at age fifty-two?"

Noah nodded. "At least you had your knitting to fall back on. I'm sure it was difficult losing your husband. That's a long time to be married."

I ran the tip of a finger around the edge of my wineglass. "It was a long time. A long time to not be aware of his secrets." When Noah didn't comment, I said, "Stephen had a propensity for gambling. Not your typical playing-the-lottery gambling." I felt the need to tell Noah all about me and went on to explain Stephen's gambling, the eviction notice, and how I happened to end up on Cedar Key.

He blew out a breath of air. "Wow, quite a story. But you seem to be doing okay now."

I raised my eyes. "That depends what you consider okay. It was difficult being the grieving widow when I found out how Stephen had betrayed me. The situation he'd left me in financially. Then I felt guilty for maybe not grieving quite as much as I should be, but it became a matter of survival. I honestly didn't know which way to turn—until Ali came to my rescue."

"Yeah, I can relate to betrayal."

My head snapped up, looking across the table at him. "You can?"

"Yeah, I'm afraid so. I was married many years ago. Simone was an art student and my model. Came home one day and found her in bed with one of my other art students. The rest is history, as they say."

It wasn't always the female that got the short end of the infidelity stick. "Any children?"

"No, and that was a blessing."

"You never remarried?"

"Nope, gun shy, you might say. But I kept myself

so busy with my art, marriage was never on my agenda. You're lucky you have a daughter."

I smiled. "Monica. You may have noticed she wasn't overly friendly toward you. I have a feeling she'll have plenty to say about this *date*. We don't agree on a whole lot."

"It's none of my business, but maybe she ought to give her mom credit for making some pretty good decisions under some difficult circumstances." Noah took a sip of wine. "Parents and family still in the Boston area?"

"My parents are both gone and I'm an only child. I'm adopted." As soon as the words were out, I had no idea why I'd told him that.

"Really? Have you searched for your birth parents?"

Without hesitation, I said, "I'm in the process of searching right now."

"I hope it works out for you. I've heard good and bad outcomes on adoptees searching."

"Thank you." I was grateful the waitress arrived with our food. Taking a bite, I said, "This duck is delicious."

"So is the pork shank. More wine?" he asked, reaching for the bottle.

"Yes, it's very good. I've never tried San Genovese before."

"One of my favorites. Now that you own a business here, what are your long-term plans? Will you be staying in the Tree House?"

I shook my head. "No, I can't stay there forever. Alison has been wonderful, but eventually I'll look for a place of my own. I doubt I could afford to purchase anything, so I'll just rent."

Noah began laughing.

"What's so funny?"

"I just realized something. We've been together over an hour and haven't had one confrontation. We're actually having a normal conversation."

I saw the grin on his face and smiled. "You're right. Apparently, we're abiding by that truce."

We managed to get through the entire dinner with more laughter and easy chatter. Finishing off the bottle of wine, we ordered coffee. It was then that I craved a cigarette.

"You've gotten quiet," Noah said.

"I'm just thinking how good a cigarette would be with this coffee."

"We're outside. Go ahead and have one."

"It won't bother you?"

Noah shook his head and grinned. "I just enjoy razzing people about smoking. A reformed smoker is the worst, you know. But . . . it isn't good for you."

Reaching into my handbag, I pulled out the pack and lit one, careful to blow the smoke away from Noah. "I know it isn't," I said, as thoughts of Sybile floated into my mind. "So you quit, huh? How long ago?"

"It has to be over twenty years now."

"Wow, I'm impressed. Maybe I'll give it a try . . . but not tonight. Tell me what it was like to live in Paris."

Noah told me about his gallery there, about restaurants, sidewalk cafés, and anecdotes of the Bohemian lifestyle living on the Left Bank. As he talked, I found I wasn't able to take my eyes from his face. I also noticed sexy mannerisms I hadn't paid attention to before. Like when he was trying to think of a name of a particular restaurant he stroked his chin with his right hand. I also found my eyes drawn to his hands—masculine, with well-cared-for nails, absent of jewelry except for an oval-shaped college ring on his left ring finger.

Realizing that he'd asked me a question, I felt heat warming my face. "I'm sorry. What did you say?"

Noah smiled. "I asked if you'd ever been to Paris?"

"No, I'm afraid not. I got married after finishing college and then Monica came along and . . . Well, it just never seemed the right time."

The waitress appeared with the check. Noah looked it over, placed his charge card in the pocket of the leather binder, and stood it up. "Thank you for a delightful evening, Sydney."

"It was fun. I really enjoyed it."

On the walk home I became anxious, unsure whether to invite him into my apartment. What does one do on dates these days? Was he expecting a drink or maybe coffee?

When we got to the top of the stairs, Noah solved the dilemma. Leaning over, he kissed my cheek. "Thanks again for a great evening," he said. Then he let his lips brush mine. "Let's do this again very soon."

I sent Dora home at 6:00, put the CLOSED sign on the door, and settled into my chair to catch up on some spinning. An hour later, I heard a tapping on the window glass and looked outside to see Sybile peering in.

"Oh, Christ. The perfect ending to the day."

Opening the door I made no attempt to ask Sybile inside. "I'm closed. We'll be open at ten in the morning."

Sending me an exasperated look, she said, "Well, I know you're closed. That's why I came here now. I need to talk to you. Alone."

My hand trembled on the door knob, but I stepped aside. Could this be it? Could Sybile really be my birth mother, and she'd come to share this at the shop? Were all my suspicions true? Thoughts tumbled in my head. "Come on in," and then I locked the door behind the woman.

When Sybile made no attempt to talk, I questioned, "Why do you need to see me?" It was then that I noticed the shortness of breath the woman was experiencing.

"I wanted to invite you to my place . . . Sunday afternoon . . . I . . . have something I'd like to discuss with you."

I heard the lack of emotion in the woman's voice. I also knew the pauses were an attempt to catch her breath that speaking seemed to rob from her. "I'm alone here. Can't we discuss it now?"

Sybile shook her head. "No. I'd rather have you come out to my house. You know where I live, right? The Lighthouse. Three o'clock Sunday afternoon. Will you be there?"

After a moment, I nodded. "Okay. I'll be there."

Without a backward glance, Sybile walked to the door, unlocked it, and was gone.

"What the hell was that all about?"

Just before 3:00 on Sunday I pulled into the spacious gravel driveway in front of the Lighthouse. Looking up at the large structure, with the blue Gulf behind it, I said, "Not too shabby." I'd driven past the house before, often wondering what it was like inside. "Well, let's get this over with," I said, and climbed the wooden stairs.

With each step upward, I became more mesmerized with the view to my left. Saw grass in the foreground, dotted with palmettos here and there—all of it leading out to the spectacular, unobstructed view of the Gulf. Patches of smaller islands could be seen sprinkled throughout the incandescent blue of the water. Reaching the top landing, I gripped the railing and breathed in deeply. Closing my eyes, I wondered what it must be like to begin each day with this panorama.

"So you like my location, do ya?"

I heard Sybile's raspy voice breaking the tranquility of the moment and turned around. "It's lovely. I can understand why you enjoy it here."

"Come on in," Sybile said, dismissing the compliment. "Yup, and someday the Marine Lab out on Twenty-four will enjoy it. I've willed it to them so they can sell it and take the money for research."

I entered the kitchen, which then flowed into an open family room. All of it surrounded by glass and light. A counter with stools filled the space across from the work area of the kitchen. A dining-room table and chairs beyond the counter, and the circular family room beyond that. It was difficult for my gaze not to be drawn to the view outside.

"Have a seat," Sybile said, indicating a leather sofa. "I've made some coffee."

I watched the woman walk toward the kitchen and then allowed my eyes to take in the interior of the Lighthouse. A metal spiral staircase led upstairs. Two rooms branched off of the family room and a black Yamaha piano dominated the far corner.

Sybile returned a few moments later with a tray containing china coffee cups and matching saucers, creamer, sugar bowl, and a crystal plate filled with oatmeal raisin cookies. "Help yourself," Sybile said, reaching for her cup of black coffee.

Adding cream, I sat back and waited for an explanation as to why I'd been invited.

Lighting up a cigarette, Sybile questioned, "Do you smoke?"

I nodded. "But I'm trying to cut back."

Sybile's sarcastic laugh filled the room. "You can't cut back. You either stop or you keep smoking. Obviously, I've chosen to keep smoking."

When I remained silent, Sybile said, "I'm not sure if you knew or not. But I have cancer of the lung," and then waited for a reaction.

"Dora mentioned that the doctor suspected this but no, I didn't know for sure. I'm sorry."

Flicking an ash into the onyx ashtray beside her, she shrugged her shoulders. "Hey, we all gotta go sometime. Some of us sooner than others."

Wondering if this was the reason I'd been summoned, I reached for a cookie and took a bite.

"This is why I wanted to talk to you," Sybile confirmed.

"I don't understand."

Sybile ground out the cigarette in the ashtray and took another sip of coffee. "I'm told that you're an RN? Is this true?"

"Well, not exactly. I was an RN years ago and didn't keep my license current after I had my daughter," I said in confusion. Was Sybile looking for a private duty nurse?

"So if you were a nurse, you're used to this kinda stuff. Dying and all that."

"Yes, I've been exposed to my fair share of it. But having cancer doesn't mean a death sentence. You'll have chemo and possibly radiation and maybe even surgery."

Sybile shook her head. "No, I won't." She lit another cigarette. "The doctor mentioned all that crap and I'm not buying into it. I refused."

"Refused?" I heard what the woman said but wanted to be certain.

"Yeah. That stuff isn't for me. So don't be like Dora and try and talk me out of it."

"I wouldn't do that. It's your life and your body, but I hope you're certain this is the route you want to go. In a month or so, you might change your mind."

Sybile's face registered surprise. "Have you met other people that decided against treatment?"

I nodded. "Not that many, but yes, a few."

"And what was it like?"

"Like?"

Sybile leaned forward in her chair. "Was the pain excruciating? I'm not brave. Not brave at all. I can't bear the thought of going through something like that."

186

"Everyone's different and it also depends on what type of cancer you have. But that's why we have hospice. Your doctor will contact them when the time comes."

"But they're limited on the amount of pain meds they can give you, right?"

"Well, yes. There's a policy and they have to go according to the doctor's orders."

Sybile took a deep breath and nodded. "That's what I thought. But you . . . you could give me those injections if you had access to the medication, right? And you could increase the amounts when I needed it."

In a split second, it became abundantly clear to me why I'd been invited to Sybile Bowden's home. Not to be told that this woman had given me life—but rather to be asked to assist this woman with her own death.

Anger bubbled up inside of me, as I stood to leave. "I'm afraid you have the wrong person. As much as I don't believe in letting people suffer, I also don't believe it's up to us when it's our time to pass on. We have no control over when that moment arrives. I can't help you with this."

Racing down the stairs to the golf cart, the word *selfish* echoed in my head.

"My God," Alison said, tucking her legs beneath her in the chaise lounge. "She actually asked you to help kill her?"

I lit up a cigarette and blew the smoke into the garden air. "Not quite so bluntly, but yes, that's exactly what she wanted me to do."

Alison shook her head. "Wow, she must be desperate."

"Selfish, is more like it. The same way that suicide is. Rather than face reality, they'd rather check out and leave the mess for those left behind."

"You have a point there. And if she is your birth mother—Sybile had probably always had a selfish streak. Maybe giving up her child wasn't for all the altruistic reasons that so many girls have. Maybe it was all about *her.*"

I nodded. "Exactly. Yeah, here I've always thought that whoever she is, she did it for me. For a better life than she could give me. Maybe that's not the case at all."

"Have you said anything about this to Dora? What Sybile wanted from you?"

"God, no. Sybile might be a total ass but I wouldn't hurt Dora like that. She doesn't need to know about this."

"I have a feeling that Dora knows that sister of hers pretty damn good."

"You're probably right," I said, standing up. "Come on, Lilly, time to head to the shop." I leaned over to kiss Alison's cheek. "You and Paul have a great weekend at Amelia Island and I'll see you on Thursday."

"Okay and don't forget Twila Faye will be here to get people checked in. If you need anything, just give her a holler."

The confrontation with Monica came that evening when I arrived home from work.

I wasn't in the door five minutes when she started. "So. Who was that guy the other night?"

I began preparing a salad for dinner. Washing tomatoes, I said, "Noah Hale."

"That's *it?* That's all you're going to tell me?"

I spun around to face her. "What exactly would you like me to tell you? That he's an artist? Has lived on the island all his life, except for his years painting in Paris? That he's a nice guy and that yes . . . He actually asked me out on a dinner date."

"Do you think that's appropriate?"

Monica stood with a hand on her hip and reminded me of myself when she was sixteen. "Appropriate? What's that supposed to mean? Millions of couples all over the world go out in public to share dinner together."

"Yeah, well, Dad's only been gone eight months."

"Ah, so that's the problem," I said, wiping my hands on a towel and sitting down at the table. "I didn't know we were back in the dark ages and there was a certain time frame before a widow could officially go out in public with a member of the opposite sex."

"That isn't what I meant."

"Then, what exactly do you mean, Monica?" I could feel my anger rising.

"I just . . . well . . . I mean I'm not sure it's *proper* to be dating at this time."

"And that's up to you to decide?" When I got no answer, I said, "Look, Monica, I've never interfered in your life, though God knows I didn't always agree with it. But I backed off. I let you make your own choices. And I trusted you to do so." Grabbing my cigarettes, I headed toward the door. "And now . . . I need you to do the same thing. Because you're not responsible for my life or my choices. I'm quite capable of figuring those out on my own, despite what you might think."

I slammed the kitchen door and headed down the stairs.

⁓20⁓

I walked to the calendar in the yarn shop and flipped the page to May. Here it was the first day of May and still no word or contact from Sybile. Dora didn't have much to report either. She said it appeared to be a closed subject.

I turned around to see Saren walking in the door. "Hey, decided to take up knitting?"

The man laughed. "Naw, 'fraid not. I sure wouldn't know what to do with those sticks you gals use."

"Don't be too sure of that. What can I do for you?"

"Well . . . I was just wondering if you'd seen Sybile lately or has Miss Dora said anything about her?"

Concern covered his face, causing me to feel bad for the old man. "I haven't seen her, and Dora hasn't said much. I have the feeling that Sybile is staying close to home lately. Just not feeling up to par."

He nodded his head. "That's what I thought. I never see her walking around town anymore. Do you think it's real bad?"

"Gosh, Saren, I really don't know what to say. She's pretty sick, I do know that."

He paused a moment before asking, "She's probably not going to get better, is she?"

I shook my head. "Probably not."

He brushed his eye with a finger and nodded. "Okay, Miss Sydney. Sorry to bother you and thanks for being honest with me."

I watched him walk out the door. Why is it that love can sometimes hurt so deeply?

Later that afternoon the phone in the yarn shop rang. "Spinning Forward," I said, and heard Sybile's voice on the other end of the line.

"Yes, hello, Sydney. This is Sybile. I'd like you to come over to my house this Sunday . . . if you have no other plans."

I refrained from asking if it was to plead her case for euthanasia again. "I can be there. What time?"

"Would around three be alright with you?"

"That'll be fine. See you then."

I realized my hand was trembling when I replaced the receiver. I also noticed two other things—it was the first time Sybile had called me by my given name and the woman had been more informal than previous encounters.

I ascended the stairs to the Lighthouse wondering if Sybile was actually willing to share the details of my birth. I heard her holler "come in" when I knocked. Stepping inside, nothing appeared different or changed until my eyes fell on Sybile sitting on the sofa. She'd definitely lost weight in the short time since I'd last seen her. Her face was taking on a look of gauntness and her color was pale.

"Come sit down. I thought you might enjoy some tea," she said, pointing toward a silver tray filled with tea pot, cups, and saucers.

"That would be nice." I sat in the chair opposite. "Would you like me to pour?"

Sybile nodded. "I imagine you know why I summoned you here?"

The aroma of exotic spices filled the room from the cup I handed Sybile. "It's about my birth."

"Dora tells me you were born at St. Vincent's in

New York City? On March nineteenth, nineteen fifty-five at two thirty-five A.M?"

I nodded.

Taking a deep breath, Sybile said, "Well, I suppose it would do no harm now. After all, I'm dying." She adjusted the folds of the black and red caftan she was wearing. "I'd say that even without both of us submitting to a DNA test for scientific proof, that yes, you're my daughter. I gave birth to a baby girl on that date, at that time, in that hospital."

There . . . she's admitted to it, I thought. Then I wondered why I felt no emotion and realized my absence of sentiment was identical to Sybile's. "I want details," I said in a monotone voice. "I have a right to know the details."

"Legally, you don't have any rights. You were adopted. But what do you want to know?"

I heard the normal sassiness return to Sybile's voice. "I want to know why, I guess. What were the circumstances that forced you to give a baby up for adoption? And who was my father? Was he married? Is that why you couldn't keep me?"

Sybile leaned forward to reach for her cigarette case but avoided lighting one. "No, that wasn't my story. I will tell you some things—but I refuse to tell you about your father. It's way too late for that now and wouldn't do anybody any good. Is that clear?"

I nodded.

"You know I grew up here. I always wanted more than this island could give me, especially in the early fifties. I wasn't like most girls of that time. I had no desire to get married and raise a family. I knew the one thing I had going for me was my looks and so—I made a plan to use those looks and make a life for myself."

"And a baby interfered with those plans," I stated.

"In a nutshell, yes. We had been careful and I was five months along before I'd accept that I was actually pregnant. I had a good friend—another model—and she took me under her wing when I told her. Molly Kisler came from money. Her father was a top attorney in Manhattan. Her parents were as kind to me as Molly was. They allowed me to stay with them in the Hamptons a few weeks prior to your birth and then they arranged for the adoption. It was the only thing I could do. I was doing well modeling and I knew I had potential."

I listened to Sybile speak. She could have been telling me about an insignificant movie she'd watched. Her voice was void of sentiment. My birth was that unimportant to her—an intrusion on the glamorous life she'd planned. An annoyance that had to be dealt with.

As if reading my mind, Sybile said, "You're probably shocked that I was deficient with maternal feelings. But I was. Not everyone is cut out to be a mother, you know. I didn't have those raging hormones or motherly instincts. Not ever."

I had a flashback of the moment Monica was placed in my arms. We might have our differences now, but I would have killed for that child—still would. But I was also aware that Sybile was correct—not every woman wants to be a mother. I'd seen plenty of examples during my training in labor and delivery.

"I don't blame you, if that's what you mean. Can I ask you a question?"

"Go ahead. But I might not answer."

"Did you ever regret giving me away? Did you ever think of me over the years and wonder where I was? Who I was? If I was safe or happy? Or did you just forget me?"

Sybile lit the cigarette she'd been holding and blew out smoke before answering. "Did I regret the adoption? No, I didn't. But I'd be lying if I said I never gave you another thought after the day I left the hospital. I did think of you, but I also knew that a couple in Concord, Massachusetts, had adopted you. I was pretty sure they'd give you a good life."

"They did," I said with emphasis. "Very much so."

"Now I have some questions for you. Did you ever wonder about your birth mother? Who she was and why she gave you away?"

I shook my head. "Except for when I gave birth

195

to my own daughter, not that much. Not until recently. I was never one of those adoptees that had a burning desire to find her roots. I guess I was very satisfied with the roots I'd been given. But yes, I did wonder about you and after I gave birth, I realized that what you did took enormous courage. You were very brave to do what you did."

Sybile took a long drag on the cigarette, snubbed it out in the ashtray and grunted. "Brave? Hell, I wasn't brave at all. Selfish I admit, but certainly not brave. I don't even have the guts to die with dignity. I'm goddamn scared is what I am."

The honesty of Sybile's words jolted me. Before even thinking I blurted, "I can help you die—but not in the way you asked me to."

Sybile's head jerked up as she stared into my eyes that were a mirror image. "What do you mean? *Help* me die?"

"Dying is simply a passing over. I can help you with the fear."

Sybile threw her head back laughing. "Now wouldn't that just be something? I sure as hell didn't live right, but I have a chance to die right? Leave it to me to get it all screwed up."

I smiled. "Your sense of humor will help."

"So where do we go from here? Will we stay in touch? Will I get to meet your daughter? Will the whole town hear about this revelation?"

"Sybile, listen. When I first started suspecting that you could possibly be my birth mother my intention was never to upset your life. I wanted to know for *me*—and for Monica. So the ball's in your court. You tell *me* where we go from here."

"I knew the first time I saw you at Cook's, you know."

"What do you mean?"

"That afternoon—when you stopped for coffee with your dog. I looked over and saw you and I knew . . . I knew you were my daughter. I didn't understand how it could be possible, but I knew it was."

I leaned forward in my chair. Did a mother always recognize her own flesh and blood, no matter the circumstances? "You did? My God, I had no idea."

"When did you begin to suspect it might be true?"

"Maybe I always did too, but I kept pushing it away." I shook my head thinking how well I'd perfected the art of denial. Never listening to that inner voice—the feminine soul. "The whole idea of it was just bizarre. I'd have to say it was really Alison that forced me to figure it out."

"I'd rather the whole island doesn't know about this right now. Dora tells me you and Monica are going to her house next weekend to meet Marin. She's also invited me to be there."

"Do I take that to mean that you'd like for us to continue being in touch?"

"That's what I mean, with one condition." For the first time that afternoon a grin covered her face. "Don't even think about calling me *mama*."

～21～

Walking into the kitchen of the B&B I found Twila Faye sitting at the table buttering a blueberry muffin.

"Hey, girl," she said. "Join me while I take my coffee break."

"Those muffins sure smell good." I poured myself a cup of coffee. "Where's Ali?" I asked, taking a bite of muffin.

Twila Faye smiled. "Probably still wrapped up in Paul's arms. She was in here pretty early, got breakfast ready, and then went back to her apartment. Haven't seen her since."

"She'll miss him when he has to leave."

"She'll miss all that lovin', no doubt."

"Shame on you for thinking such thoughts."

Twila Faye raised her eyebrows and laughed. "Yeah, right. Honey, it's the natural way of things. Nothin' wrong with lovemakin' if you love the one you're with."

I joined her laughter and recalled a song by that title.

"Why, Twila, if I didn't know better, I'd say you had a special someone in your life."

"Nah, 'fraid not. But the rumors I've been hearin' tells me that *you* might."

"Me? Where'd you hear that?"

"Yeah, you. Word travels fast on this island, ya know. Heard Mr. Noah sent you some mighty pretty flowers for your birthday and seems you were spotted out and about having dinner with him."

"Geez, it's true. Nothing is sacred around here." Getting up, I rinsed my cup in the sink. "He did send flowers . . . and we did have dinner."

"And?"

I laughed. "And that's all I have to say. Tell Sleeping Beauty when she emerges that I'm going into work and I'll see her this evening."

The Monday-evening knitting class was a social as well as a learning session. The women varied each week but the regulars included Twila Faye, Polly, Raylene, and Dora. We sat sipping tea, needles clicking, while exchanging local gossip.

"Land sakes alive," Raylene contributed. "Have you heard the latest? The conductor's uniform at the Historical Museum is missing."

"What on earth do you mean?" Dora questioned. "How can it be missing? Did somebody steal the mannequin?"

"No, not quite that easy. I'm afraid Miss Lottie

offered to take the uniform and get it cleaned. It was getting a bit dusty and needed sprucing up. But now poor Miss Lottie can't remember which cleaners she took it to."

I let out a chuckle. "Are you serious?"

Raylene nodded her head emphatically. " 'Fraid so. We've called every cleaning shop in Chiefland, Ocala, and Gainesville and we can't locate it."

I knew that Lottie Sullivan was well into her early nineties and one of the oldest docents at the museum. She was loyal and enjoyed sharing island history with everybody, but she was also forgetful.

"Well, maybe you'll be lucky and an honest person from the cleaners will call to let you know they have it," I said.

Raylene sniffed. "That uniform is an antique and worth some money. So that'll probably happen when pigs fly."

"Raylene, you're always doom and gloom. Sydney's right," Dora said. "That uniform could very well be returned. By the way, Sydney, I'm not sure you know but Cedar Key was famous for the cross-state railroad in the eighteen hundreds. It ran from Fernandina Beach on the east coast over here. The tracks are still there off Twenty-four in the area we call Kiss Me Quick and Hug Me Tight."

I threw my head back laughing. "Why do you

call it that?" I asked, putting my knitting in my lap and leaning forward for Dora's explanation.

"A conductor for the railroad lived in that section of the island and upon boarding the train near his house his wife would kiss him before the train departed and a short way down at another stop, she'd run to hug him before he left for his scheduled run."

I smiled. "What a cute story. You have such great folklore on this island. I love hearing all the stories."

Twila Faye concentrated on the raspberry sweater she was making for her granddaughter, then asked, "Did anyone hear what happened out at the cemetery the other day? Remember when Jack Patterson died a few months back? Well, his wife Ethel had a big fight with the funeral parlor because they wanted to charge her an outrageous price for the urn to put Jack in. They ended up putting him into a metal box and sent her on her way." Twila Faye paused to sip her herbal tea. "Ethel wanted to spread Jack's ashes on the family plot at the cemetery, but that's against the law. So last week she felt she'd had Jack in the house long enough—she called all the family and friends, told them to bring folding chairs and meet her at the family plot. They got there, set up their chairs, said a few words about Jack and tried to open the box, which was darn near impossible. They tried everything and finally somebody produced a crow bar—but the thing is, when they finally forced it open, poor Jack flew everywhere. And there was Ethel grasping at the air, trying to save as much of Jack as she could."

Laughter filled the knitting shop. "Serves her right," Raylene said. "Ethel always was a tightwad. Bet she has the first dollar she ever made."

Polly wiped the tears from her eyes while shaking her head. "So I'd say it's pretty safe to assume that ole Jack Patterson's now a free spirit."

I shook my head laughing. These women were a delight to be with. Unassuming, down-to-earth, and outspoken.

"I'm not sure about the next set of instructions on this pattern," Twila Faye said, confusion covering her face.

Getting up to reach for the pattern I heard Raylene say, "So what's goin' on, Dora? Is that sister of yours sick? Somebody said they saw her at Shands last week."

"Lord above," Dora said, a sarcastic edge to her tone. "Does everybody know everything on this island? She's had a bit of a cold and if you must know more, you'll have to ask Sybile yourself."

Properly chastised, Raylene tossed her head in the air. "Well, I was only asking. But then, Sybile always was the one on this island with the most secrets."

"This isn't too difficult, Twila Faye. I'll explain it to you, but let's stop knitting for a few minutes while we enjoy some of that delicious blueberry cobbler that Raylene brought," I said, swaying the conversation in a different direction.

After passing out the plates, I joined the other women in front of the fireplace.

"How's the business going?" Polly questioned.

"It's actually begun to pick up a little the past few weeks. And with Dora helping me out, I found time to do a Web site. I got a few more mail orders this past week. I'm hoping in a month or so, I might be able to cut back my hours at the restaurant."

Dora threw me a grateful smile and I wasn't sure if it was for the compliment or the fact I'd changed the subject about Sybile.

"Hey, has anyone been into Noah Hale's new gallery?" Twila Faye questioned.

"I popped in the other day," Polly said. "I have to admit he's quite the artist. I was very impressed. And his looks aren't hard to take either."

Everyone but me laughed.

"Oh, got your eye on a new beau, do ya?" Raylene asked.

Polly chuckled. "No, 'fraid not. He's not my type—too artsy, if you know what I mean."

"Well, with his looks and charm I don't think he'll stay available for long on this island," Twila Faye replied.

Noticing my silence, Raylene said, "Now there's a man for ya, Sydney. I'm sure a little flirting with him would go a long way."

"Yeah, except I don't happen to be looking for a man. Come on," I said, gathering up the plates. "Time to get back to knitting. I'll help you with the pattern now, Twila Faye."

I saw the smiles that crossed the women's faces.

S aren, that was absolutely delicious," I said, wiping my mouth with the linen napkin. "You're quite the chef." I'd been flattered when Saren had invited me to dinner at his home.

He laughed. "Oh now, it was only mullet, a baked potato, and salad. Far from a gourmet meal."

"Well, I enjoyed it very much. Now let me help you clear this table," I said, getting up to fill the dishwasher.

"It's such a nice evening I thought we'd have coffee on the screened porch."

"Great idea."

I settled into a patio chair and sniffed. "Is that honeysuckle?"

"It sure 'nuff is. I have a large bush of it further back in the garden."

"I love it. Makes you realize spring is almost here."

Saren took a sip of coffee. "I'd like to ask you something, Miss Sydney. Now I'll understand if you don't want to answer." Without waiting, he said, "Is Miss Sybile dying?"

The question caught me off guard. But that one question left no doubt in my mind that this man still carried a torch for his long-ago love. "Why do you ask?" I said, while trying to formulate an answer in my head.

"Sybile's different lately. I know she's been going to Gainesville a lot and I'm pretty sure it's to Shands. She doesn't look good either. Almost like the spark is goin' outta her. You know what I mean?"

I nodded. When a person was seriously ill, most times it was difficult to hide. Especially from those that loved them. "She is pretty sick, Saren. But I just don't think it's my place to explain any more. Why don't you pay her a visit? Maybe she'd like you to make the first move."

Sadness crossed the man's face. "I think you've answered my question, Miss Sydney, and I thank you for that." He let out a deep sigh. "You know, she's one woman that can aggravate me more than any other I've met. We were mighty close years ago, but that all changed once I came back to this island. And her highfalutin ways only made me angry. We had some harsh words a year or so after I moved back here. And ever since then, we pretty much keep our distance. I don't think she'd be appreciatin' a visit from me now."

I leaned over and patted Saren's hand. "Don't

be too sure of that. People change, especially as they get older."

He shook his head. "She's a tough ole bird. Sick or not, I can't see Sybile Bowden changing for the better."

"How's Miss Elly been lately?" I questioned, searching for another topic.

His face broke out in a genuine smile. "Oh, now, there's one woman any man would be proud to call his. She's just fine, Miss Sydney, and thank you for asking." He paused to take a sip of coffee. "You know, a lot of people would think I'm nuts. But I'm not, and I know what I see in that living room every evening."

I couldn't resist asking, "Do you think she'll pay a visit while I'm here?"

"Well, now, she could, I 'spose. But she never has. I don't know why that is. But she only seems to visit when I'm alone."

I nodded. Who am I to judge his level of imagination? Hell, I had suspected a total stranger of being my birth mother. Standing up, I patted Saren on the shoulder. "Well, she's pretty lucky to have such a nice gentleman to visit. Thank you so much for supper. I really enjoyed it, but I'm afraid I need to be getting home."

Walking me to the front door, he said, "Miss Sydney, it was entirely my pleasure. You pop by anytime to pay me a visit, you hear?"

"I will, Saren. Thanks."

· · ·

Monica was spending a week in Fort Lauderdale with her friend Bree, when Dora called to invite me to her home on Sunday afternoon. She expressed disappointment that Monica wouldn't be joining us, because she'd also invited Sybilc and Marin.

"I think she'll be sorry to miss the gathering," I told her, "but I'll be there and I'm looking forward to meeting Marin."

I pulled the golf cart into the driveway on Andrews Circle. Ringing the door bell I took a deep breath wishing that Monica was at my side.

Dora opened the door with a smile. "Come on in," she said, embracing mc and putting me at ease. "It's so lovely today, we're sitting out back having coffee."

I followed Dora through the house to the patio and saw a woman of medium height stand up and come toward me.

"I'm Marin," she said, taking me in her arms. "And I'm so happy to meet you."

She reminded me of Courteney Cox from *Friends*—nicely styled brunette hair, an inviting smile, and she also reminded me of an older version of Monica. "I'm happy to meet you too," I said, returning the hug. Sybile was sitting in a chair observing the greeting. "How are you?" I asked, taking a seat opposite.

"As good as can be expected, I suppose."

Dora reached for the carafe, poured coffee into a cup, and passed it to me.

"Thank you," I said, feeling awkward with the situation.

Marin sat down, leaning forward in her chair. "I'm so happy to learn I have a cousin. And I'm dying to hear all about you. Of course, Mom told me about your yarn shop, which I think is great. I'm ashamed to say I didn't get any of her talent with knitting. I'm afraid you got all those genes," she said, grinning.

I realized that hearing this caused me to feel foolishly pleased. It seemed important to suddenly have a connection—to be validated as one of them. Their blood runs through my veins, I thought. We are a part of each other, just as Monica is a part of me.

"Your mother is an expert knitter, but we can't all enjoy the same things. What do you enjoy doing?"

"I'm an avid reader when I can find the time. I teach at the university so I'm kept pretty busy. Tell us about your daughter."

"Monica's twenty-six. She graduated college as a teacher also, but she'd been working for a publishing company in Boston. Unfortunately they downsized, so she's looking for a position in the area. She's on the East Coast with a friend right now, but she can't wait to meet you."

"How nice to have another girl in the family. I have two boys. Jason is twenty-three. He graduated college last year and works for a company in Atlanta. John is twenty-one and attends the university in Gainesville, but lives in an apartment with a few other fellows. So Cal and I have the house to ourselves. It's your girlfriend that owns the B and B, right? And you live there?"

I was grateful that Marin had a good personality and kept the conversation going because Sybile hadn't participated, which was making me feel uncomfortable. I nodded. "Yes, Alison is the owner. We've been friends since college. I live in the second-floor apartment of the Tree House."

"It's certainly quite a story, isn't it? Coming here to the island and finding out Sybile is your birth mother."

The elephant that had been lurking in the corner now jumped out, plunking itself down in the middle of us. I shot a glance at Sybile's face—she was wearing the familiar sunglasses and offered no input. "It is pretty amazing. Especially since I wasn't really searching when I first arrived here."

"Well," Sybile replied, her gravelly voice causing us to look in her direction. "Just goes to show ya— sometimes things come after us when we least expect it. They say everything happens for a reason, 'tho I'm not sure I always agree with that."

Marin got up from her chair, walking toward Sybile. Bending down she hugged her tightly.

"Aunt Sybile, you're such a crusty ole gal. You need to lighten up a bit and go more with the flow. Be grateful you've got such a nice daughter and enjoy her. I know I'm going to enjoy having a girl cousin." She turned toward Dora. "Want me to bring out the peach pie?"

"Yes, that'll be nice. Thank you, Marin," she said. "Strange, isn't it? The things we do in life and many times they come back to haunt us."

"If you're referring to my past indiscretions, I wouldn't exactly consider myself a sinner," Sybile replied with an edge to her tone.

"Oh, for goodness sake, Sybile. Lighten up like Marin said. That isn't what I meant at all. It's just when you think what were the chances of Sydney coming to this island. They were pretty slim—and yet she did. Many times our past catches up with us, whether we want it to or not. And in your case," Dora leaned forward to pat her sister's hand, "I'm sure glad it did. Sydney, you're exactly what we needed in this family."

The compliment brought a smile to my face. "Thank you. But maybe Sybile told you—we'd rather the whole town doesn't know about this."

Marin walked out with the pie on a tray and passed around plates. "Doesn't know about what?" she questioned.

"Looks like Sybile is going to continue keeping Sydney a secret," Dora said. "No, I didn't know that."

"Oh, now, don't go gettin' yourself in a snit. I didn't say we weren't ever going to say anything. Besides, what do ya want me to do, call up the newspaper and place a birth announcement?"

Both Marin and I giggled, but Dora's face remained passive.

"It's just that under the circumstances, I would think you'd want to let people know that you have a daughter."

"If you're referring to those circumstances being the fact I'm dying, whether this news is revealed or not, it doesn't change my longevity."

"God, Sybile, you can be so exasperating."

"Well, at any rate," Marin said, intervening. "I'm glad at least we know the truth, Aunt Sybile."

Picking up on Marin's attempt at mediation, I said, "This pie is delicious. Did you make it, Dora?"

"I'm afraid I can't take credit for this one. It's Marin's creation."

"Jason brought me back some Georgia peaches and I couldn't resist making some pies."

I laughed. "Now that's one gene I didn't get from you women. Cooking."

"You mean to tell me you don't cook? Having had a family and all?" Sybile's face registered surprise.

"Oh, I always made the usual—meatloaf, chicken dishes, that sort of thing. But I was never one to collect recipes and experiment."

"Well, maybe it's high time you did, girl. No Southern woman owns any less than five cookbooks and a tin full of recipes. You come see me this week and I'll pass on some of our legendary family recipes."

Marin, Dora, and I looked at Sybile and smiled.

"Start her off with something easy like Mama's biscuits," Dora offered.

"It's a date, Sybile, and I'm looking forward to it," I told her.

Alison threw her head back laughing. "Are you serious? Sybile Bowden's going to teach you to cook? I'm surprised the woman even knows *how* to cook."

I shook my head. "Yup, that's what she said. Said she'll pass on the family recipes to me."

"God, wonders never cease to exist, I guess. So are you going over there?"

"Yeah, Friday morning. Dora covers the shop for me till noon. So why not? I'll give it a shot."

"It might be nice to get to know her too, Syd. I mean—she's not going to be here forever. Maybe you have questions, things you'd like to know about. Now's your chance. You might even come to find out you actually like her."

I laughed. "I seriously doubt that. She's a little too spirited for me."

"Can I ask you something?"

"Sure."

Alison pushed her dinner plate away from her. "Now that you have your confirmation on your birth mother, are you giving any thought to your father?"

"I am. More than I ever have before. But Sybile was adamant—said she didn't want to discuss him and she wasn't going to tell me who he was."

"I betcha he was married."

"I asked her that and she did admit that he wasn't. I don't think she'd lie about it. There'd be no reason to now."

"Yeah, true. But gosh, Syd, what if he's still out there? Like up in New York? He's probably about the same age as Sybile, so he'd only be in his seventies and chances are he's still alive. Maybe you can get her to open up with you."

"I'll give it some time and who knows, maybe when Monica meets her she'll be able to get more out of Sybile than I can. The more thought I give to all of this, the more I'm wondering if it could be Saren."

Surprise crossed Ali's face. "God, do you *think?*"

"I don't know, but they did have a love affair. That much is obvious. I'm just not sure about the time frame and neither one has admitted to having an intimate relationship. He did see her in Manhattan though the day before he flew to Paris—and that was June. The month she got pregnant."

The ringing telephone ended our discussion and Alison answered. "Yeah, she's right here. We've just finished supper. Hold on."

Noah, she mouthed, handing the phone to me.

"Hey, how're you?" I asked.

"I'm great, thanks. Listen, I was hoping maybe you could meet me for an early lunch on Friday morning?"

"Oh, Friday morning? Gosh, I'm afraid I can't. I have something planned."

"Then how about dinner at my place on Friday evening?"

What? Did everyone on this island, including men, cook except me? "You're cooking?"

Noah laughed. "Yeah, I've been known to grill a mean steak. Will you join me?"

I smiled. "That sounds good. What time and what can I bring?"

"Why not come about seven and if it's not too much trouble, how about a dessert? A baker I'm not."

"Sounds great. I'll see you then."

I disconnected the line and dialed Sybile's number. "Any chance you can help me bake a dessert Friday morning? Just tell me what we'll need and I'll bring the ingredients."

23

O kay, now pour the batter into the springform pan," Sybile instructed.

I used the spatula to scrape the sides of the bowl. "And the oven's all set?" I asked.

"Ready to go." Sybile opened the door while I slid the cheesecake inside.

"Well, that's that," I said, wiping my hands on a towel. "I sure hope it comes out good."

"Of course it'll come out good. Mama's cheese-cake recipe hasn't ever failed. It's foolproof."

If all else fails, I suppose I could buy cookies at the market, I thought.

"How about some coffee?" Sybile asked, reaching for the coffeepot.

"Sounds good." I sat on the counter stool and swiveled around to take in the breathtaking view. "Do you ever tire of looking at that?"

Placing two mugs on the counter, Sybile shook her head. "Not ever."

"Sybile, thanks for helping me with the cheese-cake. I appreciate that."

"Not a problem, but next time we'll do bis-cuits."

"Tell me about what it was like to leave here and go to New York when you were eighteen."

Sybile stared across the counter. "You don't wanna hear all that old stuff."

I caught the lack of conviction in her voice. "Yeah, I do. I'd like to hear about when you were younger."

"Well . . . maybe you'd like to see my albums," she said, getting off the stool and heading to her bedroom.

Waiting for her to return, I thought about how easy the time with Sybile had been. As soon as I arrived we began preparing the cheesecake. It seemed odd—an age-old ritual, mother and daughter cooking together. Something I had never done growing up. I'd shown no interest being in the kitchen with my mother and yet this morning I found a certain sense of satisfaction sharing this event with Sybile.

"Here we go," she said, returning with albums in her hands.

I fingered the leather covers, opening the first one Sybile passed me.

"These pictures here," she explained, "were my portfolio photos. The ones that got me accepted to the modeling agency."

I saw an exceptionally attractive younger woman. All different poses—smiling, serious, sultry. But there was no doubt they were Sybile. She hadn't changed that much over the years. Tall and slim, wearing fifties-style dresses with Peter Pan collars, narrow belts, fitted jackets, and a few wearing strapless evening gowns.

"Wow, you were gorgeous," I said.

"It was a fun time. Living at the Barbizon, doing photo shoots all over New York. All of us girls—we were like one big family. See here," she said, opening another album. "Here's some of the girls that had rooms on my floor at the Barbizon."

I saw a group of young women piled on a bed, wearing cotton pajamas, pin curls in their hair, laughing and clowning for the camera. I also noticed how Sybile's demeanor had become more relaxed since bringing out the albums. Her face had softened as she flipped through the pages explaining who the girls were and relaying anecdotes of those long-ago days. She's in her element, I thought. That was a part of her life that she'll never lose.

"Why'd you decide to come back here? Rather than stay in New York?"

Sybile shrugged her shoulders and snapped the album shut. Lighting up a cigarette her gaze went to the water beyond the glass doors. "Well," she said, sitting on the stool. "Guess there comes a time when we realize that maybe Dorothy was right. There's no place like home."

Hadn't Saren said that very same thing to me? "But you returned and then pretty much cut yourself off here."

"I won't lie. I like being alone. Always enjoyed my own company. Besides, a lot of people resented me comin' back with some financial security behind me. Thought it was better if I just pretty much kept to myself. And that's what I've done."

"What was your husband like?"

Sybile seemed surprised by the question and took another drag off her cigarette. "Oh, he was a charmer, he was. Tall, dark, and handsome—that was Gerald. Trouble was, he knew it."

"Did you love him?"

Without hesitation, Sybile replied, "No. Does that shock you? So you're wondering why I married him? I married him because although I didn't love him, I did care for him. I also knew that since he was my agent, I'd have a much better chance of getting top modeling jobs."

So she married him to further her career. Which is also the reason she gave me up for adoption. "Were you sorry about the divorce?"

Sybile shook her head. "Nope. The time had come for us to part ways. Gerald was a good man—he just wasn't a faithful one. He made sure I was well taken care of with money. But he didn't want to be tied down."

I thought back to my own marriage and Stephen. Had I truly ever really *loved* him? At that very moment, I wasn't certain. I'd never given it much thought before. At the time, I thought I was in love and getting married was the logical result. "Have you ever been in love with a man?"

Sybile twirled her coffee cup in a circle, contemplating her answer. "Yes. . . . Once."

Had I chosen to ask the identity, I knew the answer would be, "Your father."

Remnants of the cheesecake sat on the dining room table, blueberry sliding down onto the plate.

"I have to say that's the best cheesecake I've ever had," Noah said, leaning back in his chair.

I smiled. "Thank you. I'm glad you enjoyed it."

"So what's next on the agenda for your cooking class?"

"Biscuits."

"There's nothing like Southern biscuits. That sure is nice of Sybile to be giving you these recipes, isn't it?"

I nodded, but said nothing.

"More coffee?" Noah asked, heading into the kitchen for the pot.

"Yes, please."

"So how do you know Sybile?" He returned to his seat across from me.

"She's Dora's sister."

He nodded. "Ah, that's right. I don't know her that well, but I'm glad the two of you have become friends."

Why did that statement feel like it had a double meaning? "Yeah, she can be a character, but I enjoy her cooking lessons."

"You look like her, you know."

The sentence caught me off guard, causing coffee to be sloshed onto the tablecloth. "Oh, I'm sorry," I said, mopping it up with my napkin.

"No, *I'm* sorry. I probably shouldn't have said anything."

"She's my mother." The words flew out of my mouth.

Noah was now the one visibly ill at ease. "Shit, are you serious?" Raking a hand through his hair, he stared at me for confirmation. "I only meant that you resemble her—especially through the eyes."

I smiled. "Well, I should and yes, I'm serious. She's my birth mother."

Noah inhaled deeply. "Christ," was all he said for a few moments. "Have you known this since you came here?"

"If you'll let me go outside and have a cigarette and another glass of wine—I'll tell you the whole story." The desire to share my experience with Noah was begging to be released.

"Wow," was Noah's immediate reaction after I had brought him up to date.

"But please," I said, "promise not to say anything to anybody else. Sybile would rather it be kept quiet for right now."

The scent of lantana hung in the air. Noah glanced over the porch railing to his back garden and sighed. "That's almost impossible to believe.

And yes, of course, I'll keep it to myself." He shook his head, attempting to piece together all he'd just learned. "When I said you looked like her, I sure never thought I'd hear a story like this. Think how fortunate you are—all the rest of your lives to get to know each other."

I remained quiet and lit another cigarette.

"Oh, maybe you don't want to get to know her."

"It's not that. Life sometimes has a strange way of working things out. Sybile is ill—she has lung cancer . . . and she's terminal."

Noah reached for my hand and squeezed it. "Oh, God, Sydney. I'm terribly sorry."

"Thank you," I said, and for the first time since learning the truth, I felt tears stinging my eyes. I felt the warmth of my hand inside Noah's and allowed the moisture to slide down my cheeks. With my other hand I wiped at the tears. "Isn't life a pisser? I never even cared for her when I first met her. Then I find out not only is she my birth mother—but she's dying." The tears continued to fall.

Noah got up and pulled me out of the chair. Bringing me to his chest, he stroked my hair and whispered, "Yeah, life has a way of making us sit up and take notice when we least expect it."

My mind was torn between sorrow for Sybile and relishing the tightness of Noah's arms around me. Being there felt so right—so reassuring.

His fingertip moved to my cheek and brushed at

the wetness. Leaning closer, he kissed me. A gentle touching of lips at first, which became deeper. Our breathing increased while I slipped my arms around his neck. I felt his body pressed against me and was aware of a floating sensation. Easing my face away, I looked up into his eyes. During that split second I saw something there that I'd never witnessed before—a deep, intense intimacy. Something I'd never experienced with Stephen.

Noah stared at my face, brushing back a strand of hair. "If there's anything, and I mean anything, at all that I can do, please let me know."

"Thank you," I said, stepping out of his embrace. "And thank you for a wonderful evening." Reaching for my cigarettes, I sighed. "But I need to get home. I'm sure it's close to midnight."

Sliding an arm around my shoulder, Noah walked with me into the house. "I'll take you home."

24

Sunlight streamed into the bedroom, causing me to fling an arm over my eyes. Snuggling into the pillow, I replayed the events of the night before in my mind. I was glad I'd shared my story with Noah. He'd been understanding—sympathetic. Caring. Turning onto my other side I recalled his kiss. Both of them. He'd kissed me again at my doorway but hadn't asked to come in. God, he was a great kisser. It was impossible at that moment to remember Stephen's kisses, but I knew they had never stirred me in the way that Noah's did. I like him, I thought. I probably like him way too much. Do I really need to be getting involved in another relationship? Between the yarn shop, Sybile, and Monica, my plate was pretty full.

Pushing my legs to the side of the bed, I reached over to pat Lilly. "Time for coffee, girl."

Opening the door, I let Lilly out to the garden while waiting for the coffee to brew. It was then that I remembered I'd invited Saren over for dinner that evening. I planned to prepare lasagna before I left for the yarn shop.

Taking a sip of coffee, I dialed Monica's cell phone. She'd left me a message the night before.

"And where were you off to last evening?"

Was that suspicion I heard in her voice? "Actually, I got invited to Noah's house for dinner."

"Oh."

"And, it was very nice. An enjoyable evening."

"Well . . . that's good. I was calling to let you know I'll be back on Sunday as planned. And . . . I got a phone call from UF. I've been offered a position in the English department beginning in August."

Based on the close relationship Monica had

always shared with her father, I was surprised at my daughter's switch in attitude concerning a man in my life. I had been fully prepared for a disagreeable confrontation. Could it be possible Monica was going to ease up on me?

"That's wonderful!" I said, truly happy for my daughter. "Congratulations."

As if she had read my previous thought, she went on to say, "Mom, I wanted to thank you for letting me stay with you. I know I haven't been the easiest person to get along with lately. It's been so difficult losing Dad . . . but I do understand how tough it's been on you. You've had some major adjustments in your life, and I haven't made it any easier. Can we call a truce?"

A truce? That's what Noah had asked of me—and I was glad I had accepted his offer. "Of course we can," I told my daughter. "I love you, Monica, and I want us to get along."

"I love you too and I'll try. I really will. How's Sybile doing?"

"About the same—no better, no worse. I haven't seen her for a couple days but according to Dora, she's resumed her crankiness. She mentioned she wished you could have joined us the other day."

"I'm looking forward to finally meeting her, so we'll set something up when I return."

I turned the cardboard sign to CLOSED. Before leaving the shop I dialed Sybile's number.

"I know this is short notice, but I just had an idea. I'm having Saren for dinner this evening. Would you like to join us?"

"Now why would I want to do that?" Sybile questioned with grouchiness.

Feeling foolish for extending the invitation, I said, "Gee, I don't know. I thought maybe you'd like to get out for a little while and socialize. But I can hear you're not in the mood for that. I'll talk to you later." I hung up the phone. God, that woman could be nasty. That's what I get for trying to be nice. "But I'm not taking her crap. Being sick isn't an excuse to be rude. Come on, Lilly, time to head home."

Saren arrived promptly at 7:15. I opened the door to find him with a huge smile and a bouquet of multi-colored carnations. "They're just beautiful. Thank you."

"Picked 'em myself. Right out of my garden."

"They're lovely. Have a seat while I put them into some water."

"Something sure does smell good," he said, taking a seat at the table.

"Lasagna and garlic bread in the oven. Thought we'd have a salad with it."

"Sure is nice of you to invite me over. It isn't often I get home-cooked meals."

I placed the vase on the table. "But you cook."

"Oh, I can do the easy stuff like fish and chicken, so I don't go hungry."

I laughed. "I don't do much more than that myself. I got Sybile's recipe for lasagna and thought I'd try it," I said before thinking. I had intended not to mention the woman's name in conversation.

Saren's head jerked up. "Sybile? Now why would you have her recipe?"

"Oh . . . well . . . Dora had mentioned it to me. So I called Sybile to see if she'd share it."

"So you've seen her recently?"

"Yeah, last week."

"How's she doing?"

I felt like I was walking a tightrope. I didn't want to betray Sybile's medical condition, but I hated not being truthful with Saren. "She's doing fairly well at the moment. You know—has her ups and downs."

He nodded. "Yeah, she's always been like that. Sometimes ya never knew which way to take her. Seems to have been born with an irritable streak in her, if ya know what I mean."

I uncorked a bottle of chianti. "Some red wine?"

"That would be nice. Thanks."

Pouring the wine into two glasses, I said, "That makes it tough in a friendship. Never quite knowing the mood of the other person."

"Sure 'nuff does," he said, reaching for the glass. "Oh, she's never been easy to get along with, that one. But . . . she sure did make life interesting." He laughed and took a sip of wine. "Very nice, thank you."

"So you have a lot of good times that you remember?"

"Oh yeah, a fair amount. Sybile was always her own person. Quite the daredevil too."

"In which way?"

"Well, her daddy would tell her to stay close to the house 'cuz there was a storm comin'. And not ten minutes later, there she was—had the boat in the water and was headin' over to Atsena Otie. All by herself. She'd wait out the storm under the trees over there. Almost like she had to prove she wasn't scared of nothin'."

She's scared of dying, I thought. "I bet she was pretty as a young girl and had lots of boyfriends."

"Boyfriends? The only one I know of here on the island was me. Guess ya could say we were a couple once she turned sixteen. Course we were always out in the open—me being eleven years older than her. I was real good friends with her daddy and he trusted me. Oh, I won't lie . . . we snatched a few kisses here and there, but no more than that. I knew how young she was, but even then, I loved her."

I smiled. Unrequited love—the most painful kind. "How about in New York? She had boyfriends there?"

"Well, if she did, she didn't tell me about them. Just told me about the one she ended up marrying."

I got up to remove the lasagna from the oven. According to Saren, Sybile may have been strong-willed but she didn't fit the character of what was called a *loose woman* back then. So could my father be Saren? Was he the one man that she'd loved and had a child with?

"Here we go," I said, placing the food on the table. "I hope you'll enjoy it."

"Oh, I know I will. Betcha it's been over fifty years since I had this here lasagna. It was Sybile's mama's special recipe, ya know," he said, taking a bite.

"So you ate at their home?"

"Lord, yes. Almost every Sunday. After church, her mama and daddy always invited me. My parents were both gone. So that was a nice treat, havin' a home-cooked Sunday meal."

I nodded. "I'm sure it was. Do you think her parents thought the two of you would end up together?"

Saren chewed a bite of food. "This sure does bring back memories. It's delicious, Miss Sydney. Sybile's mother would be proud of you." He wiped his mouth with a napkin. "Yeah, I reckon her parents thought once she got out of high school her and I might end up gettin' married. But like I told ya—she had bigger fish to fry and those fish weren't here on this island. Life is real funny like that, ya know. You think it's all headed one way and then boom—just like that, it changes."

Don't I know that. "Yeah, we never know from day to day what's around that next corner."

Saren nodded. "Yup, look at you. You come here for a little vacation and now you're a full-fledged resident. With some people, this island has a way of holdin' on and not lettin' go."

I smiled. "And I was one of those people. I've been here almost six months now and it feels like I've lived here forever. More lasagna?"

"Goodness, no, but thank you. I sure did enjoy that, Miss Sydney."

"Well, I hope you left room for dessert—lemon pie."

"Oh, my. Don't see how I could turn that down. Just a small piece, please."

I cut two wedges and returned to the table.

Saren took a bite, smacking his lips. "This sure is good."

"I'm afraid I can't take credit. It's a Mrs. Smith's."

He laughed. "She's a good baker. I'm real glad you decided to stay here, ya know and I'm real glad we became friends."

I looked across the table at this sincere and caring man. "Well, I'm real glad too."

He remained quiet for a few minutes while eating the pie. Blotting his lips with the napkin, he folded it, placed it on the table, and leaned forward. "Can I ask ya somethin', Miss Sydney?"

"What is it?"

"Well, I was wonderin'. You seem to be in touch with Sybile lately." He paused, shifting in his chair. "I was just wonderin' if maybe you could put in a good word for me. You know, mention me to her. Tell her I was askin' for her and such. And . . . see if maybe she'd be willin' to let me stop by and pay her a visit. I got to thinkin' about you saying that. Maybe you're right. Maybe the time has come to let bygones be bygones. That is . . . if Miss Sybile would be agreeable. Would ya see what you could do?"

I inhaled deeply blowing the air back out, then finished off the last sip of wine. Getting up from the table to remove the dishes, I patted Saren on the shoulder. "I can't promise anything. And I don't want to see you disappointed. But yes. . . . I'll talk to her. I'll see what I can do."

25

My chance to honor Saren's request came the following week. Sybile called Spinning Forward and asked if I could come that evening for dinner. No apology, no mention of her rudeness the last time we'd spoken.

I fought down the urge to decline. "What time?" was what I said in a brusque tone.

"Seven o'clock," Sybile stated without asking if that was convenient.

"I'll be there." I hung up the phone. No doubt about it. This woman was annoying. I glanced up to see Noah walk through the door.

Lilly ran to him for her requisite pat. "Hey girl," he said, looking up to flash me a smile. "And how're you doing?" he asked.

"Annoyed, at the moment," I said and explained about the conversation with Sybile.

Noah shook his head. "Have to admit—she can be difficult."

"She makes me wonder if she's incapable of any emotion. Like she doesn't care whether people like her or not, so she'll just be as damn rude as she can."

"Or is it that she might care too much? A lot of people put up that wall—it protects them. Keeps them from being hurt."

Was that what she'd done? Erected a wall to protect herself from further hurt? Noah could be right. If Sybile remained aloof, refrained from displaying emotions, she guaranteed herself not to be hurt. Not hurt—but possibly very lonely.

"You have a point there."

Driving to Sybile's house, I noticed the air was filled with a sweet fragrance. Must be one of those Southern flowers that bloom in the spring. Bushes of vivid reds, pinks, and purples adorned front lawns. Pulling into the gravel driveway of the Lighthouse my nostrils were assailed with the scent of salt water. Stepping from the golf cart, I inhaled deeply and headed up the stairs.

"I'm here," I hollered, sliding the screen door open. Stepping inside I found Sybile at the kitchen counter putting the finishing touches on a crabmeat casserole. Her illness hadn't tamed down her clothing style. Wearing white eyelet capris and a lemon-yellow top, her hair was held back with a lime-green scarf. I noticed the woman carried a few less pounds.

"I'll just pop this in the oven and we'll have a glass of wine before dinner," Sybile told me.

My trained ears heard the increased shortness of breath, but I refrained from commenting. "Sounds good," I said, settling on the sofa.

Sybile joined me carrying two glasses of chardonnay. "So what have you been up to? How's that new beau of yours?"

Cripe, even a woman who hardly ventured from her home seemed to know the latest gossip on this island. "I wouldn't exactly call Noah Hale my *beau*. I've had dinner with him, that's all."

"Well, seems he'd be a mighty fine catch to me."

"I suppose if one was out there fishing he might be."

"So you plan to spend the rest of your life alone?"

"Like mother, like daughter," I retorted, not sure I believed what I was saying.

Sybile threw her head back laughing. "Touché."

"Look, Sybile, I doubt you summoned me here to discuss my love life—or the lack of one. So what's up?"

"You get right to the point, don'cha? I like a no-nonsense type of woman." She slowly took a sip from the wineglass. "You're right. That isn't why I wanted you to come over. Seems you've become pretty chummy with Saren."

"If you mean we're friends, yes, we are."

Sybile nodded. "Then maybe you could do me a favor. I'd like to invite him to dinner but I'd like you to do the asking, and I'd also like you to be here if he accepts."

Was Sybile-the-Lion-Heart having a change of mind? She'd been loathsome to poor Saren over the years and I wasn't about to let her off the hook easily. "Now why would I want to do that? More important, why would *you* want to do that?"

Sybile avoided eye contact and remained silent for a few moments. "Well, I'm on my way to checkin' out—why not make amends with people before my grand departure?"

"Ah, I see. . . . Now that you're close to dying, why not stir up all those emotions that Saren once had for you? Yes, that sounds like something you'd do. Refuel his feelings and then poof! You'll be gone once again—but this time, permanently. Yeah, that sounds like a very nice thing to do."

Sybile's eyes flashed anger. "You think you know everything. You don't know a damn thing—you with the pampered and cultured upbringing. Forget it—forget I even asked you to do this."

My annoyance escalated to match Sybile's anger. "How dare you think you know me. And how dare you comment on my upbringing. You don't know a thing about me—and let's not forget, that was *your* choice. You got exactly what you wanted out of this life, Sybile, and that includes the loss of Saren."

Sybile inhaled deeply, resting her head against the back of the sofa. "You're right," she said softly, staring up at the ceiling. "I created my own destiny. But it doesn't mean that the way I shaped it was the right way."

My anger abated in proportion to Sybile's. Was the woman admitting to regret now that her days were truly numbered?

As if hearing my thought, Sybile continued, "I meant what I've always said—I have no regrets. But that doesn't mean I sometimes haven't wished that things could have been different."

"Are you referring to your modeling career or to Saren?"

"Both. He's a good, kind person. I know that. I've always known that. But I admit it just wasn't enough for me. I craved more and I tried to take the necessary steps to make it happen. I never,

ever, intentionally hurt Saren. I didn't mean for that to happen."

I interpreted this to be as close to an apology that Sybile would ever verbalize. "But why didn't you bother with him after you returned to the island? Obviously you both cared for each other—if not as lovers, then definitely as friends. All these years wasted, with no contact."

Sybile nodded. "You're right," was all she said.

"Okay, listen. I'll do what you're asking, but you have to make me a promise."

Sybile's face took on a wary expression but she remained silent.

"You have to tell Saren the truth. He has a right to know your medical situation and the prognosis. If you're going to let him back into your life, it's the right thing to do."

"I agree. I'll tell him."

"Oh, and one more thing. You have to be *nice* to him. There's no sense renewing a friendship if you're only going to be mean."

Sybile's feisty demeanor returned. "What're you talking about? I haven't been mean to him. I am who I am—and Saren knows that. So don't go givin' me orders, like you're the mother and I'm the daughter."

I stifled a grin. There was some truth to that statement. "Well, just be nice. I like Saren—a lot. And I won't stand by and watch you hurt him again. Understand?"

"Yes, Mom. So when will you ask him?"

"When do you want to arrange this dinner?"

"How about Monday evening? That is, if you're not busy with your—that guy."

"You should start working on that sassiness of yours right now and maybe you should also be more concerned with your own beau."

Sybile grinned and tilted her wineglass toward me. I wondered if that streak of sassiness could be inherited in the genes.

26

Driving to pick up Saren, I recalled the man's excitement that Sybile had actually invited him for dinner. "Dinner?" he'd said. "She really wants me to her place for dinner? That's sure more than I coulda hoped for. Of course I accept. You tell her, 'Yessiree, I accept.'"

A grin crossed my lips as I pulled up in front of Saren's house on the golf cart, gave two little toots on the horn, and waited. Within seconds he appeared on the front porch clutching a huge bouquet of red roses. Getting into the cart he smiled sheepishly.

"Those are lovely, Saren. I have a feeling Sybile will be impressed."

"I sure hope so, Miss Sydney. I went into Chiefland earlier today to the florist there. Told him to give me a big bouquet of his best roses."

I smiled and headed in the direction of the Lighthouse. Pulling into the gravel driveway, I noticed Saren hesitate before getting out. "Anything wrong?" I asked.

"Naw, just a little nervous, I guess."

I patted his hand. "Come on. It'll be fine."

Knocking on the screen, I walked in without waiting for Sybile. "Hey, we're here," I hollered.

Sybile approached us from her bedroom, clad in a long, flowing silk caftan. Black background with white lightning bolts matched the turban covering her head. I thought the only thing missing was a long, mother-of-pearl cigarette holder straight out of the forties.

"Saren—I'm glad you could make it."

I detected a subdued but courteous tone.

Outstretching his hand filled with roses, he nodded. "These are for you and thank you for inviting me."

"They're lovely. I'll get them into a vase. But don't be thanking me till the night is over. You might be sorry you came. Well then, have a seat, both of you, and I'll uncork some wine."

I led the way to the family room and chose the leather chair. Saren walked to the glass doors and stood looking out to the marsh and ocean beyond. "Quite a view you have from here. I can see why you wanted to live here."

Sybile joined us carrying a tray with three crystal glasses filled with white wine. Handing one to me, she replied, "Can you now? I tend to doubt that you truly understand why I wanted to cloister myself here in my ivory tower."

I caught the snappish tone in the words. Maybe this wasn't such a good idea after all.

But Saren overlooked Sybile's brusqueness. "You always were like Rapunzel, Sybi. I imagine you came here to finally let your hair down."

Missing what was obviously a private joke between them, I was astounded to see a smile form on Sybile's lips. And *Sybi?* Where did this Sybi come from?

"But instead of letting it down, I've cut it off, haven't I?" Taking her wineglass she clinked it against the rim of his. "Here's to past memories, Saren. Sometimes they do have a way of catching up with us." Turning toward me, she repeated the gesture and said, "And my daughter here has finally caught up with me. An indiscretion I've kept secret."

Shock registered on Saren's face as he stared at Sybile.

"You should be mighty proud of her, Sybi. You have a fine woman there for a daughter. I'm glad you've found one another," he said, but refrained from asking any details.

Observing the interaction before me, I felt inordinately pleased with what Saren said. Hearing his words made me feel like that school kid running home with a good report card to soak up the compliments from her parents, but I loathed the tactless way Sybile had chosen to explain me.

"Yes, well, I guess it was meant to be. Lord knows I lived my life keeping it a secret."

I took a deep breath. How was it this woman was capable of taking a well-intended compliment and belittling it. The fact wasn't lost on me that Sybile had also neglected to agree with Saren.

"Maybe keeping it a secret was your downfall, Sybile. Seems you still have that peculiarity of not appreciating the good things that are right in front of your nose."

I braced myself for the nastiness I was sure would spew forth and was surprised when it didn't. I was also surprised to observe that Saren seemed to have the ability to say it like it was with Sybile and not be the recipient of her backlash.

Brushing off his statement, she said, "I have some Brie and crackers to go with this wine before dinner," and headed to the kitchen.

I began to feel as if I were observing a stage play—where the characters were unfamiliar to me. Although I couldn't quite define the difference, I knew that Saren and Sybile together were different than they were separately. Silly as it seemed, Sybile appeared more docile—the feistiness in a holding pattern. Saren struck me as the bolder of the two—a take-charge demeanor had come over him that I hadn't witnessed before.

Saren reached for a cracker, looking Sybile right in the eye. "So what's this I hear about you being ill?"

Hesitating for a second, she then snapped, "Ill? Hell, I'm not *ill*. I'm dying."

I could almost see that proverbial elephant sitting directly in front of us and glanced over to catch Saren's reaction.

He bowed his head and remained silent for a few moments. Looking up at Sybile, his eyes glistened with moisture. "I was afraid you were going to tell me that. You know I'm sorry, Sybi. I'm terribly sorry this is happening to you."

Recovering her sardonic nature, she snapped, "Yeah, well, it has to happen to all of us at one time or another, doesn't it? Not like we can escape it." She took a long sip from her wineglass. "So there ya have it. I felt it. . . . Actually, Sydney felt it was only proper to tell you myself."

I caught the barb Sybile had tossed at him. Making him realize that if she'd had her way, she wouldn't have told him at all.

"And I thank you for telling me. So now—now what are you going to do to fight this?"

Sybile threw her head back laughing. "Same ole Saren. Wants to save the world. Well, you can't save me. I'm afraid it's too late for that."

"It's never too late. Remember that fat woman? It ain't over till she sings."

"Yeah, well, I can hear her singing in the distance. Saren, back off. I've had enough of this from Dora. It isn't going to amount to a hill of beans if I have the treatment or not. Sure, it might prolong my life by a few months—a few miserable months at that. I don't want that and I refuse to go that route."

I shifted in my chair, took a sip of wine, and waited for Saren's reaction.

After a few minutes of silence, he nodded. "Okay."

Sybile's head shot up, surprise covering her face. "Okay? You mean you're not going to fight me on this? Try to talk me out of it—like you did with so many things when we were young?"

Saren expelled a deep breath and shook his head. "No. Maybe I was wrong back then to do that. I'll never know for sure. But I do know that as we get older we can more easily understand where the other person is coming from. We might not agree with it—but I find it easier to accept."

Sybile remained silent.

"The only thing I ask, Sybi, is that you let me share whatever time you have left. Will you do that? Can we be friends like we were as kids? Can I take you out on my boat again? Will you let me be a part of your days? Will you allow me to celebrate this life with you—as you never would for all these years?"

I looked over to see Sybile's head was bent, fingering the stem of her wineglass.

Swiping a finger across her eye, she sniffed twice and took a deep breath. "I reckon that would be okay, Saren." Tossing her head and sitting straighter in the chair, she retorted, "Just don't go getting clingy on me. I won't stand for that, ya know. And don't even think about us moving in together or any such nonsense. Understood?"

I felt I was getting a glimpse of the young girl Sybile used to be. Even her language and voice changed as she laid down the rules for Saren. Glancing over, I saw a grin cross the man's face.

"It surely is understood, Miss Sybile. I've always understood you. You just never wanted to admit that."

Getting up from her seat, Sybile stood in front of Saren, hand on her hip. "Don't you go gettin' know-it-all on me either like when we were young. 'Cuz I ain't young anymore and I stand up for myself. So if you wanna be friends, you'd better be mindin' those Ps and Qs of yours. Ya hear?"

Saren got up quickly from his chair, appearing suddenly much younger than his stated age of eighty-two. Grasping Sybile by her shoulders, he looked into her eyes as a smile crinkled his face. "Oh, I hear, alright. I sure enough do. I always heard you, Sybile. It was you that cut off the words for *me* to hear anymore."

Leaning toward her, he kissed her cheek.

Accepting the kiss, Sybile then quickly brushed him away with her hands. "Okay, enough of this canoodling. I have a roast pork in the oven that needs tendin' to."

I watched my mother walk toward the kitchen and then glanced at Saren. I had no doubt that I'd just witnessed a momentous episode in the life of two people who had somehow lost their way and were now reconnecting.

Dora was waiting on the pavement when I arrived at the yarn shop to open on Tuesday morning. "Are you here to purchase something? You're off today, remember?" I said, holding Lilly's leash with one hand while inserting the key with the other.

"I do need some yarn, but I came over to get the lowdown on that dinner last evening."

I laughed as we walked inside and I unclipped Lilly's leash. "You mean to tell me your sister didn't share all the details with you?"

"She's as bad as she was in high school. Making me grovel for every piece of information."

"Just another thing I missed not having a sister, I guess." I began preparing the coffeemaker.

"Well?" Dora demanded.

I heard the impatience in my aunt's voice. "Well—now, I'm not sure I should be the one to relay the evening to you," I replied, turning my back so Dora wouldn't see the grin.

"It's times like this that you remind me so damn much of Sybile."

I threw my head back laughing. "I won't torment you any longer. What exactly did Sybile tell you?"

"That the roast pork turned out to perfection. Beyond that, not much else."

I shook my head. "She *is* a tough one, that woman. She didn't tell you that she and Saren have, shall we say, renewed old acquaintances?"

"What's that supposed to mean?"

"Well, he asked if he could be her friend again. Take her out in his boat, do things together, I imagine."

This time it was Dora that shook her head. "That man always did seem to have a way with her. Until she went to New York, that is. No amount of talking could convince her otherwise."

I poured the carafe of water into the coffeepot and turned around to face Dora. "Did you think Saren was good for Sybile back then?"

"Good for her?"

"Yeah, I mean you said everyone on the island thought they'd end up together. Did you think that would be a good thing for her?"

Dora took a moment to think over the question. "Yes, I'd have to say I did. I know Mama and Daddy thought he'd be able to tame her down a bit."

"But that's just it. Maybe Sybile didn't want to be tamed down at that point in her life."

"Obviously," Dora retorted.

I knew Dora was referring to my birth. I also knew I had no idea where these thoughts were coming from. I hadn't considered it at all until I saw Saren and Sybile together. "What I mean is, maybe Sybile needed to pursue her own path in life. Not Saren's. Maybe she needed to figure out who *she* was before she could commit to another person." Realizing I could be talking about myself, I blurted out, "Maybe she felt she was being smothered by Saren. Every relationship involves a certain amount of restraint—but it has to be when the person is ready."

"And you're saying she's ready now? After all these years?"

"Her time's running out, Dora."

"Hmm, you could be right. Well, then, I'm happy for her. And Saren too. If they're going to resume their friendship, I'm all for it."

I put the finishing touches on the salad, replacing it in the fridge to chill, and nodded in approval at the table set with yellow place mats in the shape of a seashell, the brightly colored yellow and blue plates, and two crystal wineglasses. Placing a vase of white carnations from Saren's garden in the center, I stepped back to assess the arrangement. Something was nagging at me. Had been all day. I realized it wasn't the table setting or even the dinner with Noah. It was the discussion with Dora earlier that day.

Lighting up a cigarette I walked outside to the balcony. Lilly was romping in the yard below attempting to catch a squirrel. Blowing out a puff of smoke, I glanced at the water. The tide was coming in. I could smell it in the air. What was this disconcerted feeling I'd had all day? And why was I suddenly coming to understand Sybile's feelings of over fifty years ago?

Lilly's playful bark drew my attention to the garden. Noah was walking along the walkway, a bouquet of flowers in one hand and a bag in the other. I had the vantage point of not being seen on the balcony. He bent over rubbing Lilly's fur between her ears. Wearing a light blue polo jersey, jeans, and loafers, I had to admit he had quite the boyish charm for a man of sixty-two. His handsome face appeared to be a deeper tan since I'd seen him on Sunday and remembered he'd planned to spend yesterday boating with the guys. Snubbing out my cigarette in the ashtray, I walked through the apartment to the door just as Noah reached the top step.

"Hey there," he said, giving me a once-over before handing me the flowers.

Happy I'd chosen the white shorts and mint-green silk blouse I smiled. "Thank you. How nice," I said, reaching for the flowers.

"And a little vino to go with the meal." He stepped into the kitchen behind me.

"I'll get these in water and then what can I get you to drink?"

"What're you having?"

"I thought a gin and tonic might be nice on a warm evening."

"Perfect. Make that two."

I turned around to arrange the flowers in a vase and could feel Noah's eyes on my back. "How was your boating yesterday?"

"Great. We did real well catching grouper. I should be cooking supper for *you* tonight."

I laughed. "I have lasagna in the oven. I'm not sure it can surpass grouper though."

"I love Italian. Thought you told me you don't really cook?"

"I didn't actually say that. I said I'm limited and only do the basic things."

"Well, I'm sure it'll be great. Hey, I'm getting my new boat."

I measured out gin pouring it into the two glasses. Reaching for the tonic water, I turned around. "Really? That's great. That must mean you do plan to stay here on the island."

"Oh yeah. I'll definitely be staying here."

Was it my imagination or had his tone taken on a sexy sound?

I sliced a wedge of lime, added it to the glasses, and passed one to Noah. Touching the rim of his, I said, "Here's to safe and happy boating."

Noah took a sip of the drink and nodded. "Very nice. Thanks. So could I entice you to join me on the maiden voyage?"

Not sure if he meant overnight, I hesitated.

"I thought I'd christen the boat right out here off shore from Cedar Key. Pay a visit to Atsena Otie, then over to Snake Key, and North Key. Eventually I'll want to take her up the Suwannee, but I want to get a feel for her first."

Of course he meant a "feel" for the boat, not me. "Sure. That would be fun. Just let me know when."

"Well, I'm heading to Crystal River tomorrow to finish up the purchase details. So it shouldn't be too long before I have her."

"Great. Let's take the drinks out on the balcony. Dinner will be ready in about a half hour."

Noah followed me outside. Sitting in the chairs opposite each other, I reached for my cigarette case and then changed my mind.

Taking a sip of his drink, Noah placed the glass on the table in front of him. "Can I ask how it went last night with Saren and Sybile?"

I laughed. "It went way better than I could have expected. It was pretty amazing to see the two of them together. Almost like they swapped person-alities in each other's company."

"What do you mean?"

I now lit the cigarette and blew smoke over the

balcony railing. "Well, Sybile was feisty, don't get me wrong. But she assumed this docile disposition that I'd never seen before."

"Interesting."

"Yeah, it was and even more so was that Saren seemed to morph into a much stronger personality than I would have thought him capable."

"Sounds like a role reversal brought on by each other."

"Exactly."

"You seem concerned about this though."

I took a long swallow of my drink. "I'm not sure. I guess I've just never witnessed a transformation like this with two people in each other's company."

"Maybe the real *them* emerges when they're together."

I nodded. "Could be," I replied doubtfully.

Noah swirled the amber cognac in his glass. I sat inches away from him on the balcony, lost in thought.

"I have to compliment you again, Syd. Dinner was outstanding."

Syd? This was the first time he'd called me *Syd*. It made me remember the pet name Saren had for Sybile. "Thanks. I'm glad you enjoyed it."

"Did you get your sign yet for the shop?"

I shook my head. "Not yet. I spoke to the company in Gainesville on Friday. They assured me somebody would drive out with it yesterday. Nobody showed up. I'll be glad when the permanent sign gets here. It'll just make the outside of the shop look even nicer."

"I can give them a call if you like. Push things along."

I took a swallow of cognac before answering. "Why would *you* calling push things along? I mean, push them along more than when I called?"

Noah turned to face me.

"Are you saying that business people pay no attention to females? But if *you* call, I'll get some satisfaction?"

"No. No, of course not," Noah mumbled.

"Good. Because I'm perfectly capable of taking care of this situation. Without the assistance of a male."

Changing the subject, Noah asked, "So how did your daughter make out with the job interview in Gainesville?"

"I think she'll accept the teaching position. She'll be looking for a place to stay there." The anger I'd felt a few moments before began to dissipate.

"I'm thinking of throwing a party in a few weeks. Just some friends and some of the locals— have a seafood buffet with what we've caught. Do you think Monica might like to come? I'd like both of you to be there."

"That sounds like fun. Of course we'll come."

Noah reached for my hand and gave it a squeeze. "I like you, Sydney. I like being with you."

I felt heat radiating from his hand into mine. This guy has incredible energy, I thought. "I like being with you too." I had to admit that being with him felt comfortable. Right. That is, when we weren't sparring. Which still seemed to happen now and again. Like this evening. But I knew he created a sense of desire in me that I hadn't experienced in years.

Noah took the last sip from his glass and stood up, pulling me up with him. Wrapping me in his arms, he nuzzled his face into my neck. "You smell good. Whatever it is, I like that perfume."

"Shalimar," I answered breathlessly.

Noah tipped my face up to his. "Can I see you again at the end of the week?"

Feeling like a schoolgirl, my legs went weak as I nodded and whispered, "Yes."

"Good," he said, kissing me with more passion than he ever had.

I felt the pressure of his lips increase at the same time his tongue entered my mouth. Lost in the heat of the moment, I didn't hear Monica clearing her voice as she stood in the doorway. Noah was the first to break away.

I stood inches away from him trying to catch my breath as I looked into the face of my daughter. Although the evening had grown cool, my entire body was flushed with heat. I knew what I'd just experienced wasn't a hot flash. It was pure lust.

"Monica," I managed to say. The second meeting wasn't going to be any better than the first.

The air suddenly got a few degrees cooler. "How're you doing?" was all she said.

"Fine and it's good to see you again. I was just telling your mother I'm having a party in a few weeks and I'd like you to join us. Bring a friend along."

Her face actually took on the hint of a smile. "Thank you. That might be fun. Well, I'll leave you two to whatever you were doing." She turned to walk back in the house.

"No, no. I really have to be going," Noah said, taking my hand as he walked past Monica. "Good night."

"Likewise," was Monica's only remark as she stepped onto the balcony.

I followed Noah out to the porch and he closed the door behind us.

"I'm sorry about that. A bit awkward for you, I guess."

"Well, I'm a big girl now and Monica has to get used to that idea."

Noah pulled me back into his arms for another kiss. But this time it wasn't as intense.

"Good night," he said. "I'll see you soon."

28

I reached for the apple that Alison passed me, took a bite, and stared at the water ebbing from the beach. Shifting for a more comfortable position on the blanket, I allowed my eyes to focus on the sun that was slowly dipping to the horizon.

"Gonna be a great sunset," Ali said, taking a deep swallow of water from a bottle.

"Uh-huh."

"Might even snow in Florida tomorrow."

"Uh-huh."

Ali nudged my arm. "What the hell is going on with you? You don't hear a word I say lately."

I jerked my arm away. "I hear you. I have a lot on my mind, that's all."

"Sybile?"

"Actually, she's status quo at the moment."

"Come on. What's up? You think I've known you all these years and I can't tell when something's bothering you?"

"I'm not sure what it is. It's just that the past few days—I'm feeling restless, I guess."

"Restless? That's a sure indication you need to have sex."

I wasn't sure whether to laugh or get upset. "Allee! For God's sake, is that all you ever think about?"

"Well, no. Not *all* I ever think about. But for

Christ's sake, Syd, face it. You're with a handsome guy, who just happens to be pretty damn sexy. It's been what? Ages since you've been with a guy. Maybe your hormones are just raging."

Hearing that, I did throw my head back laughing. "Yeah, right. I'm going through another puberty at age fifty-three. Did you ever think it's a *lack* of hormones we have at this age?"

Ali got a sly smile on her face. "Hmm, can't prove it by me."

I shook my head. "I don't know what's going on. I only know I feel restless. Not stable. Shifting. Do you know what I mean?"

"You're coming into your own."

"What's that supposed to mean?"

"Think back to where you were a year ago right now. Last May."

I went back in my mind to the previous spring. Stephen was alive. I was in a stable marriage. Cared for. No financial worries. But—was I really happy? Lately, I'd been giving that question some thought. I did know one thing for certain. Stephen had never stirred my passion and desire as Noah so easily did. Just being in the same room with Noah made me feel good. And his kisses—no doubt about it, they made me want more. Stephen and I were together till death do us part, but looking back it wasn't death that actually severed our relationship. I was beginning to see that my marriage had been severed long before Stephen died. He was a husband that I thought I knew when I really didn't know him at all. Sitting on the beach in Cedar Key, Florida, I had to honestly question the definition of love. And I knew that honesty had to be at the top of the list—something I'd never had in my marriage to Stephen, and something I'd only recently come to understand.

I blew out a deep breath. "Okay, I know where I was a year ago right now. I've moved forward with my life. I'm going on. So what?"

"Sydney, Sydney, Sydney," Ali said, shaking her head. "You always were a late bloomer when it came to catching on. Yeah, you *are* moving forward and you've come a helluva long way, baby, as the Virginia Slims commercials used to say. But it's a process—this moving forward. You came here to find yourself. You might not have realized it at the time, but you did. And think about it. Look at how much more you've found than just yourself."

"Sybile?"

Alison nodded. "Yeah, Sybile and that added to the overall process of finding *you*. And now—now you need to figure out exactly *who* you are. It takes time, Syd. You need to reach down inside yourself and figure out what you like and don't like about *you*. What are your strong points? Your weak points? What makes you deliriously happy? What causes you profound sadness? Where do you want to be twenty years from now? It's one thing to go seeking, Sydney. It's quite another to figure out exactly what you're going to do with what you've found. You're now entering the process of getting to know *you*—for the first time in your life."

I leaned over to hug Alison. "How'd you get to be so smart? How come you know all this shit and I don't?"

"Because I've already gone through it and as your best friend, I can't do it for you. But I can be here to try and pave the way. Remember Ariadne's thread? You need to grab that thread, hold on, and allow it to lead you to your feminine soul. Like many women around our age, you've had your awakening. Throughout history women normally go to men for help. But when you're on a feminine journey to recover the essence of you—that's when you need other women to guide you."

I recalled the myth about Ariadne and the ball of thread she'd given to Theseus when he entered the labyrinth beneath the palace to slay the Minotaur. Looking out to the water and sky beyond, I began to sense that this island was my labyrinth—my place to connect to the earth and hopefully recover my authentic female self. The thought crossed my mind that perhaps even my choice of opening the yarn shop was symbolic for my journey—spinning yarn that was enabling me to form new stitches resulting in the freedom and power I'd lost years before.

Monica had found a condo to rent in Gainesville and I won't lie, it was nice to have my place back to myself. After the recent encounter with Noah, I had expected her to be standoffish with me. But the opposite had happened. She seemed to be lightening up and was more conducive to friendly conversations. I wondered if perhaps a new love interest in her own life might account for her change of attitude. *That might be part of it,* I thought, but I also understood that much of her nastiness had been brought on by the sudden loss of Stephen. In her own way, she was attempting to go through the grieving process.

When the phone rang, I thought perhaps it was Monica but answered to hear Sybile's voice say a curt hello.

"Well, stranger. How're you doing? I seldom hear from you anymore."

Sybile's tone had a touch of arrogance. "That's not true and you know it. I've been busy."

"Busy with Saren?" I asked playfully.

"As a matter of fact, yes. He took me shopping yesterday in Gainesville and then for lunch. Today we're going out on the boat."

I smiled. "I'm happy for you, Sybile. That's great. And what a perfect day for boating." Looking out the kitchen window, I saw the thermometer outside read seventy-eight degrees and the water at the beach glazed like glass.

"So when am I going to get together with that granddaughter of mine?"

I had left the ball in Sybile's court. I figured when she was ready to meet Monica, she'd let me know, and apparently she was.

"Well, she's living in Gainesville now. Got her own place. But name a day and I'll see if she's free."

"Will you both come to lunch on Thursday?"

"I'll check with Monica, but I think that might be okay. I know she's anxious to finally meet you."

"Really?"

I smiled again. "Yes, really. I'll call her right now and check and oh, say hello to Saren for me."

I had no sooner replaced the phone in the cradle when it rang again. This time I answered to hear Noah's voice. "What do you think of the name Boston Beauty?"

Laughing, I replied, "For a child, outrageous. For a boat—pretty cool." Before my mind had a chance to wonder to the meaning, Noah explained.

"The new boat that I'm getting, it's a really snazzy pontoon. The previous owner was from Boston. Hence, the name. They say it's bad luck to change it." He paused for a fraction of a second. "Besides, that's the area you hail from."

Although I felt honored, I wasn't sure how to respond. "Well, I hope it'll bring you lots of good fishing."

"I know it's a bit late to be asking, but would you be free tomorrow evening? The tides are perfect to go out and watch the sun set. Plus, there's a full moon."

"It sounds like fun. Sure, what time?"

"I'm keeping it at my friend's dock for right now. How about I get the boat and meet you at the city dock about seven?"

"Sounds great. I'll bring some wine and cheese to christen it."

I breathed in the fresh salt air and exhaled. Curled up on the leather seat, I watched Noah expertly take the boat through the channel and out toward Atsena Otie. "Ready for some wine?" I asked.

"Sounds good. If you take the wheel, I'll uncork it."

I got up, reaching for the bottle and cork screw. "I think I can manage."

He shot me a sideward glance but said nothing.

Uncorking the cabernet I filled two glasses and passed one to him. "Cheers," I said. "And many happy moments enjoying your *Boston Beauty*."

Touching his plastic cup to mine, he said, "I'll drink to that."

I remained standing beside him as he maneuvered the pontoon in the water. The sun was doing a lazy descent in a vibrant shade of orange, while streaks of pink and purple surrounded the orb. Taking a deep breath, I said, "Gorgeous, isn't it?"

Noah turned, touching my face with his hand. "Incredibly gorgeous."

I smiled. "You know I meant the sun and—all this," I said, gesturing with my arm.

"It *is* beautiful, but being out here on the water with you makes it all more special."

Taking a sip of wine, I returned to my seat in back of him. Once Noah arrived between Atsena Otie and North Key, he released the throttle and the engine quieted.

"This seems like a good place to drop anchor." Walking to the side, he lifted the heavy boomerang-shaped metal attached to rope and let it fall into the water.

"There," he said, sitting beside me. "Now we can enjoy the sunset."

"I'll fix the cheese and crackers." Passing the plate to Noah, I settled myself into the corner, my back resting against the cushion, bending my legs up in front of me. Leaning my chin on my knees, I stared straight ahead as the speed of the sunset increased. "Almost gone," I murmured and felt Noah's hand stroke my upper thigh.

"Only to return tomorrow," he said. "That's just one of the things we can always depend on. Sunrise and sunset."

Within a matter of seconds the orange ball dipped below the horizon out of sight.

"Ah, another day gone." I stretched my legs out in front of me and looked around. "It's so quiet and pretty out here. I love seeing the island from the water. It looks different, doesn't it?"

I followed Noah's gaze toward the shore and saw the tall water tower with Cedar Key written on it. To our right was Piney Point.

"Yeah," he said. "Being on the water changes one's perspective in many ways, I think."

I continued staring at the sky, which had now become a canvas with streaks of bright pink, slashes of purple, and a deepening blue. "I've heard many people used to go to sea to think things out. Find answers. Do you think that's true? That they found their answers, I mean?"

Noah let his hand remain on my leg. "I believe that most of life's answers are right here," he said, pointing to his chest area with his other hand. "I think we all have to go within when we're searching."

What he said reminded me of what Alison had said. "Have you done that?"

"I think I did without consciously realizing it. When I went to Key West. I've come to realize that the years I spent there weren't just about painting."

"And did you find your answers?"

"I'm not sure yet," he said softly, turning to pull me into his arms.

That familiar heat radiated through my body as Noah bent his head to kiss me. This time I didn't pull away, but allowed myself to sink into the feeling that was filling me. Returning Noah's kiss, the thought occurred to me again that I'd never been kissed in quite this way. Certainly my body had never felt this consumed. I felt like I was riding a roller coaster and was quickly approaching the peak. Feeling Noah tug on my lower lip between kisses only increased my passion. When his tongue wrapped around mine, I pushed closer to his body. I could feel his erection through his jeans.

No words were exchanged. While continuing to kiss me, Noah managed to remove my blouse, reaching for the clasp on the front of my bra. Lost in an intimacy I'd never experienced, I slid down on the long leather seat and removed my shorts. Noah's face hovered above me as passion raged between us. "I want you," I heard him whisper in a voice filled with huskiness, as I felt him remove his jeans.

"Yes," I whispered back. His weight was on top of me, filling me with an ecstasy I never thought possible. As his body merged with mine, I felt like I was diving down into the very core of my being. A place I'd never been taken before. A place that had no beginning and no end. That place in time that simply *is*.

I realized that the moaning I heard was coming from deep inside of me. I heard Noah scream out my name as his thrusts increased and he grabbed my shoulders. And I knew that he had joined me in that single spot of the universe that suspends one's body and one's soul for the most exquisite of moments. Breathing heavily, I felt him lower himself onto me and bury his face in my hair. We stayed that way for a few minutes, savoring the oneness we had just shared. Turning on my side, I allowed him to stretch out the length of my body.

"Oh, God, Sydney," he moaned. I felt the impact of his words and understood their meaning as he pulled me tighter.

The diving sensation had now transformed to that of floating. It was a few minutes before I realized we were on the boat and it was gently rocking from side to side. My finger traced the outline of his back. I expelled a deep breath and still, I didn't speak. I stayed in his arms replaying in my mind the pleasure he had given me, while he indulged my solitude.

Unsure how much time had elapsed, I felt a cool breeze drift across my body and shivered. Was it caused from the wind or my own contentment? "I never knew," I whispered against Noah's face. "I never knew that making love could be like that."

In answer, he held my face between his hands and kissed me.

≈29≈

A dream about water, cardiac surgery, and babies woke me at 5:00 A.M. I stayed in bed for a few minutes trying to hold on to shreds of the dream, but was unable to piece it together. My mind drifted to the night before.

Making love with Noah had been an almost mystical experience—suspended in space. The water caused a placid swaying of the boat while the full moon created silver shadows above and around me. I'd lost track of time. We'd remained locked in each other's arms and I had been shocked to see that three hours had passed since we'd left the dock.

Turning on my side and burrowing into my pillow I smiled, remembering the intimacy we'd shared. Heading back to the dock I'd stood beside Noah, his arm around my shoulder. He'd left the boat at the city dock overnight and walked me back to my apartment holding my hand. I invited him in and we shared a cognac together before he returned home, telling me he'd call today.

The ringing phone startled me, causing me to jump. I answered to hear Dora's voice.

"Sydney, I'm so sorry to bother you this early in the morning."

My eyes rested on the bedside clock. 5:25. "No, it's fine. What's wrong?"

"It's Sybile. She's in the hospital and I'm really sorry to bother you—but I just needed somebody to talk to."

"I'm glad you called. Will she be alright?" I asked, before realizing what a silly question that was.

"Well, she had a very bad time breathing last night. Saren was at the house with her and when it got worse around midnight, he insisted on driving her to Shands. I just spoke with him, and he said she'll be there another day or so and they've started her on some new medication."

"Okay. Listen, I was half awake when you called anyway. I'll throw something on and I'll be over your house shortly, alright?"

"Oh, that would be nice, Sydney. I'll make breakfast for us."

I arrived at Dora's front door, with Lilly's leash in one hand and two blueberry muffins in the other. "I brought a couple of Ali's muffins," I told her. "Thought it would be good with coffee first."

Dora hugged me and led the way through the house to the patio. "This is so nice of you to come over," she said, pouring coffee from the carafe she had on a tray.

"So Sybile's not doing so good, huh?" I asked, accepting the coffee mug and taking a sip.

Dora shook her head. "Not really. I could see

her breathing was getting worse, but oh no, she wouldn't listen."

"Seems she listened to Saren."

"He always did have a way with her. I'm glad he was able to convince her to go to the hospital." Dora absently patted Lilly's head and stared out at the water. The air was thick with the scent of lantana. "How much longer do you think she has? The truth, Sydney."

"At this point, I honestly don't know. She seemed to be doing pretty well. She's been going out with Saren and I think that's been good for her. The doctor had told her nine months to a year without treatment, remember?"

"I still think she's crazy not to at least try chemo. She's just signing her own death certificate is what she's doing."

I sighed, reaching over to pat Dora's hand. "It's *her* death certificate to sign. You have to allow her this. Unfortunately, it's very difficult for you."

"Do you know what Saren told me yesterday? That's she's planning her own funeral. Did you ever hear of such a silly thing?"

Despite the seriousness of the subject, I smiled. "Actually, I have heard of this, Dora. Some people want to make sure their wishes are carried out—even after they're no longer here. And you have to admit, Sybile plans to end her life the way she lived it. On her terms."

"Always trying to be in control. That's Sybile."

"What does she have planned?"

"I told her I didn't want to hear about it, so I don't know. Except that she wants to be cremated and her ashes scattered off Cedar Key."

I nodded, but the irony wasn't lost on me. The woman who did everything possible to leave the island and forget everything about it now wanted to be a part of it forever.

"Dora, the best thing we can do is support Sybile. Be there for her. We have no way of knowing how much time she has left."

Dora wiped her eyes with a tissue. "I know and I'm sorry to dump this on you."

"Don't be silly. What're nieces for?" I asked, eliciting a smile from Dora.

"Come on. Sit with me in the kitchen while I make us a nice breakfast."

I perched on the bar stool and watched as Dora scrambled eggs, prepared grits, and buttered English muffins to place on the grill. The smell of sausage cooking filled the kitchen.

"So Monica agreed to meet Sybile on Thursday?" she asked, while adding shredded cheese to the grits. "Marin's excited about meeting her. Sybile invited both of us to the lunch, you know." She stopped preparing the food. "Oh, gosh, do you think she'll be home by Thursday?"

"Sure she will. You said just another day or so, right?"

Dora nodded. "But maybe we should have the lunch over here. It might be easier on Sybile."

"Let's wait and see how she's feeling. I think she'd like to meet her granddaughter for the first time in her own home."

"Yes, of course. You're right. Well, we'll leave it open as an option."

Dora piled a plate with eggs, grits, and sausage and placed it in front of me.

"Gosh, I'll have to call this brunch. I don't usually eat this much for breakfast. It looks great."

Dora joined me at the counter. "So how's Noah lately?"

I felt heat radiating up my neck. Feeling like a schoolgirl with a secret, I mumbled, "He's okay, I guess."

Dora's eyebrows shot up. "I thought you were seeing him last night on that new boat of his."

I put my fork down and shook my head. "How the heck did you know that?"

"Oh, I'm sorry. I didn't think it was a secret. I called you last evening and when I couldn't reach you, I called Ali. I wanted to let you know that Sybile wasn't doing good. I'm sorry if I intruded. Ali told me."

Dora's feelings were hurt. "No, no, you're not intruding," I said, attempting to soothe my aunt. "I guess I'm just still not used to everyone knowing your business before you hardly do yourself."

"One of the scourges of living in a small town"

was all that Dora said and continued eating.

"It was nice. The sunset is even more spectacular from the water and it was a full moon. A perfect night to be out on a boat."

Dora nodded. "When I was younger, how I loved going out there. Being on that water clears a person's head. Makes you feel like you're alone in the universe," she said.

Not quite alone, I thought. "Well, then, you'll have to take a ride with Noah and me sometime."

Dora's face brightened. "Now that would be a lot of fun. I like Noah. Granted, I don't know him very well, but he seems like a kind man. Not to mention pretty darn handsome." Her face wore a sly grin.

I laughed. "Why, I do declare," I said, attempting a poor imitation of a Southern drawl, "if I didn't know better, Aunt Dora, I'd say you have a crush on this man."

Dora waved her hand in the air. "Oh, don't be silly," she admonished, enjoying the teasing.

I had a sudden flashback of Noah's face hovering above mine—filled with desire. "But you're right. He is pretty darn handsome, isn't he?"

While Saren was making Sybile comfortable on her return home, Noah was preparing supper for me in his garden.

"This was really nice of you," I said, watching as he turned chicken on the grill.

"My pleasure. I figured with you being at the shop all day, it might be nice if you had a break tonight."

Noah went in the house, returning with a tray containing salad and rice pilaf. I removed lids from the plastic bowls. Taking a sip of wine, I smiled. I'd wondered if I'd feel awkward seeing Noah again after Saturday night. We took the boat out Sunday afternoon for some fishing and the moment I saw him pull up to the dock I realized it wasn't awkwardness at all that I felt. Instead, warmth had spread through my body. Watching Noah performing the mundane tasks of preparing a meal, familiarity washed over me. Stephen had never attempted to cook a meal for us in our entire twenty-eight years together. Even when I wasn't feeling well, he opted for takeout. Yet, observing Noah in this role created a feeling of *rightness*.

"Soup's on," Noah said, joining me at the table. He flashed me a smile while placing the platter of chicken between us.

That killer smile of his was as much of a turn on as his physical looks.

"It smells wonderful."

"A very simple recipe. Lemon chicken." Taking a breast, he placed it on my plate.

Instinctively I felt myself biting my lower lip. Why did he do this? Make me feel like a five-year-old at the dinner table. It reminded me of my mother doing this when I was a child. Like I wasn't bright enough to figure out which piece of meat to take. "Thanks," was all I said.

"How's Sybile doing since she got home?"

I picked up my knife, thinking, *It's a wonder he doesn't cut the chicken for me,* but said instead, "She's a bit weak and tired. Overall she sounded pretty good when I spoke to her on the phone this afternoon."

Noah nodded. "This has to be so tough on everybody, especially you."

"I'd say it's probably much harder on Saren and Dora. They've known her a lot longer than I have."

"True. But it's never easy preparing for somebody's death. I imagine Monica is looking forward to meeting her grandmother."

"She is. I'm beginning to realize it was more important to her than she let on over the years. I also think losing her father has made gaining a grandmother even more special."

Noah looked up from his plate. "But *you're* happy you found Sybile, aren't you?"

"Yes, of course. I just don't have any mother-daughter feelings toward her. It's like she's—like one of the patients I used to have in nursing. I can relate to her medical situation, but beyond that . . ."

"That might change. And if it doesn't, at least you've been given a chance to meet her and spend some time with her."

Changing the subject, I said, "So your party is next Sunday evening, right?"

Noah nodded. "They'll be about twenty people coming, if they all show up. By the way, I saw Paul today and invited him and Alison."

"Great. Yeah, I'd mentioned it to Ali this morning."

"And just to make it official—you will be my date, won't you?"

I smiled. "Hmm, can I think about that?" I teased.

"As long as your answer will be yes."

30

"That's a pretty shade of blue. Who's that sweater for?" Alison asked. When I remained silent, she said, "Oh, gee, let me guess. Could it be that male you've been keeping company with lately?"

"You know damn well it's for Noah," I snapped.

"I know. I just love getting a rise outta you. Isn't it getting kind of warm for a sweater?"

"Well, it won't be this winter."

"Ah, now that sentence has volumes of meaning. So, I take it you plan to still be seeing Noah when winter comes?"

I slipped my stitches onto a cable holder. "Who knows? We haven't signed a contract to that effect, Miss Nosey."

Alison laughed. "Cripe, you were better in college at telling me your secrets. Now you keep everything to yourself. You're no fun."

I joined Alison's laughter. "That's because I didn't know any better back then. But really, who ever knows which way a relationship will go and where you'll end up?"

"Very true. Just always remember, Syd, you have to know where you're *at* before you can end up where you're going."

I glanced toward the gate and saw Noah walking toward us. Fluttering raced across my chest as I stuffed the knitting back in the bag.

"Hey," he said to both of us and without missing a beat, leaned over and touched my lips with his. "I was on my way home from the gallery and just wanted to stop and say hi."

I smiled up at him, but not before I caught the knowing look on Ali's face. "Well, that was nice of you."

"I also wanted to wish you the best on the meeting with Monica and Sybile. I hope it goes well and Monica won't be disappointed."

"I have no clue how that'll go, but thanks."

"I have a few students coming by at seven, so guess I should get going," he said, leaning down once again to kiss me.

I watched him walk out of the garden and then my gaze shifted to Alison, who was sitting, chin in hands, looking like the cat that swallowed the canary. "What? Now what are you staring at?"

Alison shrugged her shoulders. "Nothing. Nothing at all. Except I know when I see a couple with very strong feelings for each other." Getting up from her chair, she ruffled the top of my hair. "And I think you're beginning to understand the definition of those words *deliriously happy,*" she said, heading into the house.

I sat staring at my daughter across the table. Monica had suggested coming to the island the day before our meeting with Sybile. It made me wonder if something was up. Alison had insisted on cooking dinner for the three of us the evening of Monica's arrival. My daughter had just finished telling us all about her new condo and how much she thought she'd enjoy living and working in Gainesville.

"So that's enough about me," I now heard her say. "Tell me about Sybile or better yet, tell me about Noah. What's developing there?"

I laughed. "There isn't much to tell about Noah. His party is Sunday evening, so you'll have a chance to get to know him a little better. You are still going, aren't you?"

"Definitely, and he said it's okay if I bring somebody. I have a new friend that I met a few weeks ago. He lives downstairs from me. His name is Ian—originally from England and he's teaching at the university also. Very proper British accent and all that. Quite handsome."

In addition to time lessening the hurt of Stephen's death, I felt perhaps a new love interest was responsible for creating my daughter's change in attitude. It had been a while since harsh words had passed between us and she was appearing a lot happier recently. My daughter was definitely becoming easier to get along with.

"Okay, on to Sybile," she said. "She's home from the hospital, right?"

I nodded. "She came home yesterday. I went over last night to check on her. They sent her home with oxygen, which she isn't happy about at all. But I imagine when her breathing gets worse, she'll be forced to use it. She's determined to have that lunch tomorrow, so I told her we'd be there about one."

Alison got up and began clearing the table. "Will Saren be there for the lunch?"

"I'm not sure," I said, picking up dishes to take into the kitchen. "Sybile didn't say."

"Time for dessert," Ali said, "and I'll have you know your mother made the blueberry cobbler."

Surprise crossed Monica's face. "I didn't know you took up baking."

"Actually, Sybile's been giving me a few lessons. This recipe belonged to your great-grandmother. From what I hear, she was quite the cook and Sybile learned from her."

"This is delicious," my daughter said. "I'll have

to get the recipe from you. How's your business going? Has it picked up any?"

I nodded. "More so than when I first opened. And enough that I was able to finally leave my waitress job last week. My feet are eternally grateful for that. Mail orders have increased a lot, so slow but sure, I'm building up my business."

"You never considered returning to nursing, did you?"

"I have to say I didn't. I love owning the shop and I enjoy all the people that stop by. But like any new business, it's just taking a while to build a clientele."

Monica stifled a yawn. "This island air really makes me drowsy. Thanks again, Ali, for letting me stay in one of your empty rooms for a few nights."

"Not a problem. I'm glad you came. I'm going to tend to the dishes, so the two of you enjoy visiting."

When Ali left the porch, Monica leaned across the table. "Okay, truth. So what do you really think of Sybile?"

I shrugged. "I'm not sure what to say. Truthfully, I feel closer to Dora than I do to Sybile. She can be a tough cookie. Sometimes almost abrasive. She says what she wants and doesn't worry about the consequences. Obviously, all her life she *did* what she wanted and gave no thought to the end result."

"Unlike you, huh?"

I sat up straighter in the chair. "And what's that supposed to mean?"

"I mean that I'm not a little girl anymore. I just think you should have been more involved with Dad. You really allowed him to run the whole show. You made it pretty easy for him to indulge his gambling addiction. I'm not blaming you, Mom, really I'm not. It's just that had you been more involved in the finances and household things, you might have realized something was wrong. But you thought it was the right thing to do, because he said so. You never challenged him. Not ever."

I inhaled deeply and blew out the air. "Because I trusted him."

"Exactly. You wanted to avoid confrontation, so you let it all slide. Look where that got you. On the street without even a roof over your head. Literally. That's the kind of person you are. I may have been close to Dad, but I never condoned his behavior. By the time I was a teen, I realized he was in charge of everything. And I swore if I ever got involved with a man, it wasn't going to be that way. Equals or nothing. Your lack of interest really pissed me off when I got older. I don't think you ever once made a decision in that marriage, Mom. Everything was decided by Dad. And it wasn't right. That's one thing I admire about Sybile—she made a decision, on her own, without any input from anybody."

"Why are you defending her? What she did was wrong—never telling my father that he had a child. Whoever he might be. And then giving away that child so she could pursue her own fame and fortune."

"So you resent that?"

I remained silent for a few moments. "No, I don't think so. I don't know what I feel. I guess I just feel she was selfish."

"One of the first things you ever taught me was that we're all different. Remember Sally in my third-grade class? How I came home from school crying because she refused to go to summer camp with me? She was my best friend—I wanted her there with me. And you told me, we're all different. We don't always like the same things, we may not agree on certain things. But it didn't mean that Sally wasn't a good person and a good friend." When I made no reply, Monica went on, "And just because Sybile didn't do what *you* thought would have been the right thing, you're judging her."

All these months I'd insisted it didn't bother me that Sybile had relinquished me for adoption. All these months since knowing Sybile was my birth mother, I had accepted that the woman made her choices in life. But is that how I really felt? And what about this nagging feeling concerning my father? Could my suspicion be true? Could it possibly be Saren? Did I really resent that Sybile refused to share that name with me? For the first time since finding out the truth, I had to be honest with myself and admit that yes, I *was* judging Sybile. And yes, I resented the woman's choices.

While admitting this in my own mind, I wasn't ready to share the truth with my daughter. Getting up, I said, "Let's leave this discussion alone for now. Come on, I'm tired. Time for bed."

Monica got up, put her arm around me, kissed my cheek, and said, "Good idea."

31

I drove the golf cart onto the gravel driveway in front of Sybile's house. "Oh, shit."

"What's the matter?" Monica asked.

"I was hoping Dora and Marin would be here by the time we arrived."

Monica patted my hand. "It'll be fine. Come on," she said getting out of the golf cart. "Wow! Look at this house and that view."

I marveled at the lack of nervousness my daughter displayed. Certainly not like me. Following Monica up the wooden stairs I realized the saying *like mother, like daughter* didn't always apply. Tapping on the screen, I slid it open, hollering, "We're here, Sybile."

She emerged from her bedroom tying a lemon-colored scarf at the base of her neck. Wearing a flowing caftan the shade of mustard, her eyes were fixed on Monica. She paused for a second, as if searing the image in her memory. "Well, so you're my granddaughter," she said, walking up to both of us. "You resemble me, you know, when I was younger."

Her gravelly voice had that familiar edge to it, making me feel uncomfortable. But Monica laughed and without hesitating, she folded her arms around Sybile.

"And *you're* my grandmother. I've been looking forward to meeting you," she said, as Sybile endured the hug for a few moments.

Pushing herself out of the embrace, she stared intently at Monica's face. "Why on earth would you be looking forward to meeting an old woman like me?"

"Maybe I wanted to see what I'd look like at your age."

Now it was Sybile's turn to laugh. "Touché," she said. "Hopefully, *your* genes will be kinder to you." Walking toward the kitchen, she returned with a tray of iced tea. "Come on, granddaughter of mine, let's go get acquainted," she said, leading the way to the sofa.

I stood watching the scene unfold in front of me, feeling like I was invisible. How could this meeting with Monica be such a drastic change from what I'd experienced the first time Sybile admitted she was my birth mother? Why did Sybile seem so relaxed? My God, I thought, my mother and daughter had been *bantering*. Bantering and enjoying it. For a fraction of a second, I felt a ripple of jealousy surge through me. Brushing it aside, I saw Monica sit beside Sybile on the sofa. Taking the club chair, I remained silent but it wasn't lost on me that Sybile hadn't uttered one word to me since I'd entered the house.

"So, granddaughter, what do you think of my island?"

I was surprised at my annoyance. I wanted to yell, "She *does* have a name, you know." But it was obvious that Monica wasn't slighted in the least.

"Well, Mom was holding back on me. I didn't realize this entire island was yours."

For the first time since meeting her, I witnessed Sybile at a loss for words.

Then the woman threw her head back laughing. "It damn well should be. Or at least it should be yours. You're fifth generation, you know. Yup, my grandparents came here from Jacksonville in the eighteen hundreds. Never left. Good fishing off these waters and that's how they made their living. I've got albums of photos I'll show you."

It occurred to me that Sybile had never told me any of this information. Had never offered to show me family photos. Only the ones of herself as a model. But then, I had never mentioned I'd like to see them either.

"That would be great," I heard Monica say. "I have a million questions for you and I want to see your portfolio photos from your modeling career."

"We'll get to all of that." And then as if seeing me for the first time, she said, "Well, you sure are quiet today."

I shook my head and shrugged. "I wanted to let the two of you have the time you need," was all I said.

Making no reply, Sybile looked at Monica, taking in her features. What she probably saw were features that reminded her of herself at that age. Same dark hair. Same almond-shaped dark eyes.

"I see a resilience, a confidence, in you. You have *spirit*. It shows." Sybile took a sip of iced tea and smiled. Taking a deep breath, she patted Monica's hand. "So are you involved with anybody?" she questioned. "Don't think I'm telling you all about me and you're not going to bring me up to snuff on your life."

Monica laughed and appeared undaunted by Sybile's abruptness. "I do happen to have a special somebody. Although it's a brand-new relationship."

I raised my eyebrows as that ripple of jealousy returned.

"Mom knows about Ian but just recently, our relationship has gotten a bit more serious."

"Serious like getting married serious?" Sybile questioned. "Or just living together serious?"

I was taken aback by Sybile's familiarity with somebody she'd only just met. That old saying about blood being stronger than water came into my mind.

"Well, now, we're not sure. For the time being we're keeping our separate apartments and we'll see what happens."

"What's he do for a living? What kind of family does he come from? Does he make good money? Does he want children?" Sybile rattled off the questions like a Jewish matchmaker.

I was interested in these answers too because Monica hadn't shared much more with me than his name.

"Now—wait a sec, I don't even know what to call you and you want all these answers."

Sybile pursed her lips. "You can call me anything you like. Sybile will do fine. I'm not sure I could get used to Grandma after all these years of not being one."

"Oh, no, Sybile won't do. What I call you has to be special. For me. I know," she said, throwing an arm around the woman sitting beside her. "Billie. That's it. I'll call you Billie—short for Sybile and it'll be my special name for you."

I waited for my mother's reaction, certain the woman wouldn't accept her new title. Instead, I saw a smile cross her face and heard her say,

"*Billie.* I like it. Nobody's ever called me that and I've never had a granddaughter. So it suits me fine."

Monica let her arm remain around Sybile's shoulders, and leaning in close, she said, "Okay, Billie, now for those answers you wanted. Ian is a professor at the university also. Teaches English lit. and actually comes from England. We only met about a month ago. He lives downstairs from me and we met at the mailboxes. It was one of those meetings where I just knew it would develop into more than being neighbors. We've been together just about every night since then. His parents live in England, the Cotswolds. So of course, I haven't met them yet, but . . . if all goes well, I just might fly over there with him at Christmas. Does he want children? We haven't really discussed that, but I'd say yes, he probably does. Ian is ten years older than I am. And although you didn't ask—he adores animals and has a cocker spaniel, Sally. He loves to go sailing, is an avid reader, and enjoys traveling through Europe. There. Did I miss anything?"

While I contemplated all that my daughter had just shared, I heard Sybile ask, "Is he good in bed?"

I sat on the sofa, legs crossed, observing the interaction surrounding me. Taking a sip of the coffee that Sybile had prepared following lunch, I silently watched the other four women talking and laughing.

Not surprisingly, the meeting with Monica, Dora, and Marin had gone very well. Embraces were exchanged, laughter filled the room, and my daughter was enveloped into the fold of family.

When I went out on the deck for a cigarette, Dora followed me outside to question my quietness.

"You seem withdrawn today. Is everything alright?"

Attempting to shake off the mood that I couldn't account for, I smiled. "Yes, of course. I'm fine."

But watching Sybile and my daughter sitting together on the sofa regaling us with stories of Sybile's modeling days and Monica's years at college and the publishing house, I wasn't so sure I was fine at all. Ever since we'd arrived, I had felt a sense of aloneness descend on me. What baffled me most was that in the company of Sybile, Dora, and Marin this emotion had been absent. Witnessing the camaraderie between my mother and daughter is what had caused this feeling to emerge. From the moment we'd arrived at the Lighthouse and Monica had met Sybile, I felt excluded. The two women seemed to have bonded immediately—like they'd known each other forever.

"Isn't that true, Mom?" I heard Monica ask.

"I'm sorry. What did you say?"

Monica repeated what I'd missed in the conversation. "It's true that I have two left hands when it comes to knitting, isn't it? I didn't get any genes for that talent from you or Dora."

I smiled. "We all have different talents."

"Don't feel so bad," Marin said, placing her cup and saucer on the table beside her. "I'm afraid those knitting genes eluded me as well. Mom tried to teach me when I was a girl, but—all I did was get tangled up in yarn."

"I'd much prefer to purchase knitted items," Sybile proclaimed. "All this hand-made stuff is highly overrated."

"Speak for yourself, Sybile," Dora replied. "Knitting happens to be quite fashionable these days."

"Hey," Marin said. "One of you tell Monica and Sydney about your blue-moon celebration when you were younger."

I sat forward with interest. "What's this all about?"

Sybile waved her hand in the air. "It's just a bunch of hooey. Silly teenage girls. That's all it was."

"Aw, come on, Billie," Monica said, nudging Sybile. "This sounds interesting. I want to hear it."

"It wasn't a bunch of hooey when we did it," Dora said. "I still look back on that gathering with nostalgia. The men on the island had their rituals—you know, to do with their fishing and male stuff. So I think it was the year I was fourteen and Sybile was sixteen. We'd heard that in June that year there was going to be a blue moon."

"There's really no such thing, is there?" Monica asked.

"Oh, but indeed, there is," Dora said. "It's the second full moon in a calendar month. The first of the full moons must appear at or near the beginning of the month so that the second will fall within the same month. And the average span between two moons is twenty-nine and a half days."

Monica nodded. "I *have* heard about this but never paid much attention to it. So how did you celebrate?"

"I think there were five or six of us girls and we'd decided to meet at the beach at City Park at dusk. We brought food and cold drinks and Polly was there. Remember she brought her flute and somebody else brought a guitar?" Dora looked over at her sister. "So we had music. We'd collected wildflowers and we sat on the beach and wove them into wreaths for our head. We danced. We sang. We were downright silly. We ran into the water with our clothes on and all of us spent the night right there on the beach. We'd brought blankets to sleep on. As I recall, not much sleeping got done that night. We watched the moon come up over the water and it turned into a celebration of the female spirit."

"Oh," Monica replied, clearly mesmerized by the story. "What a wonderful thing to do. Women should do that more often."

I was surprised when Sybile nodded and said, "It *was* fun. You're right, Dora. It was a magical night that I haven't thought about in years."

I detected wistfulness in my mother's voice.

"Well, then," Monica said. "We'll just have to do it. When will we have a blue moon again?"

"Late July," Dora said. "Two months from now."

I remember Polly telling me that story when I first moved here. The blue-moon celebration for the girls," Alison said, kicking off her sandals and curling up in the chaise lounge next to me. "The most remarkable part of the story was the nostalgia that seemed to come over Sybile."

"I can understand that. It took her right back to a time in her life when she was content. Before the urge to leave this island had set in." Alison sipped her iced tea thoughtfully. "So? Are you guys going to do this in July? Did Monica say she'd come to the island for it?"

I nodded. "Yeah, apparently. She seems pretty excited about it. Told me she'll be the director and coordinate all of it."

Alison laughed. "Leave it to Monica."

"You're invited, you know. I want you there."

"Absolutely. I've heard of women's rituals before, but I've never participated in one. I think it'll be fun." Leaning her head back, she closed her eyes. "So . . . it's safe to say that Monica liked Sybile?"

"They really did seem to hit it off pretty good. But then, Monica has that way about her. She seems to click with everyone instantly."

Alison sat up on the lounge. "What's that mean?"

I shrugged.

"Okay, I know you well enough to know something's going on. What's up?"

"I guess I'm just surprised at how well Sybile and Monica got on together." Running a hand through my hair, I let out a deep sigh.

"Well, for Christ's sake, isn't that what you wanted to happen?"

"Yes, of course. But—I sure as hell never thought that from the moment they met they'd act like they'd known each other forever. You should have seen the two of them together. Laughing, joking, ribbing each other. I never would have expected that."

Alison nodded. "Hmm, I see what you mean. And that left you feeling—how?"

I remained silent.

"Ah, possibly left out?"

"No, don't be silly."

"Look, Syd, you've never been overjoyed with

the fact that you even found Sybile. That was the last thing you could have known would happen when you came here last November. And even when she confirmed this fact, you've admitted you don't really care for her. Isn't that true?"

"Well, yeah. . . ."

"Okay, so don't be so hard on yourself. Nobody said you have to have daughterly feelings toward her. That's just the way it is."

"Yeah, well, how is it that Monica meets her and they both instantly seem to develop this rapport with each other?"

"Monica's not you, Syd. Two different personalities. And I don't mean that in a derogatory way. But you have to admit, Monica's much more outgoing and confident than you are."

Although I knew this to be true, it didn't make me feel better.

"Maybe you need to lighten up a little bit, Syd. Maybe you're harboring some resentment toward Sybile that you're not even willing to admit to yourself. And if that's the case—then the resentment is preventing any good feelings you might have for her." Alison took a sip of iced tea. "In other words, Syd—chill out."

I jumped up so fast from the lawn chair that it tipped over. Shoving my feet into sandals, I grabbed my knitting and headed toward my apartment. "Go to hell, Alison," I hollered over my shoulder. "You don't always know everything."

Walking into the kitchen, I slammed my knitting bag onto the table. Reaching into the fridge, I removed a bottle of chardonnay and poured a glass. Taking the wine, I plunked into the bedroom chair, sprawling my legs onto the edge of the bed. Letting out a burst of air between my lips, I gripped the stem of the wineglass.

How dare Alison accuse me of being resentful. I was never bothered about being adopted. I had a great life. Searching for my biological mother wasn't a priority.

And was that because you were fearful of what you might find? I heard a voice in my head ask. *Fearful that the woman who gave you life wasn't what you wanted her to be? Just like Stephen wasn't really what I'd hoped for in a husband?*

Taking a sip of wine, I realized that for the first time in my life maybe I'd never been the wife I had hoped to be either. Instead of confronting Stephen and demanding that I be included in household decisions and finances, it was easier to sit back and allow him to take control. And now— now I resent the non-judgmental attitude that my mother and my daughter share. "I don't accept Sybile," I said out loud. "So why is it that my daughter so easily can?"

The ringing telephone caused me to jump. I picked up the receiver to hear Noah's voice.

"Hey, there, beautiful. Just calling to make sure everything's all set for tomorrow evening."

"Yes, Monica and I will be there about six-thirty. Are you sure I can't bring anything?"

"Just yourself. I've got everything under control. Okay, I'll let you go. See you tomorrow evening."

I hung up but continued to stare at the phone. Where was this relationship with Noah headed? I wondered. I had no answers.

Halfway to Noah's house, I realized I'd forgotten the clam dip I'd made. "You go along," I told Monica and Ian. "I'll just run back and get it."

I smiled recalling the introduction to Ian earlier. I wasn't sure where their relationship would end up, but it was obvious my daughter had found somebody special.

Walking up Noah's front steps, I heard conversation drifting through the house from the back garden along with a song playing by Bob Seger. Stopping to place the clam dip in the fridge, I glanced through the French doors hoping to spot Noah in the crowd. I wasn't prepared for the tableau that played out before my eyes. Placing the bowl on the counter, I saw Noah holding a very attractive blonde in his arms. The woman's hands were wrapped tightly around Noah's neck as she kissed him. From where I was standing, it certainly looked like he was returning the kiss. Noah then pulled his face back and began laughing as he walked to a chaise lounge and deposited the woman gently on the seat. It was then that I realized the other guests were beginning to hover around the lounge staring at the woman's ankle. Noah straightened up, turned around, and saw me standing in the doorway watching the scene unfold. Another woman rushed past me into the kitchen, whipped open the freezer, and filled a towel with ice cubes. By the time she'd run back outside, I had turned my back on the garden and opened the fridge to place the clam dip on a shelf. My body stiffened as I felt Noah's arms around me.

"Hey, beautiful, I'm glad you're finally here."

"A little too soon it seems."

"What? Oh, that—that's Valerie. I'm afraid she's had a few too many margaritas. She tripped coming down the steps to the garden. I think she may have sprained her ankle."

"What a shame," was all I could manage.

Noah attempted to pull me tighter toward him. "Come on outside so I can introduce you to the rest of the crowd here."

Wanting nothing more than to leave and go home, I stood rooted to the floor. Any doubts I'd had about our relationship surfaced. Who the hell *was* this Valerie? She sure acted like more than a business acquaintance toward Noah.

"Hey, Mom, you're here," I heard Monica say from the doorway.

Moving away from Noah's embrace, I forced a

smile. "Yeah, I'm here. And I'd love a drink."

"Well, come on. I'll introduce you to Cameron. He's behind the bar," Monica said, leading the way out to the garden.

I followed my daughter and saw Ali and Paul engaged in a conversation with another couple. A bar had been set up in the corner and a very handsome young fellow was talking and laughing with a young woman Monica's age.

Out of the corner of my eye, I noticed the crowd around Valerie had dispersed. Only the woman who'd come running for the ice cubes sat at the bottom of the lounge holding a towel to Valerie's ankle.

Monica made the introduction to Cameron. "Nice to meet you. What's your pleasure?"

I smiled in acknowledgement. "A white wine, please."

"Geez, you missed all the commotion," the young woman said.

"Not quite." I accepted the wineglass. "What happened?"

The girl began laughing. "It seems Miss Hoity Toity over there had one too many margaritas from Cameron. You naughty boy, you," she said, shaking a finger toward him.

"Hey, not my fault that she probably had a few before she even got here."

"I guess she tripped on the steps and down she went. The whole thing looked like a staged pro-

production to me. I've never seen anyone fall so gracefully."

"Really?" was all I said. Taking a sip of wine I looked across the garden where Noah was busy at the grill. It wasn't lost on me that as Valerie reclined on the lounge the woman's eyes never left Noah's face.

"There you are," I heard Ali say. "What took you so long getting here? You missed the show."

"What? Is she the entertainment for the evening?"

"Hmm, maybe you didn't miss it after all. Why the sour mood?"

I shrugged my shoulders. "I'm not *in* a sour mood," I said as I felt Noah's hand on my shoulder.

"I've got the shrimp under control, so let me introduce you to some people."

Unable to comfortably decline, I allowed myself to be led around meeting Noah's friends. They all became a blur until we came to the chaise lounge.

"This is Valerie, who I'm afraid had a bit of a mishap. And this is her friend, Carol."

My first thought was that the woman reclining on the lounge like Cleopatra was strikingly beautiful. Early forties, she reminded me of an older version of Paris Hilton. Blonde, flashy and very expensively dressed in a black-and-white sundress with thick gold accessories at her neck, earlobes, and wrists. Carol was a petite brunette who appeared genuinely concerned about her friend's injury. She smiled up at me as she continued to hold the ice in place.

"So," Valerie said, waving a perfectly manicured hand in the air, "you really *did* have a date. Shame on you, Noah. For not asking me first."

I raised my eyebrows but remained silent. Saying it was nice to meet her was out of the question.

Noah laughed. "Valerie, behave yourself. How's that ankle feeling? Do you think you need to see a doctor?"

She lowered her eyes demurely. "Only if you'll drive me there, handsome."

Noah shook his head as he took my hand and walked me away from the lounge. "I'm sorry about her. She's really had too much to drink. Just ignore her. The more attention she gets the better she likes it."

"It was pretty obvious she sure liked that kiss you gave her."

"Are you serious? I didn't kiss her. When I picked her up to take her to the lounge, she latched on to me. It was nothing."

I didn't feel like it was nothing. To witness a man I'd recently made love with kissing another woman was more than I was willing to accept. All I wanted to do was go home but unlike

Valerie, I didn't want to cause a scene in front of Noah's friends.

"Can I get you another wine?" Noah asked. "I have to get back to that grill. Everything should be ready in about ten minutes."

"No, I'm fine," I replied, walking toward Alison and Paul.

"That food sure does smell good," Alison said. "And what a gorgeous garden Noah has."

"Lovely," was all that I offered, causing Ali to glare at me.

"What the hell is up with you?"

"I don't want to talk about it."

"Suit yourself," Ali said, taking Paul's hand and walking away.

"Are you okay, Mom?"

I took a deep breath. "I'm fine. So who's this Cameron?"

Monica smiled. "He works out at the Marine Lab on Twenty-four. And he's living on the island for the summer. He's a grad student at UF. I think he has a thing for that girl hanging around the bar."

"I swear this island breeds romance," I replied sarcastically.

Monica laughed. "Oh, Mom, lighten up."

That was the second time in two days I'd been instructed to do that.

"Soup's on," I heard Noah yell.

A long table had been set up for the guests complete with tablecloth and a vase of fresh flowers in the center. There was seating for twenty and as I attempted to sit on the bench beside Monica, I felt Noah's hands around my waist.

"Oh, no you don't. Up here next to me," he said, pushing me further down the table.

"Noah, be a dear and get me some of your famous shrimp, will you?" Valerie's whiny, slurred voice filled the garden.

"I have it under control," Carol said, filling a plate with shrimp, pasta salad, and grilled vegetables.

"How's that ankle of yours doing?" somebody hollered.

"It'd do a hell of a lot better with another margarita," she tossed back.

I saw Cameron look over at Noah, who held up his index finger and thumb in answer. Noah had prepared my plate and I stared down at the shrimp, steamed clams, mullet, and grouper that stared back at me. He did it again. How the hell could he just assume that's what I wanted to eat?

"Something wrong?" I heard him say.

"No," I said, picking up my fork.

Conversation flowed around the table. I had to admit that except for Valerie the crowd seemed to be friendly and under different circumstances I would have enjoyed getting into the party atmosphere. I also had to admit the seafood was superb. Noah did have a knack for cooking.

Following dinner I attempted to help with the cleanup but Noah wouldn't hear of it. "Go see Cameron," he said, "and have him fix us an after-dinner drink. I'll join you shortly."

Standing at the bar sipping a Stinger, I noticed Carol assisting Valerie into the house. The blonde was leaning heavily on her friend's arm but stopped to chat with everyone along the way. My eyes scanned the garden to see where Noah was and saw him with Paul stacking dishes to take inside. *God, I'm acting like a shrew,* I thought. *Why the hell should I even care?*

When Noah joined me, he slipped his arm around my waist and kissed my cheek. Picking up his glass, he touched the rim of mine. "Here's to a pretty good party, I think. Are you having a good time?"

I made an effort to be sociable and nodded. "The seafood was delicious. Very nice."

"Great drink," he said, nodding his head toward Cameron.

"Where's your playmate?" I asked, and then could have bitten my tongue.

"Playmate?" Noah threw his head back laughing. "I'm afraid she's passed out on the sofa. Carol said she'll let her doze a little and then she's driving her home."

By ten o'clock the guests were beginning to leave and I had managed to give myself a headache. Before finding Monica to tell her I was going, I walked into the house to use the bath-room. Coming out I heard Valerie's voice call to me from the living room. The woman was sitting on the sofa, her leg propped up with a pillow.

"Hey there, Sydney, I'm sorry we didn't get to talk more this evening. I'm afraid my little spill put me out of commission."

More like the margaritas put you out of commission, I thought. "How's your ankle feeling?"

"Not much better, actually. I might just tell Carol to go on back to Gainesville. I could spend the night here at Noah's." She waited for my reaction and getting none, she said, "Well, it wouldn't be the first time, you know." My face must have showed the surprise she was hoping for. "Oh, you didn't know? Noah and I used to see each other. It wasn't that long ago that I thought I'd be residing in this house permanently," she said, gesturing her hand around the room. "But you know Noah. He likes to dabble here and there. Never quite sure of what he wants. So one just has to be patient."

I stood there looking at the confident, composed blonde as a flashback of the acquiescent house-wife came to me. Never wanting to have a con-frontation. Never saying if something bothered me. Always willing to let things go. Hurt, anger, and humiliation filled me. How could I have been so stupid with Noah? You'd think at my age I'd know better and be able to tell a playboy from the real thing. You'd think I would have seen through

300

him and realized none of what we'd shared had been sincere. None of what he'd told me had been the truth. But this time I wasn't about to accept it. No, this time I'd be the one calling the shots.

"Well, honey, then I wish you luck," I tossed over my shoulder as I walked out of the room. "He's all yours."

≈33≈

A week had passed since Noah's party. During that time I had managed to evade repeated phone calls from him. I knew a confrontation was imminent. Both Monica and Ali had attempted to reason with me, to no avail. They saw Valerie for the flirt and troublemaker that she was, but for me there was no turning back.

"I don't want to discuss it," I yelled, when Alison tried defending Noah.

"You're being foolish. For Christ's sake, he did nothing wrong. We were there. We saw her little scheme unfold," Alison yelled back.

"It's a closed subject," I had snapped, putting an end to any further discussion.

Unlocking the door at Spinning Forward, I walked inside with Lilly. Unclipping the dog's leash, I patted her smooth fur. "Well, girl, here we are. Back to work again. Minus Noah in our life."

Spooning coffee into the filter, I knew I couldn't avoid Noah forever. Avoiding his phone calls would only last so long. Watching the coffee drip into the carafe, I caught myself biting my lower lip, and realized all the stress I'd left behind in Massachusetts almost seven months before seemed to be returning. Between my unsettling emotions toward Sybile and my misgivings about Noah, I found the tranquility of the island moving further and further away.

Hearing the tinkle of the wind chimes I turned around to see Dora enter the shop.

"That coffee sure does smell good," she said, stooping down to pat Lilly.

I smiled while filling two mugs. "Here ya go, Dora."

"Marin was very fond of Monica. Do you think she'll really come back for the blue-moon gathering next month?"

I nodded. "Definitely. She called me last night, and she has all kinds of ideas and plans in the works for the gathering."

"That's great. Sybile will be really pleased about that."

I took a long sip of coffee. "Were you surprised how much the two of them seemed to hit it off?"

"Not in the least," Dora replied, without hesitating. "Were you?"

"Very much so. Sybile sure didn't act like that with me when we first met. Still doesn't."

"She's my sister and I love her dearly, but I've always said she's an odd duck. Sybile sees her younger self in Monica. Didn't you catch on to that?"

"Yeah, probably, but . . ."

"Sybile doesn't have a lot of tolerance for people with a lack of passion. She's always considered me a very dull person. Not willing to take risks. More content with the solidness of life. The total opposite of what she is."

"So you're saying she sees me as dull and Monica as frivolous?"

"Not in so many words, but I think she saw that spark in Monica that she had herself as a young girl. And now that she knows her own life is coming to an end, I think it makes her feel that a small part of her will continue on in Monica."

I had never thought of it in that respect. Dora could be right. "So what you're saying is, I ended up being more like you?"

Dora smiled. "I'm sure that's how Sybile sees it." Walking around the counter Dora pulled me into an embrace. "That's not so bad, is it?"

I laughed, returning the hug. "No, Aunt Dora, that's not so bad at all."

The confrontation came that evening. I returned from work, had just finished up the supper dishes, and was about to relax with a cup of tea when I heard a knock on the door. Opening it, I saw Noah leaning against the railing, arms folded across his chest. The expression on his face was neutral.

"In most civilized societies, when one knocks on a door, one gets invited in," he said.

I stepped back, opening the door wider. "Come on in."

"Okay, what's going on? I've tried to call you all week and all week you've avoided me. What have I done? The least you can do is give me an explanation as to why you're acting like a bitch."

"A *bitch?*" This was definitely not getting off to a good start. "How dare you call me a bitch."

Ignoring my anger, he pulled out a kitchen chair and sat down. "You owe me an explanation. So tell me what's going on with us."

"Us? There is no *us*. Why would you assume there's an us? You're free to do as you please. And I don't owe you a thing."

Rather than sit, I began pacing back and forth in the small kitchen area.

"Aha," Noah said, slamming his hand on the table. "That's it. This all has to do with Valerie and the way she acted at the party, doesn't it?"

Receiving no response, he said, "I thought so. But I really didn't think you'd be foolish enough to pay attention to her antics."

I stopped pacing to stand directly in front of him, hands on hips. "Oh," I screamed into his face, "so now I'm a bitch *and* foolish."

"What the hell is wrong with you? Couldn't you see what she was doing?"

"Are you going to sit there and deny there's anything going on between you and her?"

"That's exactly what I'm doing—telling you there's nothing between us."

"Hmm," I said, lips pursed together, nodding my head slowly. "So I guess this is a question of semantics."

"What the hell is that supposed to mean?"

"Are you now going to tell me there was never anything between you? And I *do* mean that literally."

The look of surprise on Noah's face was answer enough. After a few moments, his anger returned. "So what—so what if maybe I was with her in the past. The past is exactly that—before I met you. Do you think I'm going to grill you on every single man you ever had sex with before me? That's insane."

No, what's probably insane, I thought, was the fact I'd have to admit there was only one before Noah.

"It might be the past but you know what they say about that. It always comes back to haunt you. And yours did—in the form of Valerie."

Noah threw his arms up in the air. "So what? What're you saying? That just because she acted like a jealous female that now you're going to act like a high school kid? That whatever we did have—and dammit, we had something—it's now over? Just like that. Because of her?"

I resumed my pacing. "No, not just because of her." I knew I'd probably be sorry for what I was about to say, but anger and disappointment were consuming me. "I'm sick and tired of you *treating* me like a high school kid. Choosing my menu, opening wine bottles for me, not allowing me to think for myself. I'm my own person. It took me a long time to figure it out—but I *know* who I am and I don't need you smothering me in the process."

I spun around to see the expression on Noah's face resembled someone who had been physically slapped.

He got up from the chair and walked the few steps to the door. Without turning around, he said, "You haven't even *begun* to figure out who you are. You don't even have a clue."

I stared at the door as it closed quietly behind him.

Within five minutes, I heard another knock on the door and opened it to see Ali standing with a bottle of Pinot Grigio in her hand.

"I was in the garden and saw Noah leave."

I shook my head and said, "Not tonight, Ali."

Pushing past me into the kitchen, Alison said, "Yes, tonight, Syd. Let's go out on the balcony."

Dabbing at my eyes with a tissue I followed Ali outside. Accepting the glass of wine, I sniffled before taking a sip. Neither of us spoke. We both sat inhaling the scent of lantana in the air, listened to the whispers of ibis flying overhead to the outer islands, and watched the pink, rose hues of the sky that was ending another day. We sat there in the silence until the western sky darkened.

I sighed and took another sip of wine. "Thank you," I said softly.

Alison glanced over at me. "For what?"

"For understanding."

"I never said I understood. As a matter of fact—I don't. Not at all."

"Neither do I. But thanks for not badgering me." Putting down the wineglass, I reached for my cigarettes, lit one up, tilted my head toward the sky, and exhaled the smoke. "I don't know what's going on, Ali. I came here in November and my whole life seemed upside down. I had no idea where I was headed or how I was going to get there. But things began to fall into place. I wasn't even sure I'd stay here and then, all of sudden I couldn't bear the thought of leaving this island. I came here hoping to find myself—that person that I never knew existed. And what do I find instead? A mother I had no desire to find and a man that I liked way more than I wanted to. I thought I had also found me—the real me. But tonight—tonight Noah told me I haven't begun to find myself. That I still don't have a clue as to who I am."

I felt the tears trickle down my face as I heard Alison say, "He's right, Syd. I'm afraid you're still seeking."

34

In late June another summons came in the form of a phone call from Sybile. "I need to talk to you. Be at my house Sunday afternoon at three. And plan to stay for supper."

No preamble, no questioning if possibly I had other plans, no thought at all for my feelings—just be there.

And yet once again I found myself obeying the command and driving to Sybile's house that Sunday afternoon.

Settling on the sofa with a glass of iced tea, I said, "Okay, so what's up?"

"More to the point—what's up with you and that boyfriend of yours?"

"Excuse me—you make me come over here to ask me that? And he is not my boyfriend."

Sybile raised an eyebrow. "Significant other? Is that what your age group is calling it these days?"

"God, you're exasperating. I assume you're referring to Noah." I shifted on the sofa, irritated with the fact that Sybile had a way of making me feel like a wayward child. "We're not seeing each other anymore. And I don't want to discuss it with you. If you don't have a better reason for making me come here, then I have plenty of things I could be doing."

"Oh, don't get your knickers in a twitch. I asked

you over so that you could help me plan my funeral."

I let out an annoyed sigh. "So we're back on that again."

"Well, it *is* inevitable and if you don't want to help your mother do . . ."

That was the first time that Sybile had willingly referred to herself as my mother. "I'll help you. I'll help you already," I interrupted, feeling a tad of remorse. "So what're we doing?"

"You know I want to be cremated, right?" Not waiting for my reply, she went on. "Okay, so I thought it might be nice if everyone gathered on Noah's boat. Drive over on the other side of Atsena Otie—and maybe you could toss my remains there."

"Me?"

"Well, you are my daughter. Actually, I thought maybe both you and Monica could do it together. You know—send me on my way. To wherever I'm going."

"I could do that," I said quietly.

Sybile nodded as she reached for a notebook. "Good. Okay, and next—I thought maybe Alison could play something nice on her flute."

My eyes widened. This woman was really getting into planning. "I don't know," I said doubtfully. "Ali hasn't played that flute in years. At least not that I'm aware of."

"Well, maybe she'll do it. So ask her. And I'd

like that song, you know, the one about being lost and now found."

" 'Amazing Grace'?"

"Yeah, that's it," Sybile said as she jotted more notes on the paper. "Marin plays the guitar and she said she'd play something for me. I'm going to tell her I'd like 'Dixie'—you know, for my Southern roots. She has a fairly decent singing voice too, so maybe she'd agree to sing the lyrics. Oh, and tell Alison I'd also like her to play 'Somewhere Over the Rainbow' at the end of the service."

I shook my head. Talk about an eclectic music selection. "I'll ask her," was all I said.

"Now, let's see, what else," Sybile said, checking her notes. "Oh, right—you could read a poem."

Oh God, this really was going overboard. "A poem? I don't know any poems."

"Well, now might be a good time for you to start doing some research and find one you think might be appropriate for the occasion."

The occasion? For Christ's sake, it's a *funeral.*

Ignoring my reluctance, Sybile continued, "So get to work on that. When you send me on my way, I'd like some gardenia petals tossed into the water with me. I think you can manage that, right? And above all, you must hold this service some-time in the afternoon. When Noah brings the boat back, I want all of you to gather here—at the

Lighthouse for a festive meal. I'll arrange this beforehand. A buffet of sorts would be nice, don't you think?"

I only nodded but for the first time it crossed my mind that it would seem odd not to have Sybile living in this lighthouse. As designated in her will, it would be given to the Marine Lab and they in turn would sell it with the money going to research. I was surprised the thought of this bothered me.

"And I plan to do invitations. I don't want the whole damn town there. Just certain people—people who've played a part in my life. There's nothing worse than false sympathy. See that drawer in the desk over there?"

I looked to where Sybile was pointing a finger and nodded again.

"The invitations will all be written out, addressed, and stamped. When I'm gone, all you have to do is fill in the date of the gathering and drop them in the mail. Got that?"

"Yes, I'll do that."

Sybile looked over her notes again, flipping pages. "Well, except for a confirmation from Noah, I'd say we covered everything. I'll get in touch with Noah myself since you're acting so juvenile. Can you think of anything else I've missed?"

Another exasperated sigh escaped my lips. "Not a thing."

"Good. Now let's talk about this spat with Noah and see if we can fix that."

"God, Sybile, I don't want to talk about it. Besides, there's no fixing it. It's over. We dated a few times, had some fun—and now it's finished."

"Uh-huh, I see. Well, you foolish girl, in case you didn't know, he has some pretty strong feelings for you."

My head shot up. "How the hell do you know that?"

"I make it my business to know things. You'd be smart to do the same. Seems you got all in a twit because of some floozy blonde at his party?" Sybile shook her head. "No daughter of mine would give up without a fight and getting what she wanted. She'd have spirit."

"Did he tell you that?"

"I don't divulge my sources. The point is you need to take a stand with that bimbo. Let her know you won't put up with her high jinks. Don't be a wimp."

"I'm not about to confront her. She can have him."

"Really? And what if it isn't *her* he wants?"

"I honestly don't care what he wants. He's slept with her for God's sake, he—"

Sybile threw her head back laughing. "Ah, now I see. Now I see what this is all about. Jealousy. You're just jealous because once upon a time he had sex with her. Well, get over yourself, girl.

That was before he met you. Maybe *you* should have experienced a bit more before you married that husband of yours."

I had visions of being raised by Sybile and turning into a promiscuous teenager. The woman's attitude on sex was a far cry from the morals I'd grown up with.

Seeing that I remained silent, Sybile went on. "I told you once before—don't make the same mistakes in life that I did. There's no going back you know. And once your chance is gone, nothing will ever make it quite the same. If you learn nothing else from me—I want you to always remember that. Some day it might make sense to you."

"Are you referring to my father? You let him go and you don't want me to do the same thing?"

"We're not talking about me. We're talking about you. You might not have gotten a lot of my genes, but unfortunately you did get my biggest fault—stubbornness. Sometimes that can be good when it's to your benefit. But the problem is, most of the time we don't know the final outcome. So then—then that's when we take a chance and risk it. Don't be a fool, Sydney. Don't be a fool like your mother was."

Getting up from the chair as quickly as her labored breathing would allow, Sybile motioned to me. "Come on, help me get that supper on the table that I promised you."

• • •

Alison raised her eyes, shook her head, and began giggling. "Are you serious? She wants me to play the flute at her memorial service? And of all things, 'Amazing Grace'?"

I had to admit, it did have a touch of humor. I shrugged my shoulders. "Hey, what can I say? The wishes of a dying woman. She wasn't a conformist her entire life—do you think she'll start now?"

"Christ, she's a character."

"So will you do it?"

Alison sat up straighter in the lawn chair. "Winston," she hollered. "Leave that poor cat alone." Turning to me, she nodded. "Yeah, I'll do it. Guess I'd better start practicing."

"So Paul left this morning?"

Alison sighed. "Yeah, gone again. He's going to make a valiant effort to get back here in the fall though. Till then I'm a woman without a man." She reached into her glass to squeeze a wedge of lemon in the iced tea. "You did know Noah left the island, right?"

"What? He's gone?"

"Ah, yup. Paul said he left yesterday," she said, holding back further information.

After a few moments I said, "Okay, and you want me to ask you for details, right?"

Alison smiled. "Not unless you want to."

"So he's left for good? Is he putting the house up for sale?"

Alison reached over and patted my hand before standing up. "No, he hasn't left for good. He's gone back to Savannah for a month or so. That's what he told Paul. Needed some time to think is what he said." She headed toward the house, then paused, turning back to face me. "But it does make ya realize, be careful what you wish for."

I was about to snap out a retort but changed my mind, chewing on my bottom lip instead.

35

I was putting the finishing touches on scalloped potatoes when Monica called to let me know she was just approaching the Number Four bridge.

"Great. I'll see you in about ten minutes. And I've invited Saren to have supper with us this evening. I know you haven't seen much of him."

"That's great. Is Sybile coming too?"

"No, she passed on the invitation. Said she wanted to conserve her energy for the blue-moon gathering tomorrow night."

Monica laughed. "Leave it to Billie. She's really enthused about this. I love you and I'll see you soon."

Rubbing rosemary onto the roast lamb, my thoughts drifted to Noah. It had been two months since we'd had any contact. As far as I knew, he was still in Savannah. Since he'd made no attempt to get in touch, I felt certain the relationship was over. Not wanting to dwell on the emptiness that his absence created, I forced him out of my mind.

"Miss Sydney, I do declare that was one of the best meals I've had in ages," Saren said, wiping his lips with the linen napkin.

"Thank you. I'm glad you enjoyed it."

"He's right, Mom. That lamb was cooked to perfection and I want the recipe for the potatoes."

I smiled. "Sybile gave it to me and I'll pass it on to you. Now it's time for the famous cheesecake."

Monica cleared the table as I measured coffee into the basket. It was easy to see that Monica was enjoying the one-on-one visit with Saren. He'd seemed genuinely interested in her life and shared anecdotes of his time in Manhattan.

"So you girls are all ready for your beach party tomorrow evening, are ya?" he asked.

Monica laughed. "It's not a beach party. It's a gathering of the female spirit."

He nodded. "I see. Very serious stuff this is. I remember when the girls did it all those years ago. Why, my goodness, Sybile was only what . . . fifteen or sixteen years old? She's just as excited about it now as she was then." His face took on a serious expression. "It's good for her, ya know? This going back in time and feeling like a kid again."

I placed a cup of coffee on Saren's place mat,

while touching his shoulder. "How are you doing, Saren? How're *you* doing with Sybile's illness?"

"Aw, I'm alright," he replied, his eyes misting. "I guess I've come to terms with the fact that Sybile will be leaving us. I'll miss her, ya know? It'll just seem real strange not to have Sybile on this earth anymore. I guess ya could say she's always been a part of my life—and pretty soon, that part will be gone."

"Well, I'm here for you, Saren," I said, squeezing his shoulder. "If you ever need to talk to somebody—now or after—I'm here for you."

A smile crossed the man's face. "And I sure do appreciate that, Miss Sydney. I surely do."

"And now it's time to try out this family cheese-cake," Monica said, bringing the plates to the table.

Taking a bite, Saren nodded. "Yup, you've got this recipe down to perfection. This is just the way Sybile's mama used to make it." Placing his fork on the dish, he leaned across the table to stare at Monica. "I hope you don't mind me saying this, but Lord above, you're a mirror image of Sybile when she was your age."

Monica laughed. "I take that as a compliment."

"You have her eyes, Miss Sydney, and you sure do resemble her—but your daughter, I do believe she scooped up every last gene that Sybile had."

I joined Monica's laughter. "Yeah, I see it too. Those genes really are amazing. The way they keep getting passed on through all the generations."

He continued to stare at Monica a few more moments, then shook his head. "Sybile sure can be proud of you two girls."

I glanced at my daughter. Monica smiled, sending me a wink.

"Gawd, Syd, we're only spending the night on the beach. Not a week. What the hell have you got there?" Alison pointed to the two tote bags and basket that I'd lugged downstairs and was ready to load onto the golf cart.

"Well, I thought it might be nice to bring a CD player with some appropriate music. And Monica said to bring a notebook where we wrote our thoughts to read to the group. I have sweaters and stuff in case it gets cool during the night." Peeking into the larger bag, I said, "And my sleeping bag. I'm not sleeping on the sand—I'm not that earthy."

Alison shook her head and laughed. "Okay, let's get this show on the road. Is Saren taking Sybile down?"

"Yeah, he wanted to be able to help her and make sure she has everything. Monica's already at the beach and Dora and Marin are on their way."

"Come on, guys," Alison said, calling to Lilly and Winston to jump in the back of the golf cart. "With all your stuff, I might have to make another trip."

"There's plenty of room," I told her, sitting on the passenger side, wedged in between tote bags and baskets of food.

"Oh, damn, I nearly forgot," Alison said, jumping out of the golf cart. "I'll be right back."

She returned a few moments later carrying a large, beautiful bouquet of flowers. Calla lilies, yellow roses, and baby's breath tied with a white satin ribbon.

"Ooooh, gorgeous," I said. "Nice touch to bring flowers."

"Yeah, except they're yours." Alison passed them to me.

"Mine?"

"Yup." Alison reached into the pocket of her skirt and passed me a small white envelope.

I laid the flowers in my lap and removed a gift card, which read:

Develop your female spirit this evening. I'll be thinking of you. Allow your soul to soar and discover your inner self. Love, Noah

With shaking hands, I replaced the card in the envelope and inhaled the fragrance of the flowers.

"From Noah, right?" Ali questioned.

"Yes," was all that I replied.

Approaching City Park and the beach along First Street, I could see Monica on the sand accompanied by Dora and Marin.

Marin and Monica came running as Ali pulled the golf cart into a spot. "We'll help you unload," Monica said, eyeing the flowers in my hands. "Nice," she said, with raised eyebrows.

Ignoring the unasked question, I gathered up some stuff and walked toward the beach. "Come on, Lilly," I called behind me. "This is our bedroom for tonight."

"Isn't this fun?" Dora said. "I think we'll be okay here on the sand when the tide comes in later."

"Perfect." I smiled at Dora's excitement. Removing cookies, bags of chips, and assorted snacks I placed them on the table Dora had set up on the sand while my mind raced with thoughts of Noah. No word from him in two months and then he sends the flowers with that note. So what was that supposed to mean? Did it mean we were at least still friends? Was just being friends all I really wanted? My thoughts were interrupted as I heard Sybile's raspy voice calling across the beach. Turning, I saw Saren escorting Sybile by the arm, a huge smile on his face.

"Let the official blue-moon gathering of the females begin," Sybile said. "I'm here."

"I'll go get Sybile's things from the car. Now you sit yourself down and I'll be right back," Saren instructed her.

Monica laughed. "I'll help you."

"Well, don't we all look as eccentric as I always

am," Sybile replied, glancing around at the rest of us.

Alison's cotton paisley skirt fell to her ankles. Her loose-fitting sheer blouse covered a bright orange tank top. Barefoot, with her customary braid flowing loose around her shoulders, she was a replica from the sixties.

My skirt was silk and fell in points skimming my calf area. My blue silk blouse was tied beneath the bust, exposing my midriff.

Dora and Marin wore brightly colored floral sundresses and each sported a straw picture hat, while Monica's outfit consisted of a sleeveless, long dress of bleached muslin.

Sybile looked down at her own multi-colored caftan and adjusted the matching turban covering her head. "Seems to me you gals have finally adopted my flair for fashion," she said, settling herself in the chaise lounge that Saren had produced. "Okay, now be off with you," she instructed him, while waving a hand in the air. "This here gathering is strictly for females."

Leaning down, Saren kissed her cheek. "You enjoy yourself, Sybile, and you have your cell phone, right? In case you need to call me during the night?"

"Oh, for goodness sake, stop fussin' over me. I'm fine. I'll see you tomorrow morning."

Nodding to us, Saren returned to the car.

"Okay, so what're we doing first?" Dora asked.

"A nice, cold drink for everyone," Monica said, as she began pouring sweet tea into glasses.

We'd arranged our chairs and lounges into a circle on the sand. After I had passed out the drinks, I turned on the CD player. The lyrics of Enya's "Only Time" filled the air as each of us sat gazing at the water with the setting sun beyond.

When the song finished, Ali said, "Let's all hold hands and breathe and feel as one. Focus on an image and state what you want to release from your life. What would you like to draw in or have more of?" With eyes closed, she reached for my hand and Sybile's hand. Taking a deep breath, she said softly, "I want to release doubt and take in joy."

After a few moments, Sybile replied, "I want to release my earthly life and take in whatever is to come next."

Dora paused for a few moments. "I want to release sorrow and take in acceptance."

Marin followed with, "I want to release conflict and take in serenity."

Monica said, "I want to release impatience and take in calm."

I felt the squeeze of my daughter's hand, indicating it was my turn. Inhaling deeply and blowing it out, I said, "I want to release fear and take in understanding."

We continued to sit for a few minutes, hands

clasped, eyes closed, until Alison's voice broke the silence.

"This completes our energy exchange. Repeat with me—and so it is."

"And so it is," six voices chorused in unison.

Picking up her flute, Alison said, "Let your minds drift. Allow yourself to go deep within and seek that for which you're searching. Allow the energy of our group to flow over you with love and acceptance. Allow your female spirit to emerge and guide you."

I closed my eyes and allowed the soothing melody from the flute to wash over me. Noah's face came into my mind. Encircled by the serenity of the group, I was able to admit that I'd been unreasonable to him. Pushing the thought aside, I inhaled deeply and forced myself to concentrate on my senses. Wiggling my toes, I felt the warm sand touch my skin. The scent of salt water filled my nostrils, while the screech of a gull could be heard in the distance.

"I have a candle for each of you," I heard Ali say, and opened my eyes to take one from Monica. Looking around at the other women, I saw their faces reflected the same calmness I was feeling.

"As you light your candle," Ali instructed, "allow yourself to let go of whatever might be holding you back. Allow your energy to merge with all of us in a ritual of healing and power."

Each woman took the matches to light their candle and six flickering flames filled the approaching darkness on the beach.

After a few minutes, Ali said, "As you blow out your candle, also blow out all that holds you back from being your authentic self. That self that your soul brought forth to earth."

When the candles were extinguished, the only light filtering onto the beach came from the lamp-posts in the park, creating a misty glow.

"Now would be a good time for you to play your guitar, Marin," Ali said, as she got up and stretched.

I heard the strains of the old Bob Seger song "Against the Wind" coming forth from Marin's guitar. Surprised by the woman's musical ability, I was even more surprised to hear Marin's splendid voice singing the lyrics. Glancing toward the water, I saw Ali walking along the shore, her feet creating splashes, her arms dipping and raising. One by one, the rest of us joined her.

Monica reached down for my hand, pulling me up. I, in turn, reached for Sybile's hand and the three of us followed behind the group, hands clasped, kicking our bare feet along the incoming tide.

Walking along the length of the beach, I watched Ali as her arms floated in the air, dipping this way and that like butterfly wings. Squeezing my mother's and daughter's hand, a sense of freedom and peace filled me. Was this the energy that Ali had promised? Was this exhilaration caused from the women in my presence? And was this visceral transformation what Ali and Sybile had called the female spirit?

⟫36⟪

By 10:00 the full moon was casting a bright glow on the beach. Satiated with food, each woman was sipping a glass of wine. We had danced, had laughed, and had exchanged stories.

I had especially enjoyed hearing the tales that Sybile and Dora had shared. Funny anecdotes about their years growing up on the island. Then Marin had told of island myths and legends, like the ghost at Shell Mound—a woman in white who could be seen wandering the beach area late at night.

Silence now descended on the group. I glanced over at Sybile and realized that the woman I was seeing tonight was bearing a strong resemblance to the Sybile that Saren must have known when they were young. She'd laughed a lot and that arrogant edge was missing. Sybile seemed to delight in all that the evening was providing. I recalled what Saren had said the evening before and for the first time, I wondered what it would be like when Sybile was no longer with us.

"Okay," I heard Alison say. "Let's read what we

wrote to share with the group. I have a large battery lantern here and I think it'll give us enough light. Who's going first?"

Marin volunteered. "May the moments we've created together always linger within us."

"For me," Dora said, "the significance of two full moons symbolize two sisters . . . separate, yet each shining brightly." Glancing over at Sybile, she smiled.

"Me next," Monica said. "Life should be like a glass of champagne . . . bubbling with shared moments, lively spirit, and lots of sparkle."

"Hear, hear." Alison raised her wineglass. "I've chosen something from Louisa May Alcott. 'Far away in the sunshine are my highest aspirations. I may not reach them, but I can look up and see the beauty, believe in them and try to follow where they lead.' " She stared directly at me and smiled. "You're next, my friend. We'll save Sybile for last."

I reached for the lantern that Alison passed to me. Clearing my throat, I said, "Stitches of a knitting pattern are joined in such a way that they produce a finished product. Much like all of you have crossed my path, enabled me to grow and, most important . . . allowed me to thrive."

I felt the squeeze of my mother's hand.

"And thrive you did," I heard her say.

"And now, the gauntlet has been passed to me. My choice is a poem by an anonymous author."

Taking a sip of her wine, she then began reading. "When I come to the end of the road. And the sun has set for me, I want no rites in a gloom-filled room. Why cry for a soul set free? Miss me a little—but not too long. And not with your head bowed low. Remember the love that we once shared, miss me—but let me go. For this is a journey that we all must take. And each must go alone. It's all part of the Master's plan, a step on the road to home. When you are lonely and sick of heart, go to the friends we know. And bury your sorrows in doing good deeds. Miss me—But let me go."

Taking a deep breath, she looked across at Dora. With tears in her eyes, her sister nodded in understanding.

Monica got up to give Sybile a hug. "That was beautiful, Billie. We'll all try to remember that."

"Okay, enough with this," Sybile said, getting up from her chair. "Come on, Marin, play us some mountain music that we can dance to."

As Marin began the first few chords of a lively song, Sybile reached for my hand. "Come on, girl. Let your mama show ya how us island girls kick up our feet."

Laughing, I joined Sybile in a two-step. A few minutes later all six women were dancing on the sand. As the song came to an end, Sybile was having difficulty breathing.

"Are you alright?" I asked with concern, leading Sybile back to her chair. "Here," I said, reaching for the inhaler. "Take a few puffs and no more kicking up your feet for you."

After inhaling the medicine, Sybile's breathing slowed down. "Damn, I used to love to dance, didn't I, Dora?"

Dora smiled. "Yeah, they called you the best dang dancer in Levy County."

Sybile nodded her head emphatically. "Those were the days," she replied, wistfulness coloring her words.

"Well, will you look at that moon," Alison cried, pointing to a large orange orb above the water. "We have our blue moon, girls. It doesn't get any better than that, so soak in all that energy the moon's sending down on us."

"It sure is gorgeous and I don't know about the rest of you, but I'm getting a mite tired," Dora said, spreading open her sleeping bag.

"If it wouldn't bother the rest of you, I'd like to just sit here and pluck away at some tunes," Marin told us, settling into her chair.

Monica joined Dora and arranged her sleeping bag. "I can't think of anything nicer to fall asleep to. With the moon up there and the water lapping at the shore, you'll probably hear me snoring within five minutes."

Alison laughed. "Not if I beat you first. Now remember, guys," she said, settling into her sleeping bag, "It'll be light around six, but if everyone is awake earlier we can pack up then and head home."

Sybile shifted on her chaise lounge and pulled a blanket around her. "Well, it's only midnight and I'm a night owl, so if y'all don't mind, I'm going to have myself another glass of wine and just soak in all this so-called energy."

I jumped up to refill the wine glass. "And I think I'll join you," I said. Passing the glass to Sybile, I got one for myself, then settled into my sleeping bag.

Both of us remained silent staring out at the reflection the moon created on the water. After a few minutes, Sybile said, "Sure is pretty, isn't it?"

I nodded. "Almost magical."

"Ah, but it is magical. Everything about this night has been magical."

"You've enjoyed it, haven't you?"

Sybile took a slow sip of wine. "More than you can imagine."

The soft sounds of Marin's music floated around us. I stared up at the silver spots that dotted the sky. "Where do you think we go when we leave earth?" I asked, softly.

"I don't rightly know, but my guess is—we go back out there. Into the Universe."

I glanced sharply at my mother. "I had no idea you thought that."

Sybile sighed "There's a lot you still don't

know about me, I guess. And we're running out of time. So what else would you like to know?"

"Who my father is."

"We've been through this before."

"And you just asked me what I'd like to know. That's what I'd like to know."

"Would it change anything? It wouldn't change one single thing about your life thus far, now would it?"

I knew the woman was right and remained silent.

"Those flowers you have over there," Sybile said. "They're from Noah, aren't they?"

I still didn't speak.

"Sure they are and you're too damn stubborn to acknowledge them." Taking a sip of wine, she shook her head. "I've told ya this before. Don't be like me, girl. Don't go throwing away what might turn out to be the best thing that ever happened to you. Noah's a good man. If you're not careful, you'll end up a crotchety old woman like I am. Alone and mean."

I nibbled on my lower lip. "I'm scared. I'm scared of being hurt again."

"Of course you are. Wouldn't be normal if you weren't. But there comes a time when ya have to let go. Let go and let that female spirit overtake you. If you're strong and you believe in yourself, then you'll know if you're making the right choice or not."

"Did you? Did you make the right choice when you left this island?"

"I thought so at the time."

"And now?"

"I told ya once, I don't have any regrets. But the closer I come to leaving this earth, the more I'm wondering if I should have been stronger with taking a risk than I was about getting away."

I sat up straighter, turning to face Sybile. "Is that what you're telling me? That I should take a risk with Noah?"

Sybile smiled. "I can't tell you to do that. Only you know. Deep down inside, if you listen to that female spirit—you know what you should do."

"It's so damn hard, isn't it? Life."

"Yeah, it is, but so's dying."

Knowing what lay ahead for Sybile, I felt like a whiny child. "I'm sorry. Here I am bitching to you and you sure don't have a bed of roses."

"But I've had a good life, Sydney. I really have. Probably shoulda done a few things differently, but still a good life. You could too. Remember that fear you let go of earlier tonight? Don't let it hang around. Purge it once and for all. Get rid of it and allow yourself to follow that destiny. Fear only holds ya back."

"Be more like Monica, is that what you're saying?"

Sybile reached over and took my hand. "Honey,

you're *you* and you're plenty fine. But there's so much more to you. Let yourself soar and find that person."

I recalled Noah's words on the card—"allow your soul to soar."

Finishing off her wine, Sybile snuggled down into the lounge and adjusted her pillow. "Now this is the best way in the world to fall asleep. Don't you ever forget it. Out here in the open, with the sky and the water. You wait and see if you don't have the best night's sleep ever."

I brought Sybile's hand to my lips. "Good night, Sybile. Sleep well."

"Oh, no doubt about that," Sybile replied, pulling my hand to her own lips. "Good night, Sydney."

Murmuring voices caused me to stir inside my sleeping blanket. Opening my eyes, the first thing I saw was a milky blue sky above. Sitting up on one elbow my gaze was drawn to the horizon where a bright red ball was inching its way upward.

"Well, sleepyhead, 'bout time you decide to wake and join us," I heard Alison say.

Coming more fully awake, I looked around to see the women sipping coffee.

"What time is it?" I asked while untangling myself from the sleeping bag and standing up to stretch.

"Six o'clock," Monica said, passing me a mug of coffee.

The robust aroma floated up to my nostrils as I took a sip of the hot liquid.

"Hmm, good. Thank you. Why didn't you guys wake me? How long have you been up?"

"Just long enough to make coffee," Dora said. "Besides, you were in a deep sleep."

"I haven't slept that good since . . ." I started to say and glanced at Sybile, who gave me a wink. "A long time. It's been a long time since I've slept like that."

"Here, help yourself to a muffin," Marin said, passing a plate.

"I'm so glad we did this. Wasn't last night just incredibly special?" Monica asked, while hugging my shoulder.

I nodded and caught Sybile staring at me. "It was very special. A night I'll always remember. Now I know why the blue-moon gathering years ago meant so much to both of you."

Sybile smiled. "And I enjoyed last night immensely. I'm glad we did it too."

"So am I," Dora chimed in. "But if you gals will forgive me, I think I just might head home to grab a few more winks."

"So how'd it go?" We heard Saren holler as he walked toward us across the sand.

"Why, we can't divulge a thing about our gathering," Sybile said. "It might damage all that female spirit that we conjured. I will say though, it was a fun time. But now I'm ready to return to my creature comforts."

I laughed as I joined the others in gathering up our belongings. "Yeah, I have to say that I'm looking forward to a nice hot shower." Walking over to Sybile, I leaned down to hug her. "And you go home and behave yourself. Take a nap and rest."

"And you," Sybile said into my ear, "you remember all that I told you last night."

~ 37 ~

Streams of rain fell into the garden while I sat knitting on the balcony. The late-August afternoon reminded me more of autumn in New England. Rain had pelted the island for two days as the weathermen talked about a tropical depression possibly ending up in the Gulf.

Laying my knitting in my lap, I pulled a cigarette from the case, lit it, and exhaled smoke into the air. The dreary, rainy afternoon prompted me to recall the day I'd been caught without an umbrella and Noah had driven me home. According to Alison he'd returned to the island a few days before but I hadn't seen him, nor had he contacted me. I had been debating whether to call him to say thank you for the flowers—but had neglected to take that step.

Sybile's medical condition had declined over the past week causing me to make frequent trips to the Lighthouse. Saren was now staying there full time to care for Sybile and both had indicated that they welcomed my visits and medical assistance.

Monica was calling daily for updates and Dora also relied on me for a nurse's opinion of what might happen next.

Based on Sybile's weakness and twenty-four-hour assistance of oxygen to breathe, I had told my aunt, "I think the end is coming."

The ringing telephone interrupted my thoughts and I answered to hear Dora's voice. "Saren had to take Sybile to the hospital this morning. She had a real bad spell during the night." The woman paused as a sob escaped her throat. "Do you think this is it, Sydney?"

Stamping out the cigarette in the ashtray, I let out a deep sigh. "I don't know, Dora. I'm not sure what to say. What are the doctors saying?"

"Saren said he'll call as soon as he knows anything."

"Then I'm afraid all we can do is wait. Do you want me to come over?"

Dora hesitated. "No, I'm alright. But if she's not coming back home, maybe we could drive to Gainesville together to see her."

"Of course we will. You call me as soon as you hear anything."

Hanging up the phone, I sat staring out over the garden while the rain continued to fall. Nine months ago this news wouldn't have affected me any more than if Sybile was simply Dora's sister. But she was much more than that—she was the woman that had given me life. A woman I had not only come to know but had developed feelings for.

"Damn her," I said out loud, as tears trickled down my cheeks. "Damn her for making me care."

"So she's coming home tomorrow?" Monica asked.

I nodded into the phone. "Yes. The doctor said there isn't much more they can do for her, but this time they're sending her home with hospice."

"How'd Sybile feel about that?"

"Ornery. Which tells me she's probably feeling a bit better than two days ago when she went in the hospital. She raised a ruckus at first—said she didn't want any stranger staying in her house while she took her sweet time leaving this earth."

Monica laughed. "Yup, she's not quite on her deathbed yet. What made her change her mind on the hospice nurse?"

"Saren. He assured her he'd stay there with her too. He does have a way with her."

"Do you think I should come to the island?"

"I'd wait a bit yet. See how she does once she gets home."

"Okay. Well, keep me posted. Love you, Mom."

"Love you too," I said, hanging up the phone.

Lilly's whining drew my attention away from the call. Glancing at the clock, I said, "Yup, time to get to the shop. Let's get your leash on."

Opening the door to leave, I found Twila Faye, hand in air, ready to knock.

"I have a little something here for Miss Sybile. Alison said she's coming home tomorrow."

Taking the gift bag, I smiled. "Thank you. I'll be sure she gets it. That's really nice of you."

"Just a little something. Two jars of my home-made blueberry preserves. Thought she might like it on toast."

"I'm sure she will," I said, placing it on the kitchen counter.

"Off to open the yarn shop?"

"Yeah, I've gotten behind in orders what with Sybile getting worse."

"I imagine poor Dora is taking time to be with her sister too. If I can help out at all, you just let me know, okay?"

"I really appreciate that, Twila Faye," I said, following her down the stairs.

Later that afternoon Polly entered Spinning Forward carrying a large box. I looked up from addressing labels for orders. "Got your hands full there," I said.

Polly placed the carton on the sofa. "All this

here stuff, it's for Miss Sybile. We heard she was coming home and a lot of the women wanted to give her a little something. Just to let her know they're thinking of her."

I got up to peek into the box as tears filled my eyes. A jar of honey. A few books. A small pillow with the embroidered words Get Well. A tin of home-baked cookies. "What a nice thing to do. I'll be sure Sybile gets this tomorrow."

"Well, we're all feeling mighty bad. Oh, she wasn't always the easiest person to get along with, but we sure didn't want to see this happen to her."

"Thank you, Polly."

"You take care now. And if there's anything we can do, anything at all, you be sure to let me know, hear?"

For the second time that day I acknowledged thanks for an offer of help.

Just before closing I heard the wind chimes tinkle and looked up to see Noah walk in. Butterflies twittered in the pit of my stomach. Dammit, but he was handsome. This man oozed sex appeal. My hand shook as I placed a skein of yarn into a packing box.

"Hi, Sydney," was all he said with a neutral expression on his face.

"It's . . . It's good to see you," I stammered while noticing once again how well he wore a pair of jeans. A deep tan created a bronze glow, making the contrast with his silver hair even sharper. Attempting to control my nervousness, I said, "Thank you for the flowers."

"It was my pleasure. How was the gathering? Did your soul soar?"

I smiled while fingering an ink pen. "I'm not sure, but it was a fun night. Magical."

"We all need a bit of magic in our life." Noah leaned over to pat Lilly.

"We do."

"The reason I came by was to tell you I'm sorry to hear that Sybile isn't doing well."

I let out a deep sigh. "She isn't. She'll be home tomorrow with a hospice nurse. I don't think it'll be much longer. . . ."

"Doesn't sound good." Walking over to the coffeepot, he poured himself a cup.

"Oh, that's been there since this afternoon." I attempted to take the cup from him. "I can make a fresh pot. It'll just take a second."

"Only if you'll join me."

I nodded and went into the back room to fill the carafe with water. Taking a deep breath and blowing it out, my thoughts raced. Was coming here just a friendly gesture on his part? Was he willing to forget my behavior about Valerie? And where exactly did we go from here?

Pouring the water into the coffeemaker, I felt him walk up behind me and the heat in the room seemed to get notched up a few degrees.

"How're *you* doing?" he asked.

Turning around, I locked my eyes with his and felt an overwhelming urge to cry. To start crying and not stop. Instead, I moved away from him and sat on the sofa. "That'll be ready in just a minute." Shoving a hand through my hair I said, "I'm okay. This has turned out to be a lot tougher than I thought it would."

Noah sat across from me in the chair. "Why's that?"

"Because in the beginning, I didn't even *like* Sybile. I thought she was self-centered and mean and . . ."

"And now?"

"And now, I still think she has a tendency to be that way, but—but over time I've gotten to know her better." Fighting to control the tears forming in my eyes, I said, "Dammit," both for the tears and for my emotion toward Sybile. "Dammit, I don't think I really intended to get close to her. Do you know what I mean?"

Noah got up and poured coffee into two mugs. Passing one to me, he said, "Yeah, I know what you mean. The same way you never *intended* to get close to me, right?"

I lowered my head, staring into the brown liquid.

"That's how life is. We can't control our feelings and emotions, Sydney. You might try—but it doesn't work." He took a sip of coffee and when I didn't speak, he went on. "We had something going between us. I'm pretty sure we still do. I care for you—a lot. You were right when you told me this wasn't just about Valerie. It was about much more than that. It was about you being unsure and afraid. Afraid to take another chance with a man. Unsure if you'd be hurt again."

Still not looking Noah in the face, I nodded. What was it I had asked to be released and taken in the night of the blue-moon gathering? *To release fear and take in understanding.* "You're right," I said softly. "I wanted a guarantee that wouldn't happen."

"And life has no guarantees, does it?"

I shook my head.

"You were right about something else. Maybe I *was* smothering you. Maybe it's an annoying habit of mine. And I apologize for that."

My face shot up to stare directly at Noah. In all my years with Stephen, he had never once said he was sorry. For anything. "I'm sorry too—for the way I've acted. You didn't deserve that."

"Neither one of us did," he said, standing up. "You're going through a hard time right now. You need some space. But if you feel the need to talk to someone, call me. It isn't my plan to pressure you, but if you need or want anything you know where to find me." Leaning over, he touched my shoulder as he kissed my cheek.

Hearing the wind chimes tinkle, I knew that what I wanted was to feel the security of his arms around me.

"I agree with Noah," Alison said. "Now isn't the time for you to be confronting your relationship with him. You have too much going on with Sybile."

I nodded while squeezing lemon into my tea. "You're both probably right."

"We are."

"I've missed him these past few months while he was gone. More than I thought I would."

"And if it's meant to be, it'll happen, Syd. You're very vulnerable right now. Don't be so hard on yourself."

"I've been a bear, haven't I? Creating such a scene about Valerie."

"More like a bitch."

"I can always depend on you to set me straight."

Alison laughed. "Hey, what're best friends for? I've never coddled you, and I'm not about to start now."

I smiled. "So what I need to do is just—let go. Just *be.*"

"Ah, now that's the smartest thing I've heard you say in ages."

I finished off the tea and stood up. Placing the cup and saucer in the sink, I said, "Thanks, Ali.

Thanks for always being there for me. You really are the best friend a woman could have."

"I won't argue with that. It's after eleven and you look beat. Get outta here and get to bed."

"Yeah, it's been a long day and who knows what tomorrow will bring."

The following day I was standing on the deck of the Lighthouse waiting for Sybile's arrival home. Taking deep breaths of the salt air, my mind wandered back to the past nine months. *Nine months.* I found the number symbolic. It had taken nine months for me to grow inside of Sybile's womb. Nine months for me to emerge from Sybile into the world and my life. And it had taken nine months for me to develop a relationship with my mother.

Sybile had given my name to hospice—the contact person to be called for information. A registered nurse from hospice had called me the day before. She'd explained that a hospital bed would be delivered that afternoon and a nurse would come by to do the initial assessment after Sybile arrived home.

My attention was drawn to the gravel driveway and the sound of Saren's car. Racing down the steps, I hollered, "Welcome home," as I approached the passenger side. Seeing Sybile caused my heart to lurch. In just a few days there had been a significant transformation. Sybile's skin had turned gray and pasty. New lines had formed on her face. She was failing. Brushing aside any sadness, I opened the door, leaned in, and said, "Well, are you ready to go dancing tonight?" as I kissed Sybile's cheek.

"As a matter of fact, I am. Did ya hire the band?" Sybile allowed me to support her out of the car and slowly up the stairs.

Saren was removing flowers and a piece of luggage from the trunk. "You girls go on ahead. I'll bring this stuff up."

Each step that I took with my mother forced the realization this was the last time that Sybile would make this ascent.

"Bed or sofa?" I asked, leading the way into the kitchen.

"What the hell is that?" Sybile asked, pointing at the hospital bed in the living room. The chrome-sided bed had been placed in a corner, looking incongruous beside the gaily polished wood of the piano.

Noticing Sybile's increased difficulty breathing, I led her to the sofa, placing the oxygen tube to her nostrils. "Exactly what it looks like. A bed."

Taking a few deep breaths, Sybile said, "Well, it sure as hell isn't *my* bed and I'm not sleeping in it."

"You don't have to," Saren said, entering the kitchen. "The doctor recommended it in case you thought it might be more comfortable."

"That's crap and you know it. He ordered it for me to die in. My death chamber. Well, I plan to die in my own damn bed."

Sybile's illness may have weakened her body but I could see it hadn't dampened her feisty spirit. "I'll make some tea. Twila Faye sent you some homemade preserves. How about some on toast?"

"I'm not hungry," Sybile replied, sounding like a whiny child.

Saren and I exchanged glances but remained quiet as I went into the kitchen to prepare the tea.

"I'm glad you're back home," I heard Saren say, followed by silence. *Damn her,* I thought, *the least she could do is be nice to him.*

When I brought the tea, Sybile looked up. "Now you have all my instructions in order, right? You know exactly what to do for my farewell?"

I noticed how the woman had used the word *farewell* rather than *funeral.* I nodded, passing a cup and saucer to Sybile. "I have your notebook. I know what you want."

"And Noah? Have you been in touch with him?"

"About the boat? Yes, he said of course he'll take us out on the water."

Sybile sighed in annoyance. "Not the boat. About you. You and him."

Now it was my turn to be annoyed. "Look, Sybile, you've been in control of everything. Your illness and your death. But it's time to stop trying to tie up loose ends before you leave this earth. Sometimes things can't be wrapped up the way you want them to be."

"Honey, as long as you're still breathing, you can make anything happen. So stop kidding yourself. So—have you been in touch?"

"God, you're impossible. But yeah, he dropped by the shop to inquire about you."

"And?"

"And he said if I needed anything or to talk to somebody to call him."

A satisfied smile crossed Sybile's face. "Now, that's more like it. Now all you have to—" A coughing spasm didn't allow her to finish.

Saren rushed to her side, while Sybile attempted to catch her breath. After a few moments, her rapid breathing resumed.

I knew that normal respirations were between sixteen and twenty. Watching the rise and fall of Sybile's chest, I knew my mother's probably hovered close to forty.

Dabbing her eyes with a tissue, Sybile asked, "And when is that nurse supposed to get here? What good is she if she'll be sleeping during the night?"

"She'll stop by later today," Saren explained. "And for right now, she won't be here during the night. Just a daily visit to check on you. And . . . when the time comes, there'll be three nurses coming to do eight-hour shifts. So she won't be sleeping on the job, Sybile."

"Oh," was all she said.

"Are you sure I can't make you some lunch? How about some fruit?" I asked.

Sybile shook her head. "Just the tea. And after I finish this, I might lay down here for a nap. I think the drive made me tired."

I saw the concern on Saren's face. "Well, then, I think I'll go home for a while. I'll be back later this evening though. If the nurse has any questions, tell her to call me. I'll be home the rest of the day catching up on things."

Leaning over to kiss Sybile's cheek, I patted Saren's shoulder. "You both take it easy. It wouldn't hurt you to doze off for a while either, Saren."

"When's Monica coming?" Sybile asked.

"She's not quite sure, but she was thinking about early next week."

"Yes, tell her to come then," Sybile replied with a bold tone. "I want her here next week."

I caught the insistence in my mother's voice. "I'll let her know," I said softly, before walking out the door.

When Monica arrived, I knew she found her grandmother had greatly deteriorated from the last time she'd seen her. I was at the Lighthouse with Dora and Marin when my daughter pulled into the driveway.

Sybile was propped up with pillows in the hospital bed. A few days earlier it had been her request to begin using it. With a smile on her face, Monica walked over to Sybile taking her hand and placing a kiss on her cheek.

"Well, if you don't just look like queen of the island with all those lacy pillows."

Joy covered Sybile's face as she gripped her granddaughter's hand. "I'm so glad you're here."

"Of course I'm here. Had to get away from all the noise in Gainesville," she kidded.

"Dora made a delicious quiche. How about a slice?"

"Sounds great," Monica said, releasing Sybile's hand to hug Marin and Dora. "Where's Saren?"

"We sent him home to get some decent sleep," Dora said. "Poor man was ready to keel over from being here night and day. Told him we women could look after Sybile just fine."

Monica laughed. "And we can."

Joining me in the kitchen, Monica whispered, "How's she *really* doing?"

I shook my head. "Not good. Sleeping more and more. Her mind is still lucid though. But her breathing and weakness is much worse."

When we returned to the living room, Sybile was pushing herself up straighter against the pillows. "I want the two of you," she said, pointing to Monica and me, "and Saren to come by tomorrow morning. Morning is my best time. When I don't feel so woozy. I want you here."

I exchanged a look with Monica and we nodded. When Sybile volunteered nothing more, I asked, "Any particular reason?"

"Yeah," Sybile replied in a strong voice. "Because I said so."

"Sounds to me like she's getting all her ducks in a row," Alison said.

Pouring milk into the mashed potatoes, I nodded and smiled. "Yeah, but her ducks have always been in a row."

"You know what I mean—the final lineup."

"I agree. She keeps asking about the memorial arrangements and driving me nuts checking on Noah and me."

Alison raised an eyebrow. "Where's it at with the two of you?"

"I'm not sure. Friendly. Civil. I haven't seen him since he stopped by the shop a few weeks ago."

"And why not?"

"Why not?" I spooned the potatoes into a serving bowl.

"Why haven't you called him like he asked you to?"

"I don't know. I don't know because . . . I really *would* like to see him and talk to him."

"You're such a damn fool, Syd. Just do it. Call him."

I placed the bowl on the table. Placing hands on my hips, I said, "You know what? You're right. You're right, Ali. I'm going to call him after we finish supper."

Alison rolled her eyes, shaking her head. "Of course I'm right. It just always takes you so damn long to figure that out."

Later that evening I sat on my balcony, a glass of cognac in my hand, and Noah at my side.

"I'm glad you called," he said, staring at the setting sun.

I looked over at him. "I'm glad I did too."

He reached for my hand. "Have you sorted things out in your mind?"

Enjoying the feel of my hand in his, I said, "Somewhat."

"Enough for you and me to resume seeing each other?"

"I think so." I paused for a few moments, clutching his hand and feeling a renewed energy course through my body. "Yes," I said, with more conviction. "Yes, I'd like that very much."

Noah leaned over and taking my face in his hands, he smiled. "Good," he said, letting his lips brush mine. "Good. Because I love a woman that knows what she wants."

If the situation hadn't been so dire, I would have chuckled. There sat Sybile, wearing a lacy bed jacket, supported by a multitude of pillows while the three of us sat quiet and stone-faced waiting for an explanation as to why we'd been beckoned. Sybile reminded me of the queen in my childhood story books—regal, efficient, and in charge. Convening this gathering to assert her power and demands on her peons, one final time.

After a few moments, Sybile broke the silence. "I suppose it isn't odd that a dying woman would summon her loved ones to her bedside. For whatever reason. You know, there was a time when I used to wonder how I'd die—would it be sudden, in an accident? Without a moment to think about it. Or would it be long and drawn out, giving me plenty of time to think over the life I was leaving? My choice was to go fast—poof! Just like that and I'd be gone. No recriminations, nothing. Just gone."

I was surprised by the vitality Sybile was displaying this morning. She appeared stronger, and some of her determination had returned to her voice.

"But I didn't get my choice. Many times in death, as in life, we don't. But I also learned to accept the hand I was dealt. I asked the three of you here this morning because there's something I now feel compelled to tell you—something that maybe I should have told you long ago."

I slid forward on my chair, waiting.

Without any preamble whatsoever, looking directly at me, Sybile blurted out, "You wanted to know who your father is—Saren's your father."

Lightheadedness overcame me as I reached forward and gripped the bed rail. It had been one thing to suspect for months the possibility that Saren was my father and quite another to now hear my mother confirm it. At the mention of Saren's name, my glance shot to the elderly man sitting on the other side of my daughter. The shocked expression on his face told me he'd had no prior knowledge of this and I heard him say, "That can't be possible."

"Oh, it's possible alright."

I was backtracking in my mind the story that Sybile had told me all those months ago about my birth. Sybile had left the island and she never saw Saren again except briefly in Manhattan before he left for Paris. Unless . . .

"It's very possible," Sybile continued. "I know you always wanted to protect my reputation, Saren, but now's the time to be honest. You know as well as I do that we slept together that one night—that one night before you flew off to Paris."

With a million thoughts racing through my

head, I felt Monica take my hand and squeeze it and I saw my daughter's other hand reach out for Saren's.

For a brief moment I was concerned that such a shock could be dangerous for him. But the look on his face was calm. Calm but bewildered.

"I don't understand," he said, shaking his head. "I don't understand why on earth you couldn't tell me. All these years, all these empty, lonely years . . ." He released Monica's hand to begin pacing around the room.

"That's why I couldn't tell you. I didn't want you to hate me. I was selfish, I won't lie about that. I wanted my career, my fame, and had I told you, you would have insisted that we marry. Marry and raise our child. And I just couldn't do that. That lifestyle wasn't for me. So I made the decision that you were better off not to know. You didn't need to know."

Saren spun around to face Sybile. "How dare you make that decision for me! It wasn't *just* your decision to make. How dare you deprive me of a daughter—and a granddaughter, that I never knew." Tears flowed down his face as he stood there not taking his eyes from Sybile.

She let out a deep sigh and nodded. "Perhaps you're right. I didn't think so then. But now—all these years later, maybe you're right."

"All these *lost* years later," Saren replied in a raised voice.

"I can't make up for those years. They're gone. You have no idea how close I came to taking this secret to my grave. But I felt it was more important to risk the hatred of all three of you—because after I'm gone, at least you'll have each other. Maybe you can have the love and relationship that I denied to all of you."

Without saying a word, Monica got up, walked to the side of the bed, and took Sybile in her arms. "That was a hard thing to do, Billie," she said softly.

Saren turned on his heels, walked outside to the deck, and I followed.

Leaning against the railing, we stood silent watching the gulls swoop over the shimmering water.

Saren—this man standing beside me—had given me life every bit as much as Sybile had. For the past nine months I'd wondered who my father was—had even suspected it could possibly be him. And for nine months Sybile refused to tell me. And all that time he was right here. A feeling of awkwardness came over me. Nothing like having the truth forced on you. What must he be feeling?

"Are you alright?" I asked.

He nodded. "I'm angry. All my life I've loved her and all these years she kept this secret from me. How could she do such a thing?"

"She's loved you too, Saren. So it must have

been a very difficult thing for her. And by telling us now, before it was too late, I think she's proved that love." I heard myself voicing the words, but the sense of understanding for Sybile surprised me. "I guess she feels now, what's she got to lose? She won't be with us much longer. If you hate her, you'll do so in death. Not for all these years she's been alive."

"You're my daughter," I heard Saren say with wonder. "My *daughter.*"

I reached for the veined hand that rested on the railing and squeezed it. "And you're my dad."

Saren turned and pulled me into an embrace. "Imagine that. You're my daughter," he repeated again.

I smiled. "She couldn't have chosen a better father for me. You're a very special person, Saren, and I'm proud to be your daughter."

He released our embrace to reach into his pocket for a handkerchief. Wiping his eyes, he said, "She's really given me a gift, ya know. The best gift possible."

"Maybe that's how she wants it. To be able to leave this world giving you a part of herself. She was never able to in life, but death has enabled her to do this."

Saren nodded slowly. "I think you're right." He patted my arm. "I have a very brilliant daughter, you know."

Putting an arm around his shoulder, I smiled.

"Of course you do. She takes after her father. Let's go inside and see Sybile."

"Well, if this doesn't beat all," Dora said, glancing around the table at Monica, Saren, and me.

"You really didn't know this?" I asked, while taking the bowl of green beans that Saren had passed me.

Dora shook her head. "No, I surely didn't. I'm as surprised as all of you. But I won't lie, there were a few times that I wondered if possibly Saren was involved. Sybile was so secretive though, I never mentioned it to her."

"That's a long time to live with a secret like this, isn't it?" Monica took a bite of the meatloaf Dora had prepared.

"My sister always was her own person. Had a knack for keeping things to herself. Makes me angry though—she just as easily could have passed on without telling either one of you."

Saren nodded. "Yeah, I thought that too. But she didn't."

"How was she when you left her this evening? Do you think she feels more at peace now?"

"I've seen this happen before in my nursing career. Once somebody shares something or maybe has a visitor they've been waiting for, it's like they can begin to let go. She's been sleeping pretty much all afternoon and when the nurse

356

arrived, she suggested getting 'round the clock coverage now." I pushed the food around my plate. "I think she does feel more at peace, Dora. I wasn't willing to understand before, but like Monica said, that's a heavy burden to live with for over fifty years."

"Well, all I can say is, our family just seems to keep growing." Picking up her glass of iced tea, she tipped it in Saren's direction. "Welcome to the family, Saren. Officially."

Smiling, he lifted his glass in salute. "I'm real grateful to Sybile. Oh sure, maybe it would have been nice if things had worked out differently. But you know that old saying, it's never too late."

"And what a bonus for me," Monica said. "Finding not only my birth grandmother, but a grandfather too. I agree with Saren—it's never too late and everything usually happens in its own time."

Following dessert and cleaning up, I glanced at the clock over Dora's refrigerator. Seven-thirty. I'd called Noah earlier to share my news with him and he'd told me to stop by after dinner.

"Well, everyone, if it's alright, I'm going to head over to Noah's."

Three smiles beamed back at me.

"Of course it's alright," Dora said.

"I'll be spending the night at Sybile's, so I'll be going back in a little while." Saren stood up from the table.

"You gave the nurse your cell number, Mom, so go and have a relaxing evening. She'll call you if there's any change."

I stretched my legs out in front of me on the lounge. Turning my head, I watched Noah at the garden bar preparing a gin and tonic for us.

"Here ya go." Passing me a glass he settled into the lounge beside me.

"To life," I said, touching the rim of his glass.

"I'll drink to that." Taking a sip he reached for my hand.

Just the touch of his hand caused heat between us. What I felt was sensual mixed with contentment. We sat in comfortable silence for a few minutes.

I rested my head back, looking up at the sky. A sweet fragrance filled the air. Above me, ibis flew past leaving the island for the night heading to a sanctuary offshore.

"Tired?" Noah asked.

"Weary. It's been a tough couple months."

"You've been through a lot emotionally. You might want to . . ." He stopped mid-sentence.

Turning toward him, I said, "What? Might want to what?"

He shook his head. "Sorry. I was about to suggest something, but I don't want you to think I'm telling you what to do again."

I squeezed his hand and smiled. "At least you're aware of it. Tell me."

"I was just thinking it might be nice for you to take some time for yourself—after. You know, take a trip for a couple weeks. Close the shop for a while to have a rest."

"Are you trying to get rid of me?"

"Never. Maybe I could be persuaded to take that trip with you."

"As lovely as that sounds, why would I want to leave all of this? I can close the shop for a while and relax right here as well as anywhere."

"Very true. You'll know what's best."

"Noah?"

He turned his head toward me. "What?"

"Would it be alright if I spent the night here with you? I think *that* would be best."

A smile crossed his face. "Have I told you that you make brilliant decisions?"

I was awakened the following morning to the sound of my cell phone ringing on Noah's bedside table. Reaching for it, I was instantly alert.

"Sydney, this is Barbara, the nurse. No need to rush, but Sybile had a restless night. She's fading in and out of consciousness. I thought you might want to be with her."

"I'll be there within an hour," I said, already swinging my feet to the floor.

It had been a long, draining day. I sat at Sybile's bedside, holding her hand, watching her sleep. Glancing over my shoulder I saw Saren and Monica sitting on the sofa. Dora had stepped outside for some air and the nurse sat quietly on the other side of the bed reading a novel.

How many times had I done this, I wondered? Sat with somebody as they made the transition and passed over? A lot. But I hadn't even been with my adopted mother or father when they died. They had gone quickly in a hospital.

Sybile's eyes fluttered open, focusing on my face. "It's a girl, you know. I've had a baby girl," she said clearly.

I squeezed my mother's hand. "I know."

Sybile's eyes closed momentarily only to snap open. "She's beautiful. Have you seen her? She's the most beautiful baby I've ever seen and I love her."

I nodded, feeling wetness on my face. "I know you do. She loves you too."

Sybile's eyes closed as she drifted back into that in-between plane. That place where she had to journey alone.

But as long as she's here, she's not alone, I thought, finding it ironic that this woman, whose blood ran through my own veins, had given me life and now . . . I sat beside this woman as life ebbed out of her.

"Why don't you take a break?" I heard Monica say and felt a hand on my shoulder.

I nodded and got up. Walking out to the deck, I saw Dora sitting at the table staring out over the water.

"Any change?" she asked.

I shook my head.

Dora wiped her eyes with a tissue. "I'm going to miss her."

"We're all going to miss her."

I was dozing on the sofa and awoke to a touch on my hand. Opening my eyes, I saw Noah kneeling in front of me. Momentarily disoriented, I looked around the Lighthouse and realized that the vigil was still continuing.

"What time is it?" I asked, stretching.

Taking my hand to his lips, he said, "Eight o'clock. Are you hungry? Can I get you anything?"

I looked to the other side of the room and saw Saren, Monica, and Dora standing around the bed while the nurse rearranged the pillows, making Sybile more comfortable.

I shook my head. "No, but thank you. Any change?"

"I heard the nurse tell them that Sybile's breathing was slowing down."

Letting out a deep sigh, I got up. "I need some air," I said, walking out to the deck.

Noah followed. Placing his arm around my waist, he said, "Birth and death. Neither one is easy, is it?"

Looking out to the purple and pink sky, I shook my head. "Not at all."

After a few minutes I went back inside and prepared another pot of coffee. Standing in the kitchen waiting for it to brew, I looked over at Saren. Leaning over the bed, he clasped Sybile's hands in his. "It's okay, Sybi, it's okay to pass on," I heard him say. "I'll be alright. I've got my girls now, ya know. The girls that you've given me. I love you, Sybi, and we'll be together again. I've always loved you."

I brushed away tears as I filled mugs of coffee. Bringing them into the living room, I saw Dora was now with Sybile, talking quietly to her sister.

Taking two cups of coffee, I joined Noah on the deck, passing one to him. "They're saying their good-byes."

"I know. That's why I came out here. I didn't want to intrude. Thanks for the coffee."

"God, I want a cigarette."

"Where are they? I'll get them for you."

I took a deep breath and shook my head. "No. I've quit."

Noah looked at me sharply. "Just like that?"

"Just like that." I took a deep gulp of coffee. "It's pure hell, I won't lie."

"You're strong," he said, pulling me close. "And I'm right here for moral support."

Finishing the coffee, I walked back in the house. Monica glanced up from Sybile's bedside and walked toward me.

"How're you holding up?" she asked.

"Okay. I'm going to sit with Sybile for a while."

Glancing over at the nurse, I reached for my mother's hand. "Thank you for telling me," I whispered. "Thank you for telling me who my father is. And thank you for being my mother. I love you, Sybile."

The bedside clock read 9:07. A sense of calm covered my mother's face. Maybe it was only a reflex, but I felt my hand being squeezed in the same moment I realized my birth time was 9:07 P.M.—and in the same moment Sybile exhaled her final breath.

"She's gone," I said softly.

Three days later Noah maneuvered his boat away from Atsena Otie and headed back to the city dock. Sybile's farewell had gone precisely as she'd wanted it. The music, the poems, the gardenia petals.

"Fly free and soar, Billie," I heard my daughter say.

Watching the flowers float by in the water,

something else caught my eye. A school of four dolphins had swum up beside the boat, jumping and diving. I smiled. "Well, Sybile didn't have that on my list of instructions, but maybe she placed this request with someone else."

Everyone came to the railing to enjoy the graceful antics. "Leave it to Sybile," Saren said.

Monica laughed. "Yup, she didn't leave a stone unturned."

"If I didn't know better, I'd say she ordered up this gorgeous day too," Dora said.

Brilliant sunshine filled the sky and after all the heat and humidity of a Florida summer, early October was proving an enjoyable respite.

Halfway between Atsena Otie and Cedar Key, I felt moisture on my arm as I looked up and realized that despite the sunshine, a cloudburst was above us. Everyone gathered under the bimini, as rain fell from the sky.

I shook my head and laughed. "I think Sybile's letting us know she approved of her farewell."

Arriving back at the Lighthouse, I saw quite a few cars already in the driveway. "I'm glad Polly said she'd come early to greet people," I said, getting out of the golf cart and running up the stairs.

Only a few weeks before, Sybile had changed her mind on a small gathering of select people. She instructed me to put a notice in the local paper inviting everyone who'd like to drop by to pay their final respects. She'd also given me a check to pay for a catered buffet lunch.

"Thank you so much for getting here early, Polly."

"It was my pleasure. The staff from Island Room has everything all set up," she said pointing to all the food covering counters and the table.

People began arriving, many carrying homemade pies, cakes, and casseroles. "So you won't have to cook for a while," they told me.

Within an hour the house was packed and guests were overflowing out to the wrap-around deck.

"Quite a crowd, isn't it?" Noah slipped an arm around my waist.

"It certainly is. I wasn't sure if it would only be the six of us or if we'd have a full house. Sybile would be pleased."

Saren was clapping his hands for attention, waving a newspaper in the air. People quieted down to hear him.

I looked at Noah questioningly. He shrugged his shoulders.

"I'd like to read y'all something," Saren said with importance. "I took the liberty of placing this here notice in today's *Cedar Key News*. And for those of you that haven't seen it yet, I'd like to read it to you."

I raised my eyebrows waiting to hear what he'd say.

"Sybile Mae Bowden and Saren Carl Ghetti

would like to announce the birth of their daughter, Sydney Lynn Webster, on March nineteenth, nineteen fifty-five and the birth of their granddaughter, Monica Webster, on October twenty-fourth, nineteen eighty-one. It is with great pride that this announcement is made."

A loud round of cheers and claps filled the room as Saren reached for a large box and began passing out cigars, a pink label attached, to everyone.

I looked at Monica and started laughing. Moisture filled my eyes as I realized that due to the reaction, most of those in attendance had already read the paper or heard the news via the infamous coconut pipeline of the island. There was no doubt that both my daughter and I were being warmly accepted—accepted as Sybile Bowden's kin. Something Sybile was never sure would happen.

I looked up at Noah standing beside me. A huge grin covered his face. "You knew he was putting that in the paper, didn't you?"

"Guilty. He asked if I thought you'd approve."

"Obviously you felt you knew me well enough to say yes." Noah pulled me into an embrace. Kissing me, he said, "Obviously."

41

A few days after the memorial service, I was at the yarn shop catching up on back orders. Although maybe Noah had been right about me taking some time off, I had a responsibility to my customers, and they had grown considerably since I'd started my business. Hearing the wind chimes, I was surprised to look up and see Alison walk through the door.

"Now don't tell me you finally decided to knit."

"Right. I'm not telling you that. I'd only manage to get myself all tangled up in that yarn. I stopped by to see you. You've been so busy lately I've missed your company."

"Let me put some coffee on. I'm ready for a break from these orders. I don't mind being busy. I'm grateful that my business seems to finally be taking off."

Alison sat on the sofa, leaning over to pat Lilly. "I bet you've felt neglected lately," she told my dog.

"Yeah, I think she has. I'm taking her down to the beach tonight after supper. Just so the two of us can bond."

I poured water into the coffeemaker. "So what're you up to? Any word from Paul?"

Alison smiled. "Yes, actually. One of the reasons I wanted to see you. He called this morning—and he's retiring in January, after the first of the year."

"That's great, but . . ." I hesitated. "Oh God, Ali, please don't tell me you're moving to Atlanta."

Alison laughed. "No, I'm not. But Paul is planning to move here to the island. Permanently."

I ran over to hug her. "That's great. I'm so happy for you. Will you be keeping the B and B?"

Alison nodded. "I'll keep it, but he wants to look at some property in the Historic District. He's thinking it might be nice to purchase a house and have me live there with him. It'll be close enough for me to keep the B and B going, but for the first time in over twenty years, I won't be living right there."

"That might be a nice break for you."

"That's what I was thinking and before you go jumping to conclusions, I want you to stay put in the Tree House."

"Really? Gosh, it's going on a year that I've been there, Ali. I never intended to stay that long. Maybe it's time for me to look for a place too and move on."

I brought the coffee and settled in across from Alison.

"Well, that's entirely up to you, but it's your home for as long as you want."

"Sometimes I can hardly believe it'll be a year next month since I arrived here."

"A lot's happened in this past year. When I

think back to that fearful, confused, and betrayed woman who showed up at the B and B, it's like you're a whole different person."

"In many ways, I am. I've had a year of tremendous growth. And so much of it is due to you. You're a wonderful friend, Ali."

"You're the one that did it, Syd. I only tried to keep you on the right track."

"Exactly—as I said, a wonderful friend."

The ringing telephone interrupted our conversation.

"Sydney Webster? This is Richard White. I'm your mother's attorney in Gainesville."

"Oh, yes. I've heard her mention your name."

"First of all, I'm terribly sorry about your loss. Miss Sybile was quite a character. Please accept my condolences."

I smiled. "She was and thank you."

"The reason I'm calling, I'm going to need you to come into my office at your earliest convenience. We need to discuss your mother's estate."

"Oh. Oh, I see. Well, yes, I guess I could arrange that." Strange, this wasn't part of Sybile's instructions. I'd been told nothing about this.

"Very good. Would Friday afternoon, say around two o'clock be convenient for you?"

Dora would cover the yarn shop. "Yes, that'll be fine but you'll need to give me your address and directions. I'm not that familiar with Gainesville."

"Not a problem," he said.

I wrote down what he told me. "Okay, then, I'll see you Friday afternoon."

I hung up the phone and felt bewildered.

"Tell me it was good news," Alison said. "We've had enough sadness around here for a while."

"I think it's just neutral news. That was Sybile's attorney. Wants to see me about her estate. I imagine it's about cleaning out the Lighthouse so the Marine Lab can take possession and put it up for sale."

"Hmm, probably. How do you feel about that?"

"Well, I never thought I'd feel one way or another. But lately I've grown attached to that place. It just seems to have Sybile's stamp all over it. You know what I mean?"

I looked up as the wind chimes tinkled again and saw Saren coming through the door, carrying a bouquet of flowers.

"These are for you," he said, passing the roses to me. "Picked them myself from my garden and thought you'd like 'em."

I reached for the flowers and stood up to give him a hug. "They're beautiful. Thank you so much. Have a seat, I'll get these in water and get you some coffee."

Since Sybile's memorial service three days before, Saren had dropped by the yarn shop each afternoon. The first day he brought me a box of chocolates, the second day a book he'd purchased about the island that he thought I'd enjoy, and today, flowers.

Returning with the vase and setting it down on the table, I heard Saren mention Miss Elly.

"What's this about Miss Elly?"

"Strangest thing," he said, accepting the coffee mug. "Ever since Sybile took a turn for the worse, Miss Elly has disappeared. Hasn't joined me at all for our usual conversation and cognac."

"That *is* strange," I agreed. "What do you think is going on?"

"I don't know. But I'd like to think she's okay."

"Did you ever consider that perhaps she found her true love after all these years?" Alison offered. "You always thought she was at your house searching. Maybe their souls reconnected."

Saren scratched his head. "Well now, Miss Ali, I never did think of that. But you sure could be right. Wouldn't that be somethin'? After all these years, if Miss Elly found her soulmate? There's a good possibility of that, isn't there?"

Alison glanced over at me and winked. "There's a huge possibility of that, Saren."

I smiled back at my friend with gratefulness.

"Your appointment's at two on Friday?" Noah asked while putting the finishing touches on the salad.

I nodded, continuing to dip chicken breast in

and out of marinade. "I'm pretty sure it's about putting Sybile's house up for sale."

"You're probably right," he said, uncorking a bottle of cabernet.

"I'll take these out to the grill for you." I headed out the door with a plate of chicken.

Standing in the garden I breathed in the crisp, autumn air. Hopefully, the agonizing heat of the summer was behind us. I turned to Noah's voice.

He passed me a glass of wine. "Here's to new beginnings for us," he said, kissing my lips.

I smiled. "To new beginnings."

I had spent the past two nights at his house—complete with Lilly, who no longer deemed it necessary to pee on the carpet. The dog had taken a genuine liking to Noah and the feeling was mutual.

"I wanted to talk to you about these new beginnings," I said hesitantly.

Noah shot me an inquisitive look as he placed chicken on the grill.

"I've stayed here with you the past two nights and I won't lie, it's been wonderful."

"You don't want to continue sleeping with me?"

"That's not exactly it." I took a sip of wine before going on. "I guess what I don't want is to be staying here permanently. What I'm trying to say is, I don't want to give up my own place. I've been on my own now for almost a year—and I rather like having my own space."

"I can understand that. Getting set in your ways, huh?" he kidded me.

"Well, you do have all those annoying habits," I said with mock seriousness.

"Like making love to you?" he asked with a grin.

"Now, *that* does not come under the category of annoying habits." Far from it. Making love with Noah was the most passionate and intimate experience I'd ever had. "No, it's just . . ."

Noah took my face between his hands staring into my eyes. "You don't have to explain to me. I *do* understand. But I just want you to know—any night you feel inclined to stay here instead of going home, I want you to. If you'd like me to stay at your place, just ask. And if you'd rather be completely alone, that's alright too—just as long as you're not alone more than we're together."

I smiled. "Thank you. Thank you for understanding."

"Okay, now I have something to ask you. But you have to promise to say no if that's really what you'd rather say."

"Promise."

"I was just wondering if maybe I could drive you to Gainesville tomorrow. I don't want to intrude, but I thought maybe we could have lunch together at a great French restaurant there. And I'll wait in the car while you're with the attorney. I won't cramp your style."

I frowned. "Absolutely not. Absolutely not you'll wait in the car. You'll come into his office with me. And yes, I'd love for you to drive me, and I accept your offer for lunch."

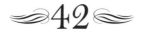

42

I accepted the menu from the waiter and smiled across the table at Noah. How *did* he find such an authentic French restaurant in a university town in north central Florida? Stepping into Chez Collette was like what I imagined a Paris bistro might be. Small, with only six white, linen-covered tables. Dimly lit after the brightness of outside. A flickering candle at each place setting. Dark wood and shining brass comprised the interior with large prints of the Champs Elysées, Montparnasse, Eiffel Tower, and the Seine adorning the walls. Completing the authenticity were the French accents of the staff.

I allowed Noah to choose a glass of French wine for each of us.

"You're quite the savvy Frenchman, aren't you?"

Noah smiled while reaching for my hand across the table.

"I spent many years in Paris. It became like a second home to me. Except for Cedar Key, it's my favorite place in the entire world."

I returned his smile and sighed. "Ah, romantic Paris. How I'd love to visit there someday."

"And you will, if you'd really like to. I suggested you take some time off from the shop."

"I'd be hopelessly lost over there. I don't speak a word of French."

"I didn't mean for you to go alone. My French is fluent and I'd love to take you to Paris—just the two of us for a couple weeks."

"God, you're really tempting me," I said as excitement filled me. "Let's do it. Let's make plans to go after the first of the year. I've already let too much life pass me by. And like Sybile told me, once your chance is gone, nothing will ever make it quite the same. I'm not passing up this chance."

Noah squeezed my hand. "It's a date."

I crossed my legs, adjusting the hem of my skirt at my knees. Glancing around the attorney's office my gaze went back to the man behind the desk. I'd been surprised that Richard White was younger than I'd imagined. For some reason I thought Sybile would have chosen somebody more her age to manage her affairs. But this fellow in the Armani suit and looking more like a soap opera star was barely forty. A smile formed on my face. Then again, it was undoubtedly those handsome looks that allowed Sybile to entrust him with her estate.

"Now then," he said, in a professional tone. "Everything seems to be in order here." He flipped through pages in a folder. "Yes, Sybile made certain of that." He smiled across the desk at me, leaning forward. "From what I understand this is to be a surprise. That's how Sybile wanted it."

I shot him a blank look causing him to continue.

"According to Sybile's will, she has left the entire bulk of her estate to you."

"What?" Now it was my turn to lean forward, my face covered in surprise. "No, that can't be possible. I know for a fact that her will states the Marine Lab is to get her house so they can sell it and take the money for research."

"Yes, well, that was what the original will stated. However, Sybile changed her will in early August. She did leave a sizable amount to the Lab."

Managing to find my voice, I said, "But I just assumed whatever there was would go to her sister, Dora."

He nodded. "She did make a small provision for . . ." He paused, scanning down a page. "A Eudora Foster and her daughter, Marin."

"But, but . . . What do you mean that she left the entire estate to me? I have to sell her house, right?"

Richard grinned. "Not unless you want to." Placing reading glasses on the bridge of his nose, he again read from a page. "I won't bore you with all the legal jargon," he said, removing his glasses and putting the stack of papers down. "But in layman's terms, you have inherited everything she owned. The house and entire contents, her stocks, her bank accounts. Oh, and she did leave some sizable stock in her grand-daughter's name." Referring to a paper, he said, "A Monica Webster."

"So you mean I don't have to sell the Lighthouse? That I could just . . . just move in there if I wanted to?"

Richard smiled again, nodding. "Free and clear. You are now the owner of the Lighthouse on Cedar Key."

With no warning, I burst out crying.

Richard jumped up to come around the desk touching my arm. "Are you alright? Can I get you some water? I know this is all a bit surprising."

My sobs quickly turned into laughter immediately followed by hiccups. "Could you just . . . just get my . . . my friend in the outer office?"

Noah was by my side within moments as I continued to vacillate between crying and laughing. "I'm the owner of Sybile's Lighthouse. Sybile left me everything."

A broad smile crossed Noah's face as he scooped me into his arms. "Congratulations to you, Miss Heiress."

During the drive back to the island, the aftermath of my jubilation had simmered to a pensive quietness. I could feel Noah's glances across the front seat. He allowed me time to absorb everything the attorney had told me. "I wonder what it says." I broke the silence waving a business-size envelope in the air. "I imagine it's a final good-bye from Sybile." I looked at the large, bold writing of my name on the envelope.

Richard had said Sybile mailed it to him two months before and instructed it be given to me after she was gone. "I'm going to read it now," I said, removing the typewritten page.

To my daughter Sydney,

I'm not much of a writer but since I'm now gone, there's a few things I wanted to say. By now you know you're the owner of the Lighthouse. Yes, I've passed the gauntlet to you. My only request is, if you shouldn't want the house, would you please then ask Monica if perhaps she would like it? I know a house is simply lumber and brick, but the Lighthouse was always much more than that to me. It was my sanctuary, my place on this island, but when you came into my life all these years later, it was also my salvation—something from my soul that I could leave to you. Due to the choices I made, I was never a mother to you in the official sense. And I certainly have no right to make requests of you, but since the blue moon gathering I feel

perhaps you've gained some understanding. Therefore, I'd love nothing more than for you to now have this house. I saw how your eyes lit up gazing out to the view on the water. I once accused you of having no spirit. Maybe you didn't, but over time you learned how to acquire it. This house has a lot of spirit—so soak it up, enjoy it and love it. Because I do love you, Sydney. And maybe over time, you learned to love me too.
Sybile

I reached into my handbag for a tissue. "Are you alright?" I heard Noah ask softly.

I nodded while wiping my eyes. "That Sybile, she was some special woman, wasn't she?"

"Like mother, like daughter," Noah said as he slowed the car to the requisite forty-five on SR 24.

I reached out to touch his arm. "Do me a favor? When you get to the Number Four bridge, could you pull off the road for a minute?"

"Sure."

A few minutes later, Noah pulled over as instructed. I got out, recalling the first time I'd seen this vista when I drove onto the island. Looking to the north, I saw clusters of lime-green patches dotting the blue water. A houseboat lazily bobbed to the rhythm of the waves. I felt Noah standing behind me, pulling me to him.

Resting his chin on my head, he said, "Breathtaking, isn't it?"

I nodded and glanced above as a flock of white ibis flew over the water. "Angel wings. Somebody once told me that in the utter silence of the island, when the ibis fly over, the whispering sound they create sounds like angel wings."

I spun around, throwing my arms around Noah's neck. "Hey, do you own a sleeping bag?"

"I'm pretty sure I do. Why?"

"Because a very wise woman once told me that there's nothing better than sleeping out in the open, under the sky and stars. And I can't think of a better spot than the deck of the Lighthouse."

Noah smiled. Opening the car door for me, he said, "Let's go test that theory."

DISCUSSION QUESTIONS

1. It has been said that after a life-altering event, such as a death, we should wait a year before making major changes in our life. Do you think Sydney should have remained in the Boston area to start over? Why or why not?

2. Sydney admitted to Alison that she should have paid more attention to financial matters in her marriage. Why do you think she didn't?

3. In college, Sydney was a strong and independent young woman. What do you think accounted for the change that resulted in her loss of identity?

4. Do you agree with Monica's opinions of her mother?

5. Did you feel Sydney harbored resentment for being given up at birth? Why do you think, at age fifty-two, her need to find her biological mother became stronger?

6. Do you think that Noah's attitude toward acquiring a lease on the shop accounted for Sydney's desire to open her yarn shop?

7. When you were first introduced to Sybile, what was your opinion of her? Did it change through the story? If so, in which way?

8. Do you think Monica was too tough on Sydney? What do you think accounted for her change toward her mother?

9. Which character do you think had the most impact on helping Sydney go forward?

10. Discuss the sister relationship between Sybile and Dora.

11. Discuss the blue-moon celebration. Why do you think it created a turning point between Sybile and Sydney?

12. What were your feelings toward Saren throughout the story? Do you think Miss Elly was only a figment of his imagination? Why do you think she disappeared at the end of the story?

13. Discuss Sybile's request to have Sydney assist in her death.

14. Do you agree with Sybile's statement "Not everyone is cut out to be a mother"? Did you think she was selfish to feel this way?

15. Sydney considers herself very different from Sybile. Did you observe any similar traits between the two women? In which way did Sydney grow and change by the time Sybile died?

Center Point Publishing

600 Brooks Road ● PO Box 1
Thorndike ME 04986-0001 USA

(207) 568-3717

US & Canada:
1 800 929-9108
www.centerpointlargeprint.com